Shamil, a young local reporter i_____o find his
editors in a state of great agita_____d that the
Russian government is building a wall to cut off the Caucasus …om the rest
of the country. Unrest is spreading through the capital city on the Caspian
Sea, with new protests and assemblies held daily by religious and ethnic
groups to respond to the crisis. The atmosphere is tense. Fear hangs in the air.
But Shamil tries to go on living as if nothing had changed. He is shocked out
of complacency when Madina, his fiancée, tells him she is going to take the
veil and follow a strict Islamist into the mountains where the rebellion is being
plotted. Even after the first people in town have been killed and his well-
educated cousin Asya tries to convince him to flee with her to Georgia and
from there on into the West, Shamil cannot overcome his hesitation. But then
events catch up with him…

More international praise for Alisa Ganieva:

"Like a latter-day Leopold Bloom, Ganieva's protagonist Shamil wanders
through his hometown of Makhachkala…[*The Mountain and the Wall*]
marks a real event in contemporary Russian literature because it tackles an
important topic—the intercultural dialogue between Russians and Russia's
Muslim population—but does so in a compelling artistic form. Ganieva
successfully avoids the trap of naïve realism but rather combines a complex
representation of the protagonist's consciousness with a high degree of
literary self-reflexivity."
—ULRICH M. SCHMID, *Neue Zürcher Zeitung*

"Alisa Ganieva has aimed to write in clear-eyed fashion about her
homeland, a region that has been racked by violence fueled by criminal
and clan elements and an Islamic insurgency."
—BBC on *Salam, Dalgat!*

"Her long story *Salam, Dalgat!* aims a merciless lens on a Dagestani town
roiling with drug gangs, Islamic fundamentalists, water-supply breakdowns,
burning garbage cans, abusive police officers and women fawning over
Gucci knockoffs."
—CELIA WREN, *Washington Post*

ALSO AVAILABLE IN ENGLISH BY
ALISA GANIEVA:

Salam, Dalgat!
translated by Nicholas Allen
(available in *Squaring the Circle*, Glas, 2010)

THE MOUNTAIN AND THE WALL

—

Alisa Ganieva

TRANSLATED FROM THE RUSSIAN BY
CAROL APOLLONIO

INTRODUCTION BY
RONALD MEYER

DEEP VELLUM PUBLISHING
DALLAS, TEXAS

Deep Vellum Publishing

2919 Commerce St. #159, Dallas, Texas 75226

deepvellum.org · @deepvellum

ISBN: 978-1-941920-15-2 (paperback) · 978-1-941920-14-5 (ebook)

LIBRARY OF CONGRESS CONTROL NUMBER: 2015935164

—

Published with the support of the Institute for Literary Translation (Russia)

ИНСТИТУТ ПЕРЕВОДА

AD VERBUM

Translation of this publication and the creation of its layout were carried out with the financial support of the Federal Agency for Press and Mass Communication under the federal target program "Culture of Russia (2012-2018)."

—

Издание осуществлено при участии Программы поддержки переводов русской литературы TRANSCRIPT Фонда Михаила Прохорова.

The publication of this book was made possible with the support of the Mikhail Prokhorov Foundation's Transcript program to support the translation of Russian literature.

—

Cover design & typesetting by Anna Zylicz · annazylicz.com

Text set in Bembo, a typeface modeled on typefaces cut by Francesco Griffo for Aldo Manuzio's printing of *De Aetna* in 1495 in Venice.

Deep Vellum titles are published under the fiscal sponsorship of The Writer's Garret, a nationally recognized nonprofit literary arts organization.

Distributed by Consortium Book Sales & Distribution. Printed in the United States of America on acid-free paper.

Contents

———

THE MOUNTAIN OF CELEBRATIONS

In noon's heat, in a dale of Dagestan…
—*Mikhail Lermontov, 1841*
(trans. Vladimir Nabokov)

Russian literature has a long and rich tradition of works set in the Caucasus. Three of the great writers of the nineteenth century— Alexander Pushkin, Mikhail Lermontov and Leo Tolstoy—all spent time in the Caucasus: Pushkin in exile, Lermontov and Tolstoy both served in the army there. This firsthand experience was put to good use in Pushkin's narrative poem *Prisoner of the Caucasus* (1820); in Lermontov's lyrics and *A Hero of Our Time* (1840), the first great Russian novel in prose; and Tolstoy's *Hadji Murat* (1904), his last major work of fiction. Importantly, these tales, set amidst the dramatic landscape of the mountainous Caucasus, are told by Russian imperial outsiders who come into contact, temporarily, with the local "noble savages" who inhabit the borderlands of the empire. Alisa Ganieva's novel *The Mountain and the Wall* (published in Russia in 2012) belongs to this tradition of Russian writing about the Caucasus, but with one major proviso: Ganieva herself is a native of Dagestan, the setting of her novel; the viewpoint is not of an outsider or onlooker, but rather of someone who has lived both in the mountains and in the capital city.

Alisa Ganieva's (b. 1985) entry onto the literary scene is a public relations team's dream. A native of Makhachkala, capital of the southern Russian republic of Dagestan in the Caucasus Mountains, she moved to Moscow for university and graduated from the prestigious Gorky Literary Institute, where she studied literary criticism—rather than prose fiction. Ganieva submitted *Salam, Dalgat!*—her first novella—for the 2009 Debut Prize, an award given to writers under the age of 25 that routinely sees 50,000 submissions from all over Russia. *Salam, Dalgat!* narrates one day in the life of young Dalgat as he travels around the city and meets with characters from diverse social classes, ethnic groups, religious confessions, and professions. This remarkably mature first story opens at a market that the reader can hear, smell, and feel; Dalgat then attends a literary ceremony, is the victim of a mugging, and witnesses a shooting at a wedding. Ganieva submitted the work under a male pseudonym, so that many assumed that the work was a thinly disguised autobiography of the male protagonist, Dalgat. At the award ceremony, when the winner was announced to be Ganieva's pseudonym, there was tremendous surprise when she stepped forward to accept the prize. As Ganieva said in an interview, "They were expecting some brutal, unshaven guy from the mountains."

Dagestan ("land of the mountains"), a republic in the southernmost portion of the Russian Federation, is situated in the Northern Caucasus region, with Chechnya and Georgia to the west, Azerbaijan to the south, and the Caspian Sea to the east. Makhachkala, the capital city characterized by Ganieva in an interview as "backward and provincial," is located on the sea and stands in stark contrast to the mountains, the nexus of traditional culture in *The Mountain and the Wall*.

Russia formally annexed Dagestan in 1813, following an agreement with Iran, but the resistance against Russian rule, led by Dagestan's Imam Shamil, among others, during the subsequent Caucasian War, forestalled Russia's complete dominion until the 1870s. It is not accidental that the historical Shamil is referenced in the novel's prologue, nor that the main character is named for the historical fighter. Russia's most heterogeneous republic, Dagestan is home to some 30 languages and unique ethnic groups, including Avar, Dargin, Kumyk, Lezgin, and Russian—but none represents a majority. Ganieva herself is an ethnic Avar, but identifies with Russian culture.

Dagestan has been a center of Islam scholastics and culture since the Middle Ages; Muslims today account for more than 80 percent of the population. Officially repressed during the Soviet period, Islam in the Caucasus has witnessed a strong rebirth since the 1990s, and today experiences the same pressures exerted by "fundamentalists" and "religious extremists" (as they are named by some in the novel) that we encounter in other parts of the globe.

In *The Mountain and the Wall* Ganieva imagines what would happen if Russia were to construct a wall to insulate itself from the strife and turmoil of its Caucasian republics, a topic of intense debate within Russia today. What we witness, primarily through the eyes of Shamil, who stands at the intersection of various storylines, is a dystopian vision of chaos and intimidation, demonstrations and mass meetings, women forced to take the veil, street shootings, and the pillaging of museums and cultural institutions. Despite the importance of the wall as plot device and the impetus for the chaos that grips the city, we never see it. Even though Shamil spends the first day at a newspaper in the city and obsessively watches television for news reports, his only source of information is rumor and conjecture. Shamil's friend Arip, freshly arrived from Moscow, also cannot fill him in. Although Arip's bus from Moscow is held up for two hours at the border crossing, he is unable to provide eyewitness testimony about the wall, because the windows on the bus are filthy; all he could see were towers and barbed wire.

The "mountain" of the book's title alludes to the "Mountain of Celebrations," first introduced fleetingly in the prologue as an "enchanted village." The reader witnesses this enchantment in Part I through the eyes of Shamil. He and Arip are hiking in the mountains and come across a village, where they meet an old man who speaks in riddles. He tells them that this is the Mountain of Celebrations (Rokhel-Meer, the same place name given in the prologue), and invites them into his house, where he feeds them. Sleepy after their meal, Shamil and Arip take a nap before meeting the other villagers. But they wake up the next day on the mountainside, no village to be seen, and not knowing how they came to be there. The two men have either shared the same dream, for they both remember the same events, or have both been the objects of the same enchantment. Arip, significantly, at one point denies that this act of enchantment took place, but later recants and assures Shamil that he remembers the peculiar incident. As the reader will see in subsequent episodes, the mountain represents a special locus of history and family, beauty and enchantment.

Shamil's family, like many of the characters in the novel, is originally from the mountains. It is no accident that when the reader is introduced to Shamil he is visiting a mountain village, collecting material for a newspaper feature on the ancient goldsmiths who have plied their intricate craft there for millennia. Shamil is entranced by the fine metalwork, but also connects it to the present—not an unusual jump for a young man. He begins writing his article in his head:

> Religious extremism is on the rise in the Republic of
> Dagestan, claiming more and more victims every day.
> It is at moments like these that you begin to value the

5

power of Dagestani culture. In order to learn the extent to which our traditions still endure, I set out for the village of Kubachi, where the local armorers have been honing their craft for twenty-six centuries.

The cultural repositories in the city are pillaged in an act of religious zeal after the alleged construction of the wall, but the mountains, the originator of this culture, remain a haven for those who flee the city to escape the chaos.

In the prologue, Zumrud recalls the time she spent as a child in her great-grandmother's "mountain home." (Ganieva herself spent her childhood with her grandmother in the mountains before moving to Makhachkala.) Significantly, Zumrud reminisces about village weddings, when the old women would sit on the flat rooftops and observe the dancing. Weddings—a central event in the life of the people of the Caucasus—are a favorite plot device in Ganieva's work, beginning with *Salam, Dalgat!* and including her most recent novel, *The Groom and the Bride*, published in Russia in spring 2015. Weddings proliferate throughout *The Mountain and the Wall*—for example, we observe Shamil's neighbor Kamilla go from the hairdresser to a lavish wedding packed with political and business elites in the city, which is interrupted by these same elites being called away, perhaps in connection with the wall. Another symbol of the changing social fabric and the status of Islam is Madina, Shamil's fiancée, who takes the veil and is married in a religious ceremony to another man without her parents' consent. A counterpoint to both of these weddings is the one recounted in the epilogue, which takes place in the mountains. Moreover, numerous tales are recounted with love as their primary subject—the most poignant of which is the story of Khandulai, the

Black Widow, from Makhmud Tagirovich's novel, which Shamil reads while standing in a neverending line to buy bread.

Interpolated tales provide respite from the dystopian gloom of the narrative—and provide an opportunity for Ganieva to entertain the reader with the introduction of styles and language that fall outside the colloquial idiom of the main narrative. In addition to Makhmud Tagirovich's novel, the longest inserted text, we are given excerpts from his much less successful poem, which freely mixes events of a half-century past with details from the post-perestroika period; and includes this immortal line of which he is inordinately proud: "The cow, a roan, went mincing past, and left a gift upon the path." Tellingly, Shamil reads the novel, still in manuscript, but is ignorant of the poem. Makhmud Tagirovich also retells at a dinner party the story of his namesake's unrequited love for the beautiful Mui, whose well-to-do parents will not permit their daughter to marry the son of a coal miner. "To drown his sorrows," Makhmud enlists in the Dagestan cavalry, comes across a Michelangelo *Madonna with Child,* is stuck by the resemblance to his beloved Mui, and pens the narrative poem *Mariam.* An example from the other end of the spectrum is the schoolbook Shamil happens upon from Soviet times with its admonitions against arranged marriages, praise for collectivization and Soviet contributions to life in the Caucasus, and its picture of the backward and dismal traditional life in the mountains. The diversity of these tales and the styles in which they are told, ranging from socialist realism to fairy-tale pastiche, comment on the histories and fates of Ganieva's characters and Dagestan more generally. The young people in *The Mountain and the Wall* are composite products of these myriad sources, which they must evaluate and balance as they make their way as adults.

The final interpolated text Ganieva introduces is the newspaper of the newly-created Emirate, which Shamil reads by the seaside. The front page features an address by the emir exhorting jihad and martyrdom. Following the quotations from the newspaper, we read: "Shamil set the newspaper aside. Darkness was settling in." Darkness here should be read in two senses, the physical and metaphysical. The darkening skies over Shamil bear witness to the darkening of society and culture in the city. Ganieva, however, does not leave her characters in the darkness that has enveloped the city. Instead, the epilogue brings us back to the mountains—and a wedding. As in the prologue, the women observe the dancing from the flat roof and the songs echo in the snow-capped mountains—a far cry from the ostentatious and showy wedding Kamilla attends in the banquet hall amidst a flurry of hundred-dollar bills. Without advocating a return to the mountain, Ganieva points to the importance of the site for her characters' sense of self and the country's history. Shamil may indeed pursue a career in journalism in the city, but he will surely maintain his family's ties to the mountains, representative of the diversity of cultures that straddle the past and present, urban and rural, modern and traditional, in Dagestan. Ultimately, Ganieva's novel is not about politics, and not about the Caucasus being separated from Russia, but about the fate of her contemporaries, the young people of Dagestan, who both seek to reclaim the traditional past that was obliterated by the Soviet regime and to make their way in the twenty-first century.

Ronald Meyer

Brooklyn, April 2015

PROLOGUE

"Anvar, go get the corkscrew!" yelled Yusup, waving his hand in the air.

Anvar darted into the kitchen and found himself in a cloud of flour. Zumrud stood at the table, shifting a sieve from hand to hand and babbling:

"Can you imagine, Gulya? I've known her for over twenty years—we went to school together. She was always so sarcastic, you know, always had some snappy answer. Ten years ago her husband turned religious, so she divorced him—she wasn't about to change her whole life around on his account. So now I run into her and she goes, 'I went on the *hajj*.' I couldn't believe it. 'Who with?' I ask. 'With my husband,' she says, meaning her ex."

"*Ama-a-an!*" drawled Gulya, settling her plump body more comfortably on her chair and adjusting her colorful sweater.

"She's started praying, keeping *Uraza*. So I go, just joking, 'Why not marry him again, then, if you're getting along so well.' He's got a new wife and children now, but she can be his second wife this time around."

"*Vai*, we've got one of those second wives living across the hall." Gulya flapped her hand in that direction. "Or rather, fourth. She's Russian, a convert to Islam, and now she goes around covered.

Her husband is a big shot at the cement plant. He comes to see her on Fridays, and brings his bodyguard along. Picture this: you open your door in the morning, you're taking out the trash, or you have some shopping to do, and some hulk is waiting out there on the stairway, twitching at the slightest sound. Then the husband shows up. I've never actually seen him in person. But you can tell when he's coming. She goes outside beforehand and licks up every speck of dirt in the entryway…"

"Anvar, that's the wrong drawer," said Zumrud, kneading the dough. "Anyway, Gulya, frankly I don't like it when they start covering themselves up like that…"

"You know, I'm worried Patya is going to start covering herself," grumbled Gulya, smoothing her shimmery skirt. She lowered her voice. "So, this distant relative of ours started coming over, a real shady character. He barraged her with instructions about how young ladies should behave. Patya was already keeping *Uraza*, and then one day she comes home in the rain, crying. She goes, 'I got water in my ears, I've violated the fast.' I really let her have it. 'So don't keep *Uraza*, then' I tell her. 'And don't let me catch you in a hijab!'"

"Where are they getting it all?" asked Gulya, scrunching up her shoulders.

Anvar grabbed the corkscrew and ran back into the living room.

They were telling jokes and laughing. Kerim slid a glass over to big-nosed Yusup and said, "This Avar dreams that he got beaten up, so the next day he takes all his buddies to bed with him for protection."

They poured a round of Kizlyar Kagor wine and clinked glasses. Tall Yusup; bald, bespectacled Kerim; stocky Maga; skinny Anvar…

"So you're not drinking, Dibir?" asked Yusup, addressing a morose-looking man with a bandaged finger, sitting in silence.

He shook his head.

"It's *haram.*"

"It's *haram* to get drunk, I agree, but Kagor isn't a drink, it's a song. Just get a whiff of that bouquet, that flavor. It's medicinal! My mother used to give it to me when I was a boy…small sips, for my heart."

Dibir seemed about to object, but said nothing and just stared at the side table, where a small metal sculpture of a goat stood.

"I remember," began Kerim, smacking his lips and adjusting his glasses, which had slid down his nose, "how we used to work in the vineyards during the Soviet days. We'd do a little work, then someone would turn over a bucket and start beating on it like a drum and the rest of us would dance the lezginka. Usman was still in school back then, he hadn't been expelled yet. He was the biggest drinker of all—he'd get drunk, and then would go around mooching, asking everyone for a ruble."

"Which Usman?"

"What do you mean, which one?" countered Kerim, gesturing with his fork. "The one who became a holy man, Sheikh Usman. After he got expelled, he worked as a welder for a while, then got into selling fur caps or something like that. And now people go to him for *barakat.*"

"*Vakh!*" Yusup was surprised.

Dibir lifted his square face and fidgeted on his chair. He cleared his throat and asked:

"Are you really an atheist, Kerim?"

Kerim dropped his fork and raised both hands in the air:

"That's all, I give up, I'm changing the subject! For the record, I used to give the sheikh his ruble…"

Anvar laughed.

"You know, brother, you have just the same *iblis* inside you as the men hiding in the forest. You're living under an eternal *vasvas*. And what kind of an example are you setting for those two?" Dibir asked through his teeth, nodding in the direction of Anvar and Maga.

"Example?" Kerim spread his arms wide. "Well, I go out and work, for example, while you're sitting around praying."

"Zumrud!" yelled Yusup, anticipating a fight. "Bring some *chudu*!"

Sounds could be heard in the kitchen. Dibir scrutinized Kerim, who had redirected his attention to his eggplants, then whispered "*Bismillah*" and started piling vegetables onto his own plate. The women came in with two steaming platters.

"Let's go work out," Maga whispered into Anvar's ear, twitching his shoulders.

Zumrud saw them in the doorway. "Come back before the food gets cold," she said.

It was already dark in the little inner courtyard. Nothing could be heard from outside the gate, not the shouts of kids playing, nor the usual music, nor the sounds of men greeting one another and clasping hands.

"It's so quiet today," noted Anvar. He sprang up, grabbed the bar with his long arms, and pulled himself up.

"Can you do a flip?" asked Maga.

"Sure, look, I'll do a flip and then a few giant swings," said Anvar enthusiastically, and he began swinging his legs from side to side, warming up.

Maga observed his maneuvers with amusement.

"Hey, you're doing it wrong, let me try."

"I'm not done yet," said Anvar, hanging by one hand.

"Listen, brother, show me your fist!" exclaimed Maga.

"All right," Anvar obeyed, clenching the fist of his free hand.

"Now clench your butthole just like that, *le!*" laughed Maga, shooing Anvar down off the bar.

Then he asked: "So who's that Dibir guy?"

"Friend of the family."

"A Sufi, right? All they do is spout *ch'anda* and then ferret out quotes from the Prophet to justify it," said Maga; after doing a few brisk pull-ups, he sprang down from the bar. "Name's Bashir, he's from our village. He took me to this rock, once. Said it's an *azhdakha.*"

"Which *azhdakha?*"

"I'll tell you: so there's this *ustaz* who tells folktales. In our village, he says, there once lived a *chaban*, a shepherd who took care of people's sheep, and this *azhdakha* started stealing rams from him. Stole one after another. But the shepherd wasn't about to run and hide. Hey, he says, give me back the rams, or people will think I'm falling down on the job or stealing them myself. The *azhdakha* wouldn't budge, no way was he going to give them back. So then the *chaban* took an arrow and shot the *azhdakha*, and the arrow hit him in the torso and came out the other side. The *chaban* went and took back the arrow and asked Allah to turn the *azhdakha* to stone."

"So? It worked? Does the stone look like an *azhdakha*, or something?" asked Anvar, springing back up onto the bar and dangling from it head down.

"There's a hole that runs straight through it. Other than that, no. Bashir believes it, though, he says that the hole is just like an arrow hole…plus, he says, the head fell off afterward anyhow."

"What, hasn't he ever seen any stones in the mountains?" laughed Anvar, still hanging upside down.

"There aren't that many in that area. I told Bashir it's *bida, bida.* So then he started calling me *vakh.* With those Sufis everyone who doesn't believe them is *vakh*."

Sounds came from the house; someone was tuning the *pandur*. Maga got out his phone and squatted on his haunches.

"I'm calling this girl I know."

Anvar tipped his head back, turning his acne-covered face to the sky. The new moon shone faintly overhead, barely illuminating in the darkness the half-finished attic, the lone light fixture by the door, and the clotheslines. A startled bat fluttered upward. Anvar whirled around in a vain attempt to see where it went. Meanwhile, the sounds of the *pandur* inside the house grew louder, sending a folk tune out into the night. Its melody lingered in the air and soon seemed to inflect, in some ineffable way, the entire spirit of the evening. "Interesting," thought Anvar. "To me it's obvious, the connection between the night and the music, but the person actually playing the instrument, and the people in there listening, don't."

"Have you heard about Rokhel-Meer? It's an enchanted village. 'The Mountain of Celebrations!' Now you see it, now you don't. They say...Hello? What's up, how's it going?" Maga interrupted himself, grimaced into the phone, and turned away from Anvar. "Why not? Hey, talk normal...So call some of your girlfriends, and come on out...What's the problem?...I know you inside and out, don't play the nun with me...What do you mean, I'm 'coming on strong?' I'm not coming on strong!...You're the one—you didn't invite me either... You're such a...!'"

Anvar went inside. Yusup was standing by the table, strumming the *pandur*'s two nylon strings and singing. Kerim chimed in, grimacing and exclaiming, "*Ai!*" "*Ui!*" "Oh, man!" and the like. Gulya was reclining on the sofa, her faced flushed; Dibir, deep in thought, was staring at his bandaged finger. Zumrud sat with her eyes closed and gave herself over to the flow of the song, silently flicking her thin fingers and sending up gentle puffs of flour.

Zumrud saw herself as a small child in her great-grandmother's mountain home. Her great-grandmother was ancient; she wore a loose, tunic-like dress, which she tucked loosely into her broad trousers. Her everyday *chokhto*, which draped all the way down her spine, concealed the flat, shaved crown of her head, liberated by right of her advanced age from its decades-long burden of braids. Every day she would go out into the mountains and climb to her meager little plot on the cliffside. In the evening she would come back down, hunched low under a sheaf of hay, her farm tools covered in dirt.

When there was a wedding in the village, Great-Grandmother would sit with the other old women on one of the flat roofs, holding Zumrud on her lap, and they would watch the dancing and listen to the *tamada*'s jokes. Their black robes made the old women look like nuns, but that was where the resemblance ended. They took snuff or even smoked tobacco, and improvised filthy rhyming couplets to one another. In the evenings they would go out visiting, with their grandchildren hoisted onto their backs like bundles of hay or water pitchers.

Zumrud pictured the neighbor's house in her mind. On its broad, thick-carpeted veranda a big loud-voiced old woman sat rocking a homemade wooden cradle with a tightly swaddled baby inside. Zumrud recalled reaching inside and touching the cradle's mattress, noting its strategically placed hole under the baby's bottom; it was stuffed with fragrant herbs, which crackled inside, and a knife was concealed under where the baby's head lay…

The song trailed off, and everyone clapped.

"What was it about, Yusup?" asked Gulya, who couldn't speak Avar.

"The capture of Akhulgo. The storming of Imam Shamil's citadel.

It goes like this: in 1839 the *miurids* held out for nine weeks resisting the Russian army's attacks against the supposedly impregnable cliffs of Akhulgo, but the enemy had too many men and too many cannons… So all the mountain women put on Circassian coats and fought side by side with the men, and mothers slaughtered the babies and cast themselves down into the chasm, so as not to fall into the Russians' hands. And the older children hurled stones at the attackers, and the fortress was taken anyway, but…Brave Shamil didn't fall into the hands of the *kafirs*, though he turned over his favorite son as a hostage. That's a rough translation."

"Back then people had *iman*, not like now," noted Dibir.

"I loved our old singers," said Zumrud, tucking unruly locks of hair behind her ears. "Now, you know, all we have is pop, and all the melodies are stolen."

"Well, I like Sabina Gadzhieva," objected Gulya.

Zumrud waved her hand in the air dismissively: "Oh I can't tell them apart. Sabinas, Malvinas…In the old days people at least had real voices, and singers wrote their own lyrics, from the heart…Now who knows what it means."

"You're never satisfied, Zumrud!" said Gulya, smiling. "How can you stand living with her, Yusup?"

Yusup laughed. "Well, you can't keep her locked up at home."

"You shouldn't need to," said Dibir. "A woman herself should understand that it's not something Allah is forcing upon her—her calling is to take care of her family, so let her stay home and do the right thing of her own free will."

"Dibir, go preach to your own wife," snapped Zumrud, only partly in jest. "I've had enough of these zealots. You can't walk down the street without someone shoving leaflets into your hands—they're even there when you get on the bus, forcing their bulletins on you."

"What bulletins?"

"Yours, Islamic ones," said Kerim. "Yeah, I'm sick and tired of those hawkers. And you can't get rid of them. One time we were sitting in a club, just hanging out and listening to music, nothing special. And all of a sudden this guy shows up. All in white, wearing a green skullcap, and holding a bundle of religious bulletins. Rustam explains to him man to man that his presence isn't really required. So he leaves, or so it seemed. But within an hour he's back. Must have forgotten that he'd already tried us."

"You should have taken one and read it! Might have done you some good!" said Dibir.

Kerim snickered. "It does me good to work out, too, though I haven't done it for a while now...but look, the hows and whens of *namaz* prayer just right aren't really high on my list of priorities. If you ask me it's all *khapur-chapur.*"

"Here you are making jokes, but you won't feel like joking around on Judgment Day," Dibir objected. "You think you're so smart, but it's not enough to study the material sciences. You need to look after your soul as well."

Zumrud went over to the window and opened it. For some reason, the neighborhood was dark; there were no lights on anywhere. It was strangely quiet for that time of evening. Then, suddenly, the sound of barking. Everyone shifted in their seats. Zumrud looked around and saw Abdul-Malik in the doorway. He was in a police uniform and there was a stranger with him, a man of around forty with a mustache. Behind them in the darkness stood Maga.

"*A-a-assalamu alaikum!*" said Yusup cheerfully, standing up to greet the guests.

———

Kerim raised his glass.

"Well, as they say, here's to the Motherland, here's to Stalin! *Sakhl-i.*"

The others joined in the toast, clinking their glasses and exclaiming "*Sakhl'i!*"

"So how are things at the front?" asked Kerim, watching Abdul-Malik serve himself the *chudu* that Zumrud had warmed up for the guests.

Abdul-Malik stiffened, then answered quietly: "May Allah punish those with blood on their hands."

"*Vallakh*, may it be so," repeated Gulya mournfully.

"They think they're so righteous and that we're just filthy *murtads*. And it's absolutely the other way around. Who are the ones sneaking around like jackals, anyway? Shooting people in the back? Mazhid was flagging down a car, and the guys inside opened fire and that was that. And then they came to Dzhamal's house and called to him by name, and when he showed his face they shot him, point blank. They blew up Kurbanov's car. And when Salakh Akhmedov was murdered, his own son was in on the plot. And how about all the cops they've killed? We really made them pay for it in Gubden…I've just come from there."

"I got a call from one of my friends in Gubden," Kerim broke in. "He says that you didn't make much of a dent at all. Just a lot of noise, as usual. While you were storming the building, a whole bunch of people were standing around outside, watching, and the local *Wahhabis* were right there in the crowd. And everyone there knew they were there. After the operation they sat there in the ruins, rehashing the details."

"What do you mean by that?" scowled Abdul-Malik.

"What I mean is that you knew who those guys were just the

same as everyone else, and you didn't make a move. And now you act all surprised."

"We didn't have an order—we can't take anyone without orders. We can't do anything on our own initiative. We're supposed to wait for troops from Moscow," answered Abdul-Malik.

"That's bullshit," said Maga. But no one heard.

"Let the man have his dinner in peace," said Zumrud. "In the meantime I want to make a toast. Here's to me and Gulya still being able to sit here and make toasts!"

Everyone chuckled awkwardly.

Through the clinking of glasses a new sound was heard, something metallic. Anvar, who had dozed off, looked up and saw that the chandelier was trembling. Then silence. Kerim was also looking up at the chandelier; he remembered the great Makhachkala earthquake. He had been just a child then; it all seemed like some great, romantic adventure. It had been exciting to sleep in a tent, to kill time gossiping with Rashid and Tolik, to rush around the town in his baggy Soviet underwear.

Later, when he was a student, Tolik had had gotten interested in minerals, and one autumn Kerim had taken him to his village in the mountains, where there was a big limestone-dolomite ridge. Tolik got on a donkey and rode up to the ridge with a local boy as a guide, inspiring snide commentary at the *godekan*, where the locals sat around for days on end warming themselves under old burkas. When Tolik gathered two bags of mushrooms in the low mountain forest and hung them out to dry on Kerim's veranda, people came over specially to view the strange sight. They didn't eat mushrooms themselves; they thought they were all poisonous.

"I have something to talk to you about, Yusup," said Abdul-Malik, wiping his lips with a napkin. "Nurik here is my nephew, and..."

He nodded in the direction of the taciturn man with the mustache; Yusup went over and sat down next to them.

"It's not a secret, really," began Abdul-Malik in a low voice, fidgeting and lowering his eyes. "It's about Kizilyurt. They're holding elections there for the Oblast Assembly, and they won't register Nurik. They keep coming up with some phony pretext. We have all his papers in order. Yesterday Nurik went to the Board of Elections with his *dzhamaat*, and security wouldn't let them through. A couple of them made it inside somehow, but the officials there ripped up their papers and kicked them back out...A real nightmare, believe me. Our guys lost patience and before you know it things got out of control and people started shooting. One of my cousins was hit in the shoulder, and another one's in the hospital. So then the younger guys decided to set some buildings on fire, and the others barely managed to restrain them. You know our *tukhum* isn't just going to stand by and allow such disrespect."

"*Vakh*, but where was the director at that point?"

"It was his own guards that did it."

"But why?"

"He's got a grudge against me. His nephew was murdered and left in his car, and then his car was blown up by a grenade, and he claims that it was our guys who did it."

Abdul-Malik looked around at the others. The women had gone off somewhere, but Kerim, Dibir, Anvar, and Maga were in the corner arguing about something, jabbing their fingers at the goat sculpture.

"Was his nephew one of the men hiding in the mountains, or what?" asked Yusup.

"He was, and we looked for him everywhere. He had slipped flash drives to some businessmen, you know what I mean. Along the lines of, 'Donate money to jihad or we'll kill you.' Anyway, we finally found the nephew, and when we did, he raised a big stink. Protests, you name it, *ai-ui*, human rights organizations, that kind of thing. And now he won't give Nurik any peace."

Nurik just nodded.

"So what does all that have to do with me?" asked Yusup.

"There's not a lot of time left for registering candidates—we have to hurry. And you know people in city government. Maybe you could put some friendly pressure on them, Yusup. I'd be eternally grateful."

"What people? Where is Kizilyurt? Where's the council?" Yusup spread his arms wide.

"I mean it, I'll do a *magarych*. Go see Magomedov, talk to him, tell him what's going on, say he has to do something, that kind of thing."

Silence. Yusup sat thinking, tapping, his fingers on his sharp knee. Abdul-Malik waited, wiping his face absentmindedly with a napkin. As before, Nurik said nothing.

"We used to find goats like this on the mountain, only they were smaller," they heard Dibir say in the corner. "We found some using a metal detector and made good money selling them. They'd been around five thousand years or something like that."

Kerim went on the attack: "So why did you sell them? Why didn't you take them to a museum?"

"We could have sold them in the museum too, to the director. But he doesn't pay too well, so we found a buyer ourselves, cutting out the middleman, as they say. Besides, if you give them to the museum for a few kopecks, they turn around and sell them to their own buyers for serious money anyway," Dibir explained. "My wife's brother found an old rifle with copper bullets…he took it to the depository and turned it in for free, and then the museum director got himself a new car on what he made from it. So go ahead brother, have *sabur*, why get all worked up about it?"

Yusup got out a second bottle of Kagor and poured a round.

"Of course I'll talk to Magomedov. But I can't promise anything…"

"Why not?"

"I don't have the connections I used to, Abdul-Malik," answered Yusup, offering him a glass. "You should try someone else. Anyway, we have to follow the law. They wounded your relatives, so you need to have them arrested and brought to trial."

"No-o-o." Abdul-Malik shook his head and refused the glass. "I'm not going to drink a toast until you give me your word. I don't need anyone's help with the law. By the way, where was your nephew last week?"

"Which one?"

"The one sitting right over there," Abdul-Malik nodded toward Maga, raising his voice. "Some guy from Kiakhulai insulted him, so he loaded up a bunch of his friends and they drove over from Alburikent in seven cars and three motorcycles. They started beating the guy up, made a lot of noise, bang, bang! and so a whole crowd of the guy's own people came running from Kiakhulai. More shooting, beatings, who knows what. One of our lieutenants tried to break it up and took a bullet in the knee."

"That couldn't have been Maga—he doesn't have a gun"

"How do you know, Yusup? He started the fight, and then he ran away."

Maga overheard them. He made no sign, waiting.

"What's all this *khabary* about you, Maga?" asked Yusup.

"I didn't lay a hand on anyone. We do get into something with the guys now and then, but no way would we gang up on someone twenty to one. I'm no chicken!"

"I'm going to have a word with your father, Maga," threatened Yusup.

"They worked everything out, made *masliat*. But still, none of it was any fun," said Abdul-Malik, getting up from the table.

"Come on, sit down, let's have another drink," Yusup tried to stop him.

"I can't, Nurik and I have a long evening ahead of us," answered Abdul-Malik.

Nurik smoothed down his mustache and rose after his uncle. They said their farewells, clasping hands with everyone. Zumrud came in with a pot of tea, but Abdul-Malik and Nurik were already out the door. Yusup went with them.

"So was there a fight or not?" Anvar asked Maga.

"He's a bullshit artist, that's what he is," said Maga irritably. "It wasn't me who started it, Zapir only called me after they'd already started fighting."

Dibir and Kerim were still standing by the little goat.

"Why are you all so upset?" asked Gulya, sailing into the room in her sparkly sweater.

"Sit down, have some tea," said Zumrud.

Yusup came back in, slamming the door.

"I wanted to see them off, but they wouldn't let me. It's dark out there, I need to change the bulb…"

As though on cue, the chandelier went out, flickered a few times, and then flared on again.

"Must be the wiring," said Kerim, and his glasses flashed.

Dibir looked at the window, saw his square face reflected there, and muttered something.

———

Zumrud sipped strong tea from a hot glass, straining it through a lump of sugar held between her teeth. The others were using gilt teacups. Dibir recalled that he'd seen cups like them in Mecca when he had been there on his first *hajj*. There had been a stampede at the Hajar al-Aswad. Dibir had tried to get close enough to kiss the black stone, but he got a rib broken in the crush. Before his second *hajj*, he went to visit the elder Said Chirkeisky for some words of wisdom. The elder instructed him and the other pilgrims on how to behave in Mecca. Then they all said a *dua* together, kissed the elder's hand, and left...

Anvar found the TV remote and clicked the power button. A local talk show was on.

"Khalid, two hundred inventions, is that a lot for our republic, or not so much?" an imposing-looking hostess in a taffeta skirt was asking a fat, round-faced guest. The guest's mouth was watering and he had to keep swallowing; he was short of breath too.

"None of my inventions are really being used in Dagestan yet, so it's not all that many," answered the man, swallowing. "I invented a mail-phone, a device that you can use to send a letter anywhere in the world. You send the letter, and a minute later the device provides it to the addressee in printed form, in an addressed envelope. The cost is a mere three or four rubles, total, can you imagine? In a regular post office the envelope alone would set you back fifteen rubles! We've got everything ready, patents, everything."

"That's just fabulous. Now what can you tell us, Khalid, about your theory of gravity?" asked the hostess, smiling.

The studio audience was getting restless. Some guy in an expensive jacket had his legs stretched out and was tapping his cellphone with a stylus.

A middle-aged woman was inspecting her shoes, which had big ribbons glued on them. The guest swallowed again and said:

"Well, Newton thought that gravity depends on mass, that space is full of ether. Einstein said that the curvature of space determines gravitational pull. I don't agree with them. Space is not empty. What generates the so-called force of gravity is the struggle between two kinds of matter—I won't go into the details now. But here's what's interesting: my son has found confirmation of my theory in the Koran. I had been skeptical about the divine nature of the Koran, but when I saw that *sura*, I was blown away. Overjoyed! So during the holy month of Ramadan my son and I started working on this hypothesis, we studied the *ayats*. And we proved that what we see in space isn't emptiness but a primeval field that exerts pressure on a body, which is agitated by this imposition, and seeks to return to its original state of rest. This is the origin of the forces of attraction and of inertia, this is why everything in this world is in constant motion! Since our treatise was published, no one has been able to refute our theory. Not a single person! And, you know, we went back to the Koran and discovered all the foundations of Creation there, everything: protons, neutrons, the structure of the electron…"

"So you've refuted Einstein—but why then is your discovery still considered a fringe theory, peripheral to mainstream science?" asked the hostess.

"What people say is that it's all just a hypothesis, that there's no proof. My answer is that the proof is there already in the Koran. I'm not one of them, see—I'm not a member of the scientific establishment, so no one wants to promote my work—no surprises there of course. First the Almighty bestowed a hundred inventions on me in the course of a single year, and only then did He give me the inspiration for our book, so that no one could say that I'm just some kind of charlatan…"

"Thank you, Khalid Gamidovich, we hope that your discovery of the scientific potential of the Koran, and your book *The Scientific Potential of the Koran*, will be taken to heart by readers around the world. And that's our program for today, thank you, viewers."

Applause was heard in the studio, followed by saxophone music and the credits. Dibir chuckled approvingly: "Good for him!"

"What a smart guy!" declared Maga.

Kerim shook his head darkly. "Why do you listen to that stuff?"

"What do you mean? You prefer Einstein to the word of Allah?" Anvar asked, not entirely serious.

"What I prefer is meat with *khinkal*," replied Kerim.

The logo for the next program appeared on the screen. Two men in skullcaps were sitting at a table in the studio, one stouter and somewhat older, the other a young man. They began with Muslim greetings. Anvar turned down the volume. Zumrud asked Yusup:

"That Nurik who was here, who is he, Abdul-Malik's nephew?"

"Yes," answered Yusup. His mind was elsewhere.

"Whose son is he, Leila's?"

"I suppose."

Yusup was thinking about how Abdul-Malik might be able to help Anvar get a job. Of course he'd already been asking around, checking out various agencies. Wherever he went, the going rate for bribes was different. Zubairu was asking 300,000 for a position in the prosecutor's office, but Zubairu was a friend, so they'd be able to work something out. Plus, he needed to save money so he could finish the addition. The ideal thing, of course, would be to call Khalilbek himself, but Khalilbek was flying so high these days, it wasn't that easy to get his attention…

The younger man on the screen was looking down at a piece of paper. "Here's a question from Khasavyurt: Alzhana asks, 'Can you pray with your eyes closed?' No, Alzhana, that is not recommended. Muzalipat from Kaspiisk writes: 'I have been married several times. Which of my husbands will I be with in Paradise?' Here's your answer, Muzalipat. If you're married when you die, then you will be in Paradise with your last husband. If your last husband dies and you do not remarry, then you will also end up in Paradise with your last husband. If all of your husbands divorced you, then on Judgment Day you will have the right to choose any one of them, and according to the hadiths, you will choose the one with the best character. And may the Almighty Allah aid you! And now we have a call in the studio. Hello, you're on the air."

"Hello, my name is Eldar, I'm from Babayurt." The voice on the line sounded uneven. "Here's my question: I got some of my baby's urine on my clothes. How should I wash it out?"

"What is your advice for Eldar?" The younger man turned to his senior colleague, who had been silent up to that point. "It all depends on whose urine it is," said the man, with great dignity. "If it's a boy's, under the age of two, then you can use plain water. If it's a girl's urine, however, then you need to wash it with great care..."

Anvar couldn't take any more, and clicked the TV off.

They drank their tea in silence. Anvar slurped from his saucer. Maga sat on the sofa with his legs crossed Turkish style, scratching his head. Kerim inspected the faded tapestry on the wall: a herd of deer drinking from a stream; behind them rose the tree-covered slope of a mountain. Kerim looked at the mountain's rocky crest and noticed for the first time that the rocks looked like an abandoned village. He had the feeling that he had been there before.

"No, he's not Leila's son," said Zumrud suddenly. Evidently she was still thinking about Nurik. "Leila has a daughter who's a student in Rostov, but her son is still very small. He's just had his *sunnat*. So Nurik is probably, what's her name, Zharadatka's son."

"How old is Zharadat?" Kerim was surprised. "She's not all that much older than I am, how could she have a son that big? Their mother was a teacher in my school—she used to ask me all the time, 'Are you going to marry Zharadatka? Are you going to marry Zharadatka?'"

Gulya laughed.

"What do you mean, a teacher? Are you talking about Aminat Pakhrimanovna?"

"Yes, the one who died."

"Really?"

"That's right," Zumrud agreed. "Aminat Pakhrimanovna's mother was from Gidatl, from a good family. One day she was out working in the field, and a man from the Urmin foothills came by on horseback. No match for anyone from Gidatl. He liked what he saw and grabbed her arm—was going to take her away with him. She wasn't too happy about it, so she reached for the knife that she kept stashed in a pouch in her *chokhto*…"

"On her head, you mean?"

"Yes, that's where they used to carry their knives, I think. Anyway, she stabbed this Urmin, and if he had died, then according to the *adats* she could have been exiled from her home village. But the Urmin survived and went back to his foothills. That wasn't the end of it, though. He sent a gang of his friends, and they managed to abduct her from that same field. She lost all of her rights, started having babies and weaving mats from swamp sedge. What are those things called? *Chibta*, is it?"

"You're getting it all mixed up, Zumrud," Kerim objected. "That's not what happened."

Yusup raised his head and interrupted: "That Nurik is probably Adik's son. Adik, the scholar, the one who died. I have some of his books in the other room…"

"Do you mean Adilkhan?" Dibir corrected him, flexing his hand—the one with the bandaged finger. "No-o-o, I know Adilkhan's sons. One of them, *alhamdulillah*, is the imam of the Urmin mosque. He and I went to the *madzhlis* at Buinaksk together. The other one, I think his name is Abdullah, is a lot younger: He's still doing his military service."

"Is there a third son?" asked Maga.

"Not that I know of."

There was another pause. The *pandur*, neglected on the sofa, tumbled to the floor with a hollow, stringy thud. Kerim picked it up and, bending over and showing his bald spot, strummed the strings a few times with his hairy hand. Then he tossed his head back, a blob of light flashing across his glasses, and said:

"Wait, Abdul-Malik doesn't have a nephew named Nurik!"

———

Before anyone could say anything, there was a rumbling outside on the street, and they heard a voice booming through a megaphone:

"Attention, your house is surrounded! Everyone inside, come out with your hands up! There are armed terrorists with you! You have three minutes! Three minutes. Come out one by one, single file!"

Yusup sat frozen in place. Zumrud's hands rose to her mouth. Dibir looked over at Maga. Maga bounded to the window and peered out from behind the curtain, trying to see through the gloom. Gulya's teacup slipped out of her hand; tea spilled onto her shimmery skirt, and from there trickled onto the floor, making a thin, watery sound. Kerim's face went white, and his hands fumbled with the *pandur*.

The light went out.

Anvar turned toward the wall and slipped his hand under his shirt.

PART I

I

Shamil had arrived in the goldsmiths' village several days before. It was already scorching hot on the Caspian but here in the foothills the evenings were cool. Shamil would throw on a parka that Mirza, his host, had lent him, and would go out walking along the crooked, winding streets of the village, peering into its inner courtyards, archways, tunnels, and under its stone stairways. Occasionally he would encounter a person whose features would be indistinguishable in the darkness and they would clasp hands and exchange a quiet greeting. Now and then he would come upon an old round fortress tower, which had been shortened many years ago and now served as a dwelling, but more often he would leave the settlement behind, descend the hill, and stare up at the houses clustered on top of one another like a beehive on the mountainside.

Shamil told no one about the rumors that were swarming through the city. Here they seemed like the ravings of a madman. Still, at night he would toss and turn in his bed in the hospitable goldsmith's home, alternatively worrying about when he would have to go back to Makhachkala, and wondering why he was even here.

After he lost his job at the committee where his uncle Alikhan worked, Shamil had eagerly seized this opportunity to visit the Kubachi armorers and write about their art. He had never tried his hand at serious writing, but his brother-in-law, who worked at one of the Dagestani newspapers, had entrusted the assignment to him without a moment's hesitation. Everyone from Shamil's *tukhum* was a good writer, so he figured he'd be able to handle it, the interviews at least.

Every house in the settlement turned out to be a treasure trove, stuffed with antique minted plates, inlaid weapons, gold and silver engraved dishes, fantastical *kumgan* water jugs, filigreed knickknacks, and domed copper kettle lids in the shape of helmets. Wherever Shamil went, he stumbled onto carved stone fireplaces, precious ornamented tableware, pistols with gold crosshatched designs of interwoven stems and leaves, and mother-of-pearl horns bearing metallic patterns. The families had kept the most valuable heirlooms in their private collections. What they sold were souvenir daggers, simple silver earrings, and jangly bracelets.

During the day Shamil would observe Mirza in his workshop, carving meticulously into silver with a burin. He would talk with the men at the *godekan* or visit the cemetery to inspect the ancient images carved on the stone slabs. He already had a good idea of what he would write in his article: "Religious extremism is on the rise in the Republic of Dagestan, claiming more and more victims every day. It is at moments like these that you begin to value the power of Dagestani culture. In order to learn the extent to which our traditions still endure, I set out for the village of Kubachi, where the local armorers have been honing their craft for twenty-six centuries. This region never had much arable land; instead of farming and gardening, the townspeople made plate armor and chain mail, kettles and stirrups, swords and spears. In the nineteenth century, the mountain armorers' fame spread throughout all of Russia and the East. Connoisseurs and collectors came and bought up the precious objects. The craftsmen here have told me that practically no Kubachi-made weapons or armor remain in the village; the majority of these were sold after the Russian Civil War under slogans like 'Beat swords into plowshares!' and 'Down with the dagger!' The last few daggers disappeared during the Great Patriotic War. Nevertheless, according to the master engraver Mirza Mirzaev…"

Here Shamil's thoughts became confused. He remembered the conversations he had heard over the local forges. Mirza and the other Kubachi artisans talked about the ongoing attempts to privatize the local craftsmen's guild; about the mercenary mindset of the young, who had begun turning out masses of primitive trinkets; about the decline of their intricate and esoteric craft. But Shamil's brother-in-law wanted an uplifting article, so Shamil decided to skip the moaning and gnashing of teeth.

For the ninth of May celebration of the Soviet victory over Hitler, the village went all out. They put on their grandfathers' jackets, studded with medals, and took up their Russian flags as well as the red flags from their museums. The young villagers draped their cars in colorful scarves, then paraded around the village, honking loudly. In the lead rode a motorcyclist, followed by an old military jeep with some young guys sitting in the open cab, firing their guns into the air; after them came a noisy, colorful parade of cars, with passengers leaning out of the windows.

They made twenty or so circuits around the village, then dismounted at Magara, the central marketplace, where again they fired off their automatics and danced the *Akushinskaya*. Then they visited the memorial pillar with its list of villagers who had given their lives in the Great Patriotic War, and again fired their guns. Afterward everyone gathered for a picnic on a green mountain slope outside the village.

The women came in their scarves and sweeping velvet and brocade dresses embroidered and decorated with coins. Shamil couldn't understand the goldsmiths' speeches, and the women's long, white, gold-embroidered *kaz* scarves were strange and exotic to him. A drummer and accordion player performed while people danced in pairs, one hand pressed to their chests or necks and the other bent behind their backs. The men drank continually but didn't get drunk. They spoke in Kubach, now and then switching to Russian for Shamil's sake. Mirza threw his arm around Shamil's shoulders and shouted "*Derkhab!*" Toward evening a fog rolled in and they all made their way home in a procession down the rough unpaved road, passing newly constructed buildings with all their windows and doorframes painted the same shade of blue.

In the village the festivities continued. At Mirza's house they ate local dumplings. They told Shamil about the last wedding that had been held in the village, when the kids had worn costumes and terrifying masks and had run amok, as local custom prescribed, carrying utensils out of people's houses and hiding them, making obscene gestures, and playing practical jokes on the wedding guests. Then the conversation turned to the subject of the jewelers' craft. How the people in the village had begun to make "antiques."

"You take an oil lamp," said Mirza, "and bury it in the earth for two years. It'll come out looking like an antique. Our master craftsmen could fake anything you wanted: Imperial medals, an eighteenth-century Persian vase. You could take it to the Hermitage and they'd believe you. Then you'd show them our craftsmen's brand and they'd laugh. 'Kubachi jokes,' they'll say."

Then they retold their grandfathers' stories about how Kubachi antiques were sold abroad before the Revolution. The ancient walls of the village were inset with a multitude of stones with interesting relief designs: fantastical, mythological figures, birds and animals and battles and scenes from everyday life, all encrusted with pewter and semiprecious stones. On moonlit nights, enterprising tradesman would pry stones out of the walls and bury them in some secluded place. They'd wait a couple of years, then send them to buyers abroad. Entire buildings had been dismantled in this way.

The conversation at Mirza's was accompanied by frequent cries of "*Derkhab!*" Many crystal shot glasses were emptied before they finally called it a night. Shamil lay in bed and let his mind wander. He and Uncle Alikhan would get their jobs on the committee back. Shamil would finish the renovations on the apartment and would finally marry Madina. Maybe he would buy her that huge silver ring that he had seen in one of the workshops today. Shamil's head sank heavily to one side and he fell asleep.

…waking in Makhachkala, in an alley near the shore. Cement dust rose in a column above the street, blinding him; there was a buzzing in his ears. Up ahead a man was running, showing the rubber soles of his shoes. Shamil ran after him, slipping on plastic bags scattered on the ground. Rounding the turn, he saw several more people running. On a rooftop someone was shouting hoarsely, "*Tokhta! Tokhta!*" Behind them something heavy lumbered across the roof, sending tiles crashing to the ground, but the people ran on, seeking shelter from whatever it was making that terrible roar. Shamil rounded one last corner, then heard nothing more.

…sitting up abruptly in bed and looking through the small, uncurtained window in Mirza's parlor. Lightning streaked across the night sky. Shamil got up cautiously and crept into the next room, where huge bronze plates hung on the walls. They swayed slightly, sending out a barely audible ringing. Shamil stood still for a minute, then went back into the parlor and sat down on the carpet. Intermittent flashes of lightning illuminated the copper, porcelain, ceramic, and brass bowls, saucers, and cups on the wall. Enormous three-legged wedding kettles made by local craftsmen lined the other wall: on the shelves stood human-shaped *muchalas* with lids like shaggy Caucasian wool hats, *nuknus* flour vessels, and other whimsical containers. On the floor between the carved hearth and the carpet, Shamil could see stone mosaic tiles with limestone caulking. Tomorrow he was leaving for the city; he needed to get some sleep. He scratched himself behind the ear and went back to bed.

2

The next day around noon Shamil went to the paper's editorial office. His brother-in-law—his elder sister's husband—met him in the sunlit corridor, looking anxious. They went straight to the conference room, a narrow hall filled with some forty people, all of them trying to out-shout one another. Shamil didn't immediately recognize the people sitting around the oval conference table, which was equipped with microphones. These were members of the editorial board, representatives of the business and academic worlds, and a couple of deputies from the National Assembly. At first nothing could be made out in all the commotion. A man in a beige jacket with a mass of unruly hair falling over his forehead was yelling:

"Not a single government agency has confirmed this information! Not a single one!"

A young man with a protruding lower lip was waving his hands in the air and looking around at the people sitting beside and behind him.

"What do you mean, not a single one? Just look at the Internet! I got a call today from Mineralnye Vody—they're building a concrete wall up there!"

Shamil looked around for his brother-in-law, but he was already making his way to the table, shouting stubbornly:

"Let Sharapudin Muradovich speak! Give Sharapudin Muradovich the floor!"

At last the room fell silent and everyone looked at a bald man who stood with his plump fingers pressed firmly onto the polished tabletop.

"All of you, every one in this room, is being duped—it's pure provocation!" he began, swallowing the endings of his words. "Listen to me, Where did this unverified information come from? Instead of sowing panic in the population, we need to—hear me?—need to deal with the ringleaders, the liars and conspirators who are spreading these rumors. Give me a crack at them, I'll tear their heads off with my bare hands!"

"Sharapudin Muradovich, what do you mean, 'unverified?'" A solidly built bleach-blonde demanded from the corner.

The bald man frowned, then turned toward her, lifting his hands from the table and waving them in the air: "Where are you getting this nonsense! Listen to me! The information I have is absolutely reliable. I'm on the phone with Moscow every minute! The Caucasus is Russia's primary defense in the struggle against terrorism, it's a buffer, hear me? A wellspring of democracy! What wall? You really believe that Internet-schminternet?"

Shamil leaned against the conference-room wall, which was warm in spite of the air conditioning. It felt as though the vague sense of apprehension that had been bothering him recently was beginning to crystalize. The contours of this mythological wall, rising inexorably on the border with the purpose of isolating the Caucasus from Russia, began to take on a frightening clarity in his imagination.

"If that's the way it is, then it's our own fault," said a thin man with birthmarks on his face, gesticulating wildly. "We didn't say a word when they started bringing in *Salafi* literature by the truckload. When they murdered our politicians, everyone knew who was responsible, and no one said a word! I'm telling you, not a word! And if the police can go around breaking the law…"

"What do the police have to do with it?" A stout man in a blue police shirt asked, leaping to his feat. "What kind of *khapur-chapur* is that? Why change the subject? When have the police ever broken the law?"

"I'm not about to go down the list," the skinny man tried to backtrack, gesturing grandly at the policeman.

"And where are you getting this garbage?"

"It's in the papers."

"So everything you read in the papers is true?"

The man in the beige jacket swept his mop of hair back from his forehead and raised his palms in an effort to calm things down.

"Friends, friends, let us have *sabur*. I've already told you that no one in Moscow has confirmed the rumors…"

"They haven't, but ordinary people have," the young man butted in, poking his lower lip out even more.

"Even if it *is* true," continued the man in beige, his palms still raised in the air, "our friendship with Russia will continue. They keep saying that we're a subsidized region. But look, so long as we don't have to pay any taxes, we can always feed ourselves. We have oil and gas, and there's copper in the south. We're a transport hub between Europe and Asia, we have a seaport that's open year round, pipelines, hydroelectric plants, heavy industry, wineries, fisheries. We're the country's number-one producer of cheese and vegetables. Not to mention the resorts: balneo—...balneotherapeutic and mud spas, beaches, mountain resorts—whatever you want, we have. Handmade carpets, lumber, ceramics by the truckload! No other republic comes close, not a single one!"

"Shamil Magomedov has just come back from Kubachi, where he was interviewing the craftsmen there," interjected Shamil's brother-in-law.

"There you go!" The man in beige said triumphantly. "How are our artists doing up there?"

"They used to make arms, real ones, but now they've started mass-producing souvenirs. Soon there won't be anything left of any value," answered Shamil without smiling.

"On the other hand, they'll get their goods onto the international market and establish trade relations." The man in beige cleared his throat. "And what about the wine industry? We produce ninety percent of the cognac in Russia—the Kremlin's entire stock of alcohol is made up of Dagestani spirits!"

"This is no time to be talking about booze," boomed a stone-faced man in a skullcap.

"Let me finish," the man in beige shook his forelock.

But the stone-faced man, his focus on something in the empty air above everyone's heads, continued: "The way you're talking now, we're supposedly going to become big oil magnates. But what makes *umma* is not oil, but faith. Maybe things here will get like they are in Chechnya: if you take a second wife, you get a one-room apartment, and if you take a third, then you get a two-room apartment. But the way things are here now, everyone condemns you for taking a second wife, and meanwhile they spend all their time at the saunas, *astauperulla*. If Moscow turns away from the Muslims of Dagestan, then what they'll do is close ranks around *tariqat*, the pathway to Allah. The people who are ruining Islam need to be told, in the words of one wise sheikh, 'Leave the forest to the wild beasts and come and join the people.' Those who have strayed need to be brought to the true faith, may the Prophet have mercy on them, *salallakhu alaikha vassalam*. School-children need to be set on the path of true knowledge. But instead they're being taught that human beings descended from the apes. What normal man would believe that? The almighty Allah began Creation with the human race, with Adam, *aleikhi salam*, made him out of red, white, and black clay. From his left rib Khava was created, and from them originated all life on earth. All the prophets, begin-ning with Adam, have brought us Islam—that is, *tawhid*, monotheism. And Allah accepts no other religion but this one. The Russians will leave, and there will come *fitna*, a time of troubles. Some who have strayed from the path call it *gazavat*, but they haven't a clue what *gazavat* really is. May Allah protect us from those who cause trouble for its own sake. The main thing is to teach our neighbors what's right, every single day. If you yourself perform *dua*, but your neighbor drinks, you must teach him. Otherwise in the next world he will tell the angel, 'Do not take me down to hell, take my friend, who failed to teach me.' And you will have to answer for the sins of your neighbor."

"What on earth are you talking about?" The bleach-blonde in the corner sprang up from her seat. "We've been betrayed, the trap has snapped shut on us—you can do whatever you want, but what do we have to be glad about?"

"Khadizha, get a hold of yourself," Shamil's brother-in-law tried to rein her in.

But she went on: "People say they aren't going to let anyone out, but my brother in Rostov has a wife and children, how is he supposed to get back home to them? You don't have anything to worry about," she said, addressing the stout policeman, "they'll airlift you to Turkey in a helicopter, but what about the rest of us?"

"Why pick on me? And what does Turkey have to do with anything?" he retorted. "Know your place, woman! Look at her, popping up like a *shaitan*, foaming at the mouth…"

"What are you afraid of?" the man in beige shouted to her.

"Those women in veils!"

The stone-faced man blinked his right eye: "It's because of those rabble-rousers discrediting Islam…"

"But they say that the ones discrediting Islam are you and the entire Muslim Spiritual Administration," the young man with the lip jumped in again.

Everyone went back to shouting at once.

Shamil went out into the hot corridor and flexed his shoulders, as though trying to shrug off what he had been hearing. Then he got out his phone and poked at the buttons. Uncle Alikhan didn't answer. He then tried his friend Arip, who worked in Moscow, but no luck there either. From the conference hall Shamil could still hear a chaos of voices, with Sharapudin Muradovich's hoarse bass the loudest of them all.

Shamil hesitated for a moment, then stepped outside. Everything still looked the same as ever. He took in the narrow intersection where cumbersome transport taxi-vans were beeping stridently, then at some girls, chattering and laughing, who were clustered around the entrance to an ugly glass-fronted building featuring a multitude of fashion posters and shop signs, then at a bread-seller's stall, with a head wrapped in a scarf poking out. The head shouted something to a gaggle of barelegged boys who were running in the direction of a wooden fence covered with ads that had been built around an abandoned construction site. Cheerful shrieks could be heard from behind the fence; a huge puddle had formed in the excavation pit, and enterprising neighborhood kids had turned it into an improvised swimming pool and were splashing around. Across the street from the editorial office stood a row of brightly colored private cottages and crooked white huts, on one of which someone had scrawled a note in charcoal: FLOUR FOR SALE.

Shamil turned the corner and went up to a table under a canopy where a woman sat limply, half-stupefied by the hot sun, selling kvass. He bought a big plastic glassful for a few ten-ruble coins, and walked over to a sun-scorched flower bed. Nearby stood a faded acacia tree, casting a meager shadow on the multicolored sidewalk slabs.

He sat down under the acacia on a bench covered with graffiti scrawled in black marker, sipped his kvass and stared thoughtfully at the street. In spite of the heat, a lot of people were outside, and the scene was alive with sound. Music blared from the little coffee shops and mixed with the buzzing of a chainsaw, the excited shouts of passersby, and the chirping of locusts. Shamil tried dialing Uncle Alikhan again, again with no success. "What am I so scared of?" he asked himself, straightening up in his seat.

He didn't want to go back to the editorial office, especially since he figured he would be getting a regular job soon. Omargadzhi had told him that he would see what he could find out about a good position for him that might be opening up in the courthouse. Shamil gulped down the rest of his kvass, crushed the plastic cup, and looked around for a trash can. Failing to find one, he left the cup on the bench. He had to see Omargadzhi right away. He stood up and started off in the direction of the waterfront, where a number of lawyers' offices clustered in old, moldy-smelling wooden courtyards.

Turning down one of the streets there, Shamil ran into Khabibula. Khabibula gave a little hop for joy, jiggling his big barrel-shaped belly, beamed, baring rows of gold teeth, and started babbling: "*Salam,* Shamil! Where are you headed? I've just gotten back from the *kutan,* I brought back milk, cottage cheese, and some other stuff. *Vallakh,* I didn't want to go, wanted to send Marat, but I had no choice. Look at the shape my shoes are in!" he said, gesturing at his tattered sandals. "I'm going to sell the milk and cheese and then I'll buy some shoes, a brand-new pair. Salimat will yell at me, but is it my fault? I tore them today, walking around the city. They're replacing the pipes on our street, there's mud everywhere, and sharp stones... Why not come along with me, my friend—where are you headed in such a hurry?"

"I'm going to see Omargadzhi, to ask him about a job."

"Which Omargadzhi? K'Iurbanizul Omargadzhi?" Khabibula chuckled gleefully, wiping his wrinkled mouth as he walked. "He came to see me at the tenth *kutan:* I beat him at chess twenty times! Twenty! When he sees me now, he takes off running..."

"Have you heard the rumors, Khabibula?" asked Shamil, slowing down and trying to match his steps to his companion's short stride.

"What rumors? Oh, you must mean about Mesedu's roof tiles being blown down in Shamkhal? Sure I have. Salimat told me. She should have asked me to install the tiles—if she had, nothing would have happened. I really put them up to stay, just ask Magomed. But Zapir, Paizulla's son, she asked him to do it. That's why..."

"No, not about Mesedu," Shamil waved his hand. "It's something else. They say we're being walled off from Russia. Border troops, you name it. Like the Berlin Wall."

They stopped at a crossroads, jammed with honking cars. Faces poked out of the car windows, frowning, and arms waved wildly in the air. Young pedestrians crowded on the curbs, photographing the traffic with their cellphones. Khabibula gestured toward his ears to show that he couldn't hear anything above the traffic noise.

"*Le*, where are they all going?" he asked, perking up at the sight. "Just look at them!"

"Must be road work up ahead."

"Come on, my friend," Khabibula proposed again. "I'll give you some cottage cheese…What's this about a wall?"

"Supposedly they're building a wall in the north, to cut us off," repeated Shamil, reluctantly.

"*Ai, astauperulla*," laughed Khabibula, "Forget about that *khapur-chapur* of yours! What are you talking about? Have you been visiting the newspaper? It's those journalists of yours making it all up. Here's our turn."

He waved his plump hand toward a long, cluttered street, littered with private shops.

"I can't, but look, don't take it the wrong way—I'll come by later, Khabibula," Shamil smiled. "I swear—but not right now."

"When can you? I have to go back to the *kutan*," his companion answered briskly and straightened his cheap shirt over his big belly.

"Maybe tomorrow," Shamil promised vaguely, looking back at the honking cars.

"I'll be expecting you!" cried Khabibula with a smile, giving him his hand. "See you then, my friend."

And off he went, limping and shuffling lightly in his tattered sandals. Shamil turned back in the other direction and followed the crowd.

"*Le*, what's going on there?" he asked a young man who was running past.

"Some kind of demonstration, I think," the man said hastily, glancing sideways at Shamil as he ran, then immediately dissolved into the mob. The Dagestani national anthem buzzed in Shamil's pocket, and he eagerly pressed his phone to his ear.

"*Salam aleikum*, Uncle Alikhan!"

"*Vaaleikum salam*, Shamil." His uncle's voice was hollow and hesitant. "I saw your calls, but couldn't answer, there's a meeting going on here in the Ministry. Have you already heard about it, about the wall?"

"Yes, they were talking about it at the paper."

"They say it's true…" Uncle Alikhan breathed heavily into the phone. "We'll be making a decision…The separatists are gathering there to talk about it too, looks like."

"At the Kumyk Theater?" asked Shamil, watching the young people flowing in a smooth stream into the square, heading toward the theater, a semicircular building with an elaborate façade.

"I'm not sure. Where are you right now?"

"I'm here too."

"You shouldn't be standing around there—anyway, we don't really know yet ourselves, we're trying to figure it out. Farid from the government, the one who…"

His uncle's voice cut out. Realizing that he'd lost the connection, Shamil put the phone back in his pocket and took a look around.

3

People flowed in from the side streets, and their bright T-shirts painted the square in a blurred, ever-changing play of color. Shamil stood on tiptoe and saw a group of people clustered around the theater entrance, where a man stood with a megaphone. He was speaking in Kumyk, and it was impossible to make out what he was saying. Shamil wedged himself through the crowd. Gradually he began to catch individual words. The crowd exclaimed approvingly:

"*Tiuz! Tiuz!*"

Then a man with a mustache took the megaphone and began to speak.

"*Aziz yoldashlar*! We've been hearing rumors that there's going to be a new government. What's going on? Why? Those *khakims* have closed themselves off in the government and decided, without consulting us, that the Kumyks are peaceful, the Kumyks will put up with anything, they can be removed from power without any fuss…"

The crowd buzzed.

"How were things before? The Avars and Dargins had the most powerful positions in the Republic's government, and they gave us the third place. And we always agreed to that. And now what? They want to change everything! Here in our homeland we always lived together with the Russians like this…" The man with the mustache clasped his palms tightly together. "…in peace! And then the others came down from the mountains and what happened? The Russians left…"

Indistinct shouts were heard from the front rows. All Shamil could make out was the word "Wall."

The man with the mustache shook his head: "I don't know a thing! Nothing at all! They're not telling us anything! One day I hear 'There's a Wall,' the next day, 'There's no Wall.' All I know is that everything is all mixed up." The man rubbed his palms together. "They want to divide everything up themselves, and keep the people out of it."

The crowd again moaned and stirred. Another man took the megaphone. He was draped in a green cloth with a slogan stamped on it, "*Tenglik*," in huge black letters.

"They're trying to force us into secondary roles! But who was the first to make peace with Russia? The Kumyks. Who suffered most of all during the Civil War? The Kumyks. Who gave more sons to the Great Patriotic War than anyone else? The Kumyks. Who revolutionized agriculture? The Kumyks. And what do we have now? They took our ancestral lands. We've lost nearly all our arable land! Do you see Kumyks at the bazaars? Not a single one! Do you see our traditional crafts anywhere? Nowhere! We've closed our eyes to it until now, because we're a wise people. But we can't put up with it anymore. I'm telling you, it's time..."

The square filled with sound, including, for some reason, shouts of *"Allahu akbar!"*

"It is time to liberate the plains from the usurpers, it is time to unite with our Turkic brothers," roared the speaker. "Long live the Kumyk republic!"

Shamil looked around. The square fell silent for a moment, then came back to life, chanting "Kumykstan! Kumykstan!"

Meanwhile a neatly dressed man with a round white beard mounted the steps to the theater entrance. He waited for the shouting to die down, gave the crowd some unintelligible greeting, then began to speak in a resonant, confident voice, glancing down now and then at some notes on a piece of paper.

"You were saying just now that Moscow gave us land, and that the Tarkov chiefs, our leaders in the past, had a good relationship with Moscow...But let us remind ourselves what that means. What exactly is Moscow—who are the Rus? The Rus are Varangians, and the Varangians are Turkic Kipchaks—they wouldn't have a language or a culture if it wasn't for us! It was the Turks, together with Attila, who brought literacy, metalworking, and the plow to Scandinavia.

It was the Turks who gave Rus the alphabet. Cyril and Methodius were our own blood brothers, who converted the ancient Turkic runic alphabet into European letters and who devised the Glagolitic script, which had forty sounds—the exact number our language needs. And Christianity? The Patriarchal seat of the Eastern Church was located in Derbent as far back as the fourth century, and it was there that the Turkic clergy ordained the Georgian, Albanian, Syrian, Coptic, and Byzantine priests! In the Middle Ages, Desht-i-Kipchak was the biggest country in the entire area of what is now Russia. The Russian ruling elite and nobility were Turks who spoke their native language. Take the word bathhouse—*banya*—know what that is? It's *bu-ana!*—our steam room. The Turks reigned for centuries in Kiev, till the Slavs swarmed over the city wearing animal skins, and the ancient state fell to ruin. Now our *kurgans* have been destroyed, our steppe plowed over, our cemeteries defiled. But we will not lose hope! We will take up the blue and yellow Khazar flag, will add the green of Islam, and make a new banner for the free Kipchak Steppe!"

The crowd erupted in delight, and voices called out: "To the Government House! To the Government!" The crowd lurched, heaved, and headed off in the direction of the main square, with the megaphone still roaring in the background. People shouted excitedly in Kumyk and jostled Shamil from behind. He retreated to the tall parapets adjacent to the Caspian Beer Hall and then began to push through the crowd, against its flow, toward the waterfront. Waves of humanity washed over him, pressed him up against a stone pillar, and finally tossed him out onto the steps leading to the embankment.

Lost in thought, Shamil wandered around the withered flowerbeds and blue spruce trees, passing the same corner several times. Then the yellow tank of a kvass stand caught his eye, and he went over to buy a glass.

"What's all the fuss about?" asked the bored-looking, disheveled salesgirl, nodding in the direction of the Kumyk Theater.

"*Khabary*," answered Shamil. "There's a rumor that we're going to be walled off from Russia. Now the Kumyks are all worked up—they want their native lands returned to them."

"*Ma!*" exclaimed the salesgirl, raising one plucked brow skeptically.

"It wasn't enough for those people from the lowlands to destroy the Union," Shamil heard a raspy voice behind him.

He turned and saw two old men in white Panama hats. The one to whom the voice evidently belonged slowly unfolded a checkered handkerchief and began mopping his sweaty face. The other man shook a wooden backgammon box and ordered two glasses of kvass.

"Our Kumyks," continued the first man, "want to unite with the Balkhars, but who's going to let the Balkhars go? The Nogais won't join with the Kumyks either—first they need to figure out what to do with the land."

"But *va*, why?" the salesgirl asked, still surprised, as she turned the gleaming gold-colored handle on the tank.

The man finished wiping his face and burst out laughing.

"That's my question, too: why?"

The second man tucked the backgammon box under his arm, took the two full glasses of kvass, one in each hand, and growled:

"We need a firm hand, like under Stalin, fi-r-r-r-m!"

Both of them glanced at Shamil, who was standing to one side with his glass. He hurried away; he had no desire to get into a conversation about the Kumyk and Nogai steppes at this point. He decided to head home, where he could think things over in peace.

4

Asya ran to Khabibula's, bought a couple of jars of fragrant heavy cream from his wife, then hurried home. From there she set off at last to Aunt Patimat's to complete her errand and deliver the cream, which would eventually thicken into sour cream. The family considered Patimat, Shamil's mother, standoffish, but from her childhood Asya had always enjoyed visiting her; she loved the particular smell that came from the copper-banded trunks in her apartment. The jars clinked against each other in the bag as she walked. Her hands began to feel numb, and scraps of meaningless tunes and advertising jingles played raggedly in her head in an endless loop, along with the strange expression "donkey salt." Asya came to her senses only when a man tiling the roof of someone's house laughed and shouted down to her:

"Hey, talking to yourself?" He snickered. "Talking to herself!"

Asya realized that she had been saying the phrase aloud, and that "donkey salt" was Avar for thyme, and that her mother had said something about thyme that very morning.

Asya's mother, Patimat's cousin, was dark-skinned from birth. Everyone assumed she was descended from an Arab soldier who'd been in one of the armies that had invaded Southern Dagestan. He'd gotten separated from his comrades and so strayed into their mountain town. The town shrank into a small settlement, and the Arab's blood became diluted through multiple generations of descendants, occasionally bestowing a dark complexion upon women of the house of Arabazul in the Khikhulal *tukhum*. Asya's father had come from a completely different region and was the exact opposite: he had reddish hair and brightly colored irises that looked like a mosaic-bottomed pool bathed in light.

It was because they were from such different regions and communities that her parents hadn't married right away. Asya's dark-skinned grandmother, her mother's mother, had grumbled that it would be beneath their *tukhum* to associate itself with *dzhurab* knitters and *chungur* makers, and her mother's father refused even to hear of it.

"They're nothing but savages. We're an educated people here, PhDs everywhere you look!" he would say, waving Asya's mother away, and would inwardly reproach himself for ever having allowed his daughter to go away to school in the city.

Asya's father's family weren't much pleased about the match themselves, showing their own share of disapproval for this dark-skinned girl from far away. They compiled a comprehensive list of local girls whom they had known from birth and thoroughly vetted in the meantime. Asya's mother's family brought her to heel and married her off to a placid and trustworthy man, a dental technician, and Asya's father submitted to his parents' wishes and married a hard-working, big-busted girl from his own village.

It ended in scandal. Seven months after the wedding the dental technician showed up at his father-in-law's place with his aloof, morose wife in tow, complaining that she not only was refusing to share the nuptial bed but wouldn't even talk with him when they were alone together. The father-in-law—that is, Asya's grandfather—lost his temper and nearly gave her a thrashing right there in front of everyone, but ultimately got himself under control and convened a family concilium. They threatened, sobbed, begged, trying to force Asya's mother to love her wedded husband. Asya's grandmother beat herself on the breast and declared:

"And all on account of this sock-maker, this *chungur* maker! Go on then, go off into the forests with clubs and sticks to hunt wild boar, see how you like that!"

It was true. Asya's father lived in a forested region where there were still wild boar, antelope, bears, and leopards. Whereas the populated, civilized areas where Asya's mother lived were bare as a bald man's head; over the centuries, night and day, winter and summer, all the trees had been chopped down and fed to the people's ancient and revered domestic hearths.

For his part, Asya's father had also failed to establish a harmonious domestic life with his hardworking wife, though she was sturdy, healthy, and boisterous as a seagull. She bragged to her girlfriends, cupping one big breast in each hand:

"Take a look at these girls of mine: I can put my husband on one and use the other one to cover him like a blanket!"

And nearly died laughing.

A year after his wedding Asya's father got a job as an accountant in the city and moved into an apartment there. He left his wife in the village and stopped visiting her. One night during a downpour that flooded the city streets, his abandoned wife's brothers broke into his apartment and, threatening violence, ordered him to bring his wife immediately to town and to show her the respect she deserved. Asya's father promised to get back together with his wife, and to do everything they asked, but the next day he installed a big deadbolt on his door and filed for divorce.

From that day on his life was an unending series of torments. His wife's relatives besieged him constantly. Day after day, her parents, sisters, uncles, aunts, and clan elders showed up at his door, one after another, accusing him of despicable, dishonorable, and shameful behavior. Ultimately his wife found her pride and put a stop to it all. She returned home to her parents and put her former husband out of her mind, permanently.

"He didn't even give me any children, what good was he?" she would say, and then with renewed ferocity would set to mowing the grass, milking the cows, and setting the tables for guests, of whom there was always an abundance.

Soon they found a more suitable match for her, a second cousin once removed, a practical, muscular man, and over the next ten years she bore for him, one after another, a teeming brood—five lusty boys and two husky girls.

So Asya's parents were liberated at last from their spouses, and were able to join together in lawful matrimony. Naturally this process brought with it its own strife and scandal. During the formal courtship, Asya's mother wouldn't even come out to greet the matchmakers, and practically no one showed up at the wedding.

On the other hand, when children began to enter the world, old offenses were forgotten, and Asya's paternal grandmother came in person to Makhachkala to dandle the babies and tyrannize the young mother. Asya was a pale, scrawny, awkward child, which brought her no end of trouble both at home and in the neighborhood. When she came to her mother's village, she didn't go around visiting like the other girls; she would close herself up in the storeroom and spend hours sorting through the basins and old carpets there, imagining that she was a princess imprisoned in a tower.

Her maternal grandmother said that Asya obviously took after her father's side of the family, but her paternal grandmother said that Asya took after her mother's side, and ultimately, after giving her a good scolding for the gray, limp *khinkal* and misshapen *kurze* she made, they left her to her own devices. So she spent her time reading books that she found piled up on the shelves, most of them non-Russian, old, and in tatters. There she found antique collections of sermons, edifying tracts, and theological poetry by Mukhammedkhadzhi from Kikuni, Khadzhimukhammed from Gigatl, Omargadzhi-Ziiaudin from Miatli, Sirazhudin from Obod, Gazimukhammed from Urib, Ismail from Shulani, Chupalav from Igali. There she found lyric poetry by Magomedbek from Gergebil, Magomed from Chirkey, Kurbana from Inkhelo, Magomed from Tlokh, Chanka from Batlaich, and his disciple the romantic poet Makhmud from Kakhabroso. Asya leafed through these books without understanding even half of the abundant ornate metaphors and exotic analogies they contained.

The margins were cluttered with check marks and notes, some of them just words crammed together without punctuation. Within an eighteen-year period Avar literature had endured a series of shocks: First, in 1920 the Arabic alphabet had been transformed into *adzham*, the new Arabic-based script, and then, ten years later, *adzham* had given way to Latin letters, and the books with Arabic script were destroyed. Eight years after that, Cyrillic replaced the Latin alphabet, with additional symbols to mark guttural sounds, and their vocabulary swelled and multiplied. Before the Dagestanis had time to acclimate to one new writing system, they had to start learning the next. There was such confusion that the new Cyrillic words were written without spaces, like Arabic script, out of pure inertia.

But Asya wasn't allowed to languish over books for long. She was extracted from her refuge and an attempt was made to force her out into society. This effort failed. Asya lurched like a crane when she tried to dance, flapping her arms wildly in the air. She avoided bright-colored clothes and preferred flat sandals to elegant, spangled high heels. Her hair was chestnut colored and thin, like corn silk, and her arms were skinnier, as her grandmother put it, than intestines. To complicate matters, on one of Asya's visits to her father's village she made a serious misjudgment. One day after lunch she went out onto the main street, where she ran into the village flirt, Chakar, who was carrying a plastic water jug. Chakar gave a friendly whistle, and set down the jug.

"Come on, Asya, join us," she whispered. "We're going out. Just put on a scarf."

"Going out where?" asked Asya. Chakar's free-and-easy manner disconcerted her.

"Just up the mountain and back with the guys. You'll be home in an hour. Please say yes—I can't go with them by myself."

Asya felt a rush of emotion, flattered that the beautiful Chakar had invited her, happy at the prospect of some unexpected adventure—anything to pull her out of the oppressive monotony of village life—but scared that her grandmother would notice her absence and would tell her father afterward. Chakar was so nice, so sophisticated, so fun-loving, that Asya agreed to join her. She rushed home, rooted around in the chest of drawers, found a gaudy aquamarine-colored headscarf, and threw it on. Grabbing a rusty watering can for appearance's sake, she ducked into the garden, and from there darted down terraced steps and climbed over fences until she reached the edge of the village, where an old brown jeep was waiting.

Asya got in front next to the driver, and Chakar sat in back, cramped between four big strong guys, giggling and joking in her soft voice. A fragrant breeze blew through the open windows. The rough road looped over ravines and abysses, threaded between huge granite boulders, forded streams, and plunged into wooded thickets, bouncing the jeep up and down as it crossed old ruts and ran over stones.

In the back, Chakar squabbled playfully with the guys, teased the driver, and jabbed Asya from behind with her finger: "I bet you don't get to ride around like this in the big city, do you, Asya?"

The driver, a big, meaty fellow, inserted a CD of folk songs into the player. The guys in the back snapped their fingers, Chakar shouted "*Vore, vore!*" and the aquamarine scarf quivered and fluttered on Asya's head. They sped up till they reached where the road turned, wheeled around the curve with squealing tires, and headed up toward the crooked groves of pine and birch and the alpine meadows scattered over the slopes there. Asya began to feel uneasy. She looked back at Chakar, who was squeezed between bulky male shoulders, then turned toward the driver. But everyone was laughing, singing along with the CD, and no one paid any attention to her. All at once her head was in her hands, and she'd burst into tears.

"Hey there, hey!" the others chorused, baffled. Chakar disdainfully commanded the group not to frighten the "little fool" any further, and to turn back toward the village.

The jeep braked dutifully, but the driver didn't turn it around, instead springing down onto the roadside and wading into the tall grass up to his knees, doing neck stretches as he went. The others tumbled out after him.

"We'll just take a little break here and then go back," Chakar reassured Asya. She took a plastic bottle of spring water from under the seat and, springing up like a wild goat, splashed it onto the men, and they wheeled around and grabbed her by the arms, jokingly bending them backward. Thus began hours of torment for Asya. The others kept making promises, but showed no signs of starting back. First the driver sat down next to Asya on the ground, which was covered with fragrant flowers in bloom, each bearing its own complicated two-part name, and tormented her with tedious questions: "Are you in school? Where do you go? Who's your father?" Then Chakar proposed a game of blind-man's-bluff, and they tugged at Asya's hands and wouldn't leave her alone, though she didn't want to play. Then they chatted with some people in a car that came by, and Asya hid her face so no one would recognize her. And even after they finally got back in the jeep and started back toward the village, the driver pulled over onto the shoulder, and the people in the back seat raised a fuss, with Chakar's honey-toned voice squealing loudest of all, "*Ch'a, ch'a!*"

Asya was terrified, and was about to jump out of the jeep and head off for home on her own, but everyone soon calmed down, and they started back down the mountain. They finally made it back to the village after dusk.

Asya's anxious grandfather was waiting for her at the road when they got back, and the "boys," as Chakar called them, launched into explanations and reassurances, blaming everything on that *k'akh'ba* and her wiles. Chakar herself slipped away, flashing her duplicitous eyes.

At home Asya's grandmother was waiting, armed and ready. She cursed and scolded, and pelted Asya with copper pitchers and embroidered pillows trimmed with pearls and stuffed with Grandmother's braids. By the next day the entire village was buzzing with rumors about how so-and-so's daughter, which is to say so-and-so's granddaughter, had gotten into a jeep with some young men and had gone on a joyride into the mountains, and with Chakar too, that trollop— a decent girl wouldn't even let herself be seen in her company, let alone engage her in conversation.

Many were the mothers who erased Asya's name from the lists of potential brides in the village that day. Claiming illness, the girl was absent from the *godekan* for an entire week.

But these tribulations were behind Asya now, and as she hurried down the street with her jars of cream, the only things on her mind were the phrase "donkey salt" and Patimat's son.

5

The waterfront was deserted. Shamil walked over to the old plastered railings in front of the black railway embankment; looking over the gleaming tracks he saw the chaos of buildings along the shore, and beyond them the dark, restless blue waves of the sea. In the distance to the left, brightly colored balloons floated in the sky, dangling their long, tangled strings, and the Test Your Strength machine was clattering on the midway, serving an as-yet invisible public. From his right came a vague rumbling sound, blending in with the hum of the surf. Shamil hesitated briefly, then headed off in that direction, looking now and then at the foamy crests of the waves, the narrow strip of sandy beach, and the pile of black stones visible on the other side of the tracks.

Gradually the rumble became a plaintive melody, punctuated by clapping and exclamations of approval, and before long a crowd came into view. People had gathered around a little man wearing a wine-colored Circassian coat with a cartridge belt across the front. The man was singing, accompanying himself on a *chungur* he had picked up who knows where. He stood with his eyes closed, oblivious to his surroundings. His voice vibrated sweetly, the mulberry-wood body of the instrument throbbed and sighed, and the hem of the man's Circassian coat fluttered and danced in the sea breeze. Next to him stood a man with a mustache, who smiled and extended a black microphone first to the bouncing strings, then to the *chungur* player's jutting chin, then back to the strings. Shamil wandered over to the crowd and stood to one side, staring at the musician's restless hands.

The song ended, and the listeners applauded and shouted in Lezgian. Bulky men with microphones appeared on both sides of the singer, and they too began shouting, waving their free hands in the air.

Their voices poured out of a big speaker that had been set up under an anemic little tree. The crowd listened in silence, sighing like a hundred-mouthed monster.

Shamil didn't understand Lezgian, but he lingered and listened. Now, above the heads of the performers, a huge poster appeared, showing a stern-looking bearded man in a white *bashlyk* and a big *papakha* with a green ribbon tied around it.

"Magomed Yaragskii?" Shamil thought out loud.

"Khadzhi-Davud of Miushkiur," a man standing next to Shamil uttered proudly, glancing briefly at him, then looking back at the performers.

The name meant nothing to Shamil, and he was about to head for a side street when one of the singers unexpectedly began speaking in Russian. From the way he spoke, Shamil realized that the man was reciting a speech that he had memorized and rehearsed many times.

"Thanks to our dear singer Yarakhmed. As you have correctly assumed, he was singing about our very own Khadzhi-Davud. And Khadzhi-Davud is the great hero of the Lezgian people!" roared the speaker, now throwing a quick glance down at some notes. "At the beginning of the eighteenth century he united all of Lezgistan and led our ancestors against the Persian garrisons! He traveled to Kaitag and Kazikumukh and persuaded their rulers to help in the war with the Iranian Shiites! From Derbent to Shemakha everything was in flames! They locked Khadzh-Davud up in prison, but he escaped and led the people forward! The Lezgians drove the Persians out of their towns and fortresses, but the Persians were greater in number! Our Khadzhi-Davud turned to Peter the Great for help, but Peter wouldn't help. Still the people loved Khadzhi-Davud and came to him from all corners of Caucasian Albania. Our men seized Shemakha, assassinated the Iranian puppet, robbed and slaughtered scores of

Persians, and took their children into captivity! Russian merchants there aided the Persians, and these merchants paid dearly. So Peter decided to take Shemakha and give assistance to the Persian shah! The Iranian rulers of Ganjaand Yerevan began to arm themselves for battle. But nothing came of it. The cowardly Persians drank and caroused all night long on the banks of the Kura, and only toward morning did they begin to prepare for a fight, and our brave Lezgians attacked them, routed them, and returned home in triumph with their booty. But they needed allies. Russia wouldn't help the Lezgians, and Khadzhi-Davud had to turn to the Turks for aid. He said to them, 'Help us, but let us keep our freedom!' And he was named Khan of Shirvan and Kuba, and made his capital in Shemakha. Russia and Turkey took the adjoining lands for themselves, and left the free lands of Lezgistan in Khadzhi-Davud's hands. But there was one serpent that wanted to destroy him. A former ally, the Kazikumukh khan, wanted to become shah in Lezgistan, so he asked the Turkish sultan to put him on the throne in the place of Khadzhi-Davud. The treacherous sultan invited Khadzhi-Davud, his family, brothers, and guests to Ganja, and when Khadzhi-Davud arrived, they arrested him and banished him to a Greek island. There our hero died, and thus did the Kazikumukh usurper begin to rule in Shemakha!"

The speaker stopped for breath and for some reason tugged on the middle button of his half-unbuttoned shirt.

"Now our Lezgian lands are again in the hands of an enemy. We must recall our worthy ancestor Khadzhi-Davud of Miushkiur and regain them for ourselves!"

The listeners cheered. A brisk, dark-skinned man elbowed the speaker to one side and began barking something in Lezgian, his voice cracking. The crowd buzzed in approval.

He then switched to Russian: "It's because of the treacherous politics of the Azeri and Dagestani authorities! Why is nobody talking about the Lezgian question? The Azeris are, believe me, Turks who have come to our ancient Albanian lands! They mean to destroy the southern Lezgians but will not succeed! No border is eternal! Let them sit on their suitcases in fear!"

The crowd roared. A young man standing next to Shamil cupped his hands around his mouth and shouted, "We'll eviscerate them!"

"These Azeris don't allow the Lezgians to study the Lezgian language, they register them as Azeris, persecute and destroy them! They won't even let them open Lezgian cafés!" The dark-skinned man slapped his thigh. "They changed the name of our ancient mosque in Baku from 'Lezgi Mosque' to 'Twelfth-Century Mosque!' How can we stand idly by and let that happen? In Karabakh they turned our countrymen into cannon fodder, and even fired on them from behind! They give them no autonomy whatsoever! And what if they start in with pogroms? What will we do then? Russia won't help us!"

"The Russians are dirty cowards!" Shamil's neighbor bellowed.

"You know, don't you, that the best Azeri poets, the best athletes, the best composers, all of them have been Lezgians who were fluent in Persian. They adapted everything to their own culture. But we must remember that we're not alone! The Talysh also want to split off from Azerbaijan! The Zakatal and Belokan Avars want to split from the Azeris! Remember how hard it is for our brothers the Udins. They may be Christians, but they're Lezgians too, their roots are here in Caucasian Albania! And there are only four thousand of them left! We've sat around long enough under the Avars and Dargins. Even the Kumyks in Dagestan have more seats in Parliament than we do, and we were here before the Kumyks! Let us unite northern and southern Lezgistan!

Those internationalists who are sitting out there on the square," the dark-skinned man nodded in the direction of the city, "are undoubtedly Azeri agents and traitors to the Lezgian people! They're making money on the backs of our unfortunate countrymen, whom the Azeris enslave and treat like pariahs."

The crowd bustled and shouted. Shamil couldn't make out what they were saying. His young neighbor bellowed through his hands: "The *tsaps* are assholes! Total assholes!"

Then there was someone new standing next to Shamil and his noisy neighbor. It was a young man with a protruding lower lip— the same one Shamil had seen at the newspaper.

"Hey, sissy, shut your trap, yelling is for grownups," he said, crowding the man to one side.

"So, are you a *tsap* too, or what?" smirked the loudmouth.

Several onlookers turned to look at them.

"Not at all, I'm a Lezgian myself, but I know the Azeris inside out. Who are they going to give autonomy to? The likes of you? You must have heard by now that Russia has closed itself off from us!"

"You, *gada*, what are you spouting off about?" drawled someone in the crowd, stepping closer.

"Brother, don't muck everything up," Shamil intervened, nudging the kid with the lip to one side and looking him straight in the eye. "Don't make a stink, they'll rip you to shreds."

Unexpectedly, the kid calmed down and obediently took a few steps back.

In the ensuing pause Shamil could hear the next speaker, a man neatly dressed in a suit jacket despite the heat:

"They drew the national border between the Russian Federation and Azerbaijan along the Samur River channel without any discussion with the people there! As a result, entire Lezgian villages and enclaves formed on the territory of Azerbaijan. I got a letter from a group of people in the village of Khrakh-Uba, complaining that for many years they've been living there like unwelcome aliens. And on their own land, too! They're experiencing the same kinds of problems as illegal immigrants in a foreign country! The people of Khrakh-Uba sent a whole series of appeals to both the central and local governments. And what was the response? All the bureaucrats sitting in Derbent can think about are their own personal waterfront properties! All they can come up with is, 'if you don't like it, then move.' But how are they supposed to move, with their family cemeteries and historical lands in Azeri hands? And what if we try to drive the Azeris from Southern Dagestan, what then? The Republic owes us an answer. Why won't they help their own disenfranchised people? Why isn't a single one of them here to speak with us?"

Someone poked Shamil in the shoulder. "What's with all the bitching and moaning? Is your pal here looking for trouble?" It was the same drawling voice that had first challenged the kid with the lip.

Shamil turned to look at the kid, who was standing tentatively to one side, staring sullenly at the crowd.

Shamil lowered his voice and laid his hand gently on the drawling man's neck.

"Don't pay any attention to him—he doesn't mean anything by it. He hit his head pretty bad, recently. You know how it is."

"If he opens his trap again, I'm going to beat the shit out of him." Shamil's interlocutor shook off his hand; he wouldn't back down.

"Must be an Azeri," the loudmouth suggested again.

"I'll keep an eye on him," promised Shamil in a conciliatory tone, and backed toward the young man with the lip.

"*Sag'rai!*" he heard from behind. He and the young man stepped off to the side.

"Are you our Magomed's wife's brother?" asked the kid.

"Yes, Magomed is my brother-in-law. You were over the line, brother!" said Shamil.

The young man paused, then answered, "They're humiliating the Lezgians. This is no time to play dumb. You've heard about the Wall, haven't you? Magomed is planning to leave for the mountains. Are you going to go with him?"

"Nah," answered Shamil curtly. "What are you doing here, are you on assignment?"

"Yes. I'm not the only one here from the paper, either. But I'm not going to listen to any more of it. I'm going to go figure out what's the problem with the mobile network. Almost everyone's phone is dead."

Shamil recalled Uncle Alikhan and nodded.

"You go on, I have to head back."

He held out his hand to the young man, who clasped it in both of his.

Shamil went back over to the crowd. Nothing had changed. The man in the suit jacket was still ranting about the border.

"Well, here's what I would tell the Russian president. In the nineteenth century the Lezgians legally recognized themselves as Russian citizens. Citizens of Russia, not of Azerbaijan or the Republic of Dagestan. In return Russia undertook the obligation to protect the Lezgians' legal rights. So then what? The Soviets created the Socialist Republic of Azerbaijan and formally established the Azeri people on Lezgian national territory, and then after the collapse of the USSR the greater part of the Lezgian people and their land was just turned over to independent Azerbaijan! There are a million of us—we are Russian citizens, supposedly under Russia's protection, and now they're slaughtering us!

Some bureaucrats simply sold us off to the highest bidder! And you know what is going on on the Golden Bridge, don't you, the amounts of money that are changing hands over there? That money is being made on the blood of the Lezgian people!"

The crowd applauded, and shouts were heard, first isolated, and then louder and louder as more and more people joined in:

"*Sadval! Sadval! Sadval!*"

The short man in the wine-colored Circassian coat stepped forward again and played another song on the *chungur*. When the song ended, the crowd resumed its clamoring. Someone gestured toward the city, and the crowd began to bubble and surge in that direction, as though they had been waiting for just this signal.

"Can they be going to the administration building too?" thought Shamil.

"To the Government House! To the Government!" howled the crowd.

Shamil started off behind them, keeping a slight distance. They left the embankment and headed in the direction of the main square. The traffic jams had already dissipated; here and there curious onlookers joined the procession. Women who worked in the food shops and newsstands came out and stood on the street, shading their eyes with their hands and watching the people as they walked by. They marched several blocks, passing throngs of onlookers who had materialized from out of nowhere, then stopped at the corner across from the main square, where the Government House stood. There they began shouting again:

"*Sadval! Sadval!*"

"It's closed off," people on the sidewalks called out. "The cops aren't letting anyone through—they just kicked out the Kumyks!"

Sure enough, the way to the square was blocked off by a gated barrier and a police cordon. A fat, severe captain came out from the cordon and waved his arms:

"No entry! Stop right there!"

"What's going on?" asked a dark-faced man, the one who had given the speech on the embankment.

Only scraps reached Shamil's ears: "An urgent meeting in there... orders not to let anyone through... street repair."

The crowd howled. Shamil felt thirsty again, and decided not to linger. Groping his way through the steamy human labyrinth, he some-how managed to make his way out onto an empty sidewalk. From there he started straight toward home. Behind him, the shouting continued:

"A united Lezgistan! United Lezgistan!"

But Shamil didn't look back.

6

The glassed-in veranda facing east was a refuge from the morning heat. On the spacious daybed, covered with a long-napped rug, fat Marya Vasilyevna reclined with her legs splayed. Next to her on a low three-legged stool sat her neighbor, hunched over nearly double and guffawing. Shamil silently sipped a bowl of beef bullion, glancing now and then at his mother's calm face as she bustled around preparing tea. Her composure seemed strange; after all, she herself had said that his sister and brother-in-law had just been by, trying to persuade her to pack up and leave for the mountains, to get as far away as she could from whatever might happen.

"The celebration is going to go on for several days," Marya Vasilyevna announced. "Everyone who's anyone is going to be there—people are even coming from other republics. The boy is twenty... they say the girl is from an ordinary family... they met when they were students at Dagestan State University."

"My Kamilla knows her," the neighbor interjected enthusiastically. "She's been invited."

Marya Vasilyevna was offended. "What, you think they didn't invite me? I've known the Khanmagomedovs for ten years. I used to wipe Bashirchik's nose with my own hand. I tutored his younger brother for his university entrance exams. They still send me presents. 'Marya Vasilyevna,' they say, 'you saved our lives!' I've ridden in Khanmagomedov's car many times. You should see their house...oh my God, everything is made of pure gold. The whole place is like a museum. I've even spent the night there—the family thinks very highly of me. When Bashir has children, they'll get them into my class. Right, Patya?"

Shamil's mother nodded. She was setting out cups.

"That's one lucky bride," said the neighbor, undoing her scarf and retying it. "She's just an ordinary girl. Her name is Elmira—she was in Kamilla's class. For whatever reason, he took a liking to her. They say he ordered a billboard for her birthday, cost him seven hundred thousand! Her portrait on it, with 'Happy Birthday.' It was right in the center of town, next to the department store."

"You're right, it was," Marya Vasilyevna agreed. "But then they took it down. Her parents asked him to."

"I thought the Khanmagomedovs only married their own people," Shamil's mother said, pouring the tea. "The elder daughter married her cousin."

"That's right," Marya Vasilyevna chimed in. "It makes sense. If you have so much money, why share it with strangers?"

Shamil finished his bouillon and stared blankly at the freshly washed windowpanes. Girls' squeals could be heard outside, and a ball banged against the iron gate.

"What a racket, just listen to those kids. Must be Naida's daughters from the second floor. It's high time for them to be inside setting the table, but listen to them running around and squealing out there."

The neighbor jumped up and hopped around in place, imitating the shameless girls.

"Our math teacher Kurbanova has a daughter like that," muttered Shamil's mother. "Some grown man is supposedly paying bribes to get her through her exams…"

The doorbell rang and Shamil's mother went to open the door.

"So Shamil, when's your wedding going to be?" asked the neighbor with a smile.

"Should be September, if…"

"*Inshallah, inshallah.*"

Asya appeared in the doorway and peered into the room. She mumbled a greeting, nodded in the direction of the women, and vanished without looking at Shamil. A rustling noise came from behind the door, and Shamil heard his mother's voice. Asya reappeared in the passageway. She had dark blue shadows under her large, tired-looking eyes, and the clip in her hair was about to come off. Again without looking at Shamil she sat down at the table, at a loss as to what to do with her hands.

Marya Vasilyevna lurched up off the daybed and waddled to the table, where a silver-gilt cup of hot, strong tea awaited her. They all gathered around and resumed their conversation. The wedding was scheduled for the next day, and the Khanmagomedovs were going all out. A special landing pad had been built for helicopters to bring in the VIPs. Shamil smirked:

"A fine time they've chosen to put on a show, with the world falling apart around us."

"Things are always falling apart around here," protested Marya Vasilyevna. "Just look what's going on at school! Tell him, Patya.

If it hadn't been for me, what would have happened there? I keep things in order. After the renovations there were five buckets of paint left over. I tell Gadzhiev, I say, 'Get those buckets and take them to my garage. Better they go to a poor schoolteacher than to who knows who.' So he took them. And he whitewashed my house. So what? I pulled his son out of a pit by the ears. And that boy is…" she rapped the table with her knuckles. "Not a single brain cell to call his own. Dumb as a shepherd."

Shamil's mother objected: "He's good at physics."

Marya Vasilyevna waggled her hand dismissively. Asya stirred sugar into her tea, clicking the sides of the cup with her spoon. Shamil looked at her neck with its taut veins and asked:

"Why aren't you saying anything, Asya? How are things?"

She blushed and mumbled, swallowing the words: "All right."

"Have you gone to the shore yet?"

"No."

It was boring. Shamil looked at his watch, and at a moment when he saw that the neighbor was preoccupied with Marya Vasilyevna, he asked his mother about his sister's departure with her husband. His mother had no idea about what was going on and was confused by all the secrecy. She hadn't seen anything out unusual on TV, and she gave no credence to the rumors about a Wall.

Marya Vasilyevna laughed uproariously, her entire heavy body heaving.

"Have you heard, Patya? That deputy Makhmud keeps one wife on Sedov Street, and another on Titov. Poor things, they live just down the street from each other, and neither of them knows about the other. And just yesterday someone saw him at the Stormy Petrel restaurant with some new pretty young thing. Go figure!"

Asya squealed and leapt up from her chair, staring in horror at her overturned cup of tea.

"Did you get burned?" asked Shamil's mother anxiously.

"No, no, I'm sorry, I'll clean it up," muttered Asya, her face scarlet, slipping out awkwardly from behind the table.

Shamil slid his cup away and left the room. He wanted to go see Madina. They hadn't spoken for a long time, and recently she even seemed to be avoiding him. But maybe she would agree to go to a café with him. He had invited her several times, but she refused each time, as though afraid of what people might think.

Shamil took out his cellphone and then hurled it onto the sofa. No service. He began fumbling around in his desk drawers, angrily scooping out computer discs, brochures, and postcards with photographs of cars. One brochure was entitled *The Meanings of the Koran*; another *The Criminal Code of the Russian Federation*; a third *The Art of the Pick Up*; the title of a fourth was illegible.

Shamil's quest led nowhere. He ran out into the corridor to where the landline phone stood on a table. The phone was old-fashioned, the kind with a rotary dial, shiny from use. Poking his finger into the dial, Shamil briskly dialed six numbers, then waited.

"Hello," said Madina.

"Hi, it's me, Shamil."

Silence.

"So I'm calling, how about we go to a café? We can sit and talk, this and that. Are your parents home?"

"No."

"Shall I come over?"

"Not now—I'm cleaning."

"When, then. In an hour?"

"All right. See you then."

She hung up. She had agreed too easily. It was disconcerting. Shamil paced the corridor, feeling the onset of something like hurt, or even scorn. "Any stranger could just call and ask her out like that, and she'd say yes," he thought.

Asya came out into the hall. She looked at Shamil sheepishly and gave a faint smile.

"Leaving so soon?" he asked brightly.

"Yes," she answered, but didn't move.

"Well then, say *salam* to everyone for me."

Asya sighed and slipped on her sandals, bracing herself against the wall. His mother came out; Shamil went back into his room.

He lay down on the sofa and let his thoughts wander. He had driven a Lada Priora to the goldsmiths' settlement. The car was his brother-in-law's, and Shamil might have been able to borrow it and drive to Madina's in style. But the timing was wrong, what with the increasing unrest on the streets, and now his sister and brother-in-law were packing to leave for the mountains, and would need the car themselves.

Shamil looked up at the whitewashed ceiling, then at the ram's horn hanging on the wall with its silver rim and chain, then at the poster of the local soccer team hanging on the wall next to it. His thoughts became jumbled.

He got up, for some reason again shuffled through the pile of disks and brochures on the desk, then let his eyes wander along the bookshelf on the wall above the computer. A thick, well-worn book caught his eye, and he took it down. The cardboard cover had a picture of a small river on it, and green letters against a beige background proclaimed: *Rye Does Not Grow in Stone*. Must have been one of his sister's schoolbooks.

Shamil glanced inside the front cover, where there was a stamp from the village school; he noticed the year of publication, which coincidentally was the year of his birth. Something about the number drew him in, and instead of putting the book back on the shelf, he took it to the sofa and opened it at random, close to the beginning.

7

The village rooster crowed hoarsely, greeting the spring. Snow still showed white on the distant peaks, but in the village gardens the lilac was already in bloom, enveloping the winding streets in an intoxicating fragrance.

Marzhana and her girlfriends were coming home from school.

How cheered you would be, reader, at the sight of this merry bouquet of girls, and, most of all, at our Marzhana! A fresh satin pinafore stretched across her ripe young breasts; her long pitch-black braids thumped merrily against her supple legs as she walked; her Komsomol badge gleamed ardently in the spring sunshine! Like fleet-footed chamois, the girls scampered from one stone to the next, from one terrace to the next, and threaded their way through the village's narrow, winding alleyways with their schoolbooks pressed to their chests. They laughed and exchanged happy glances as they went. So many hopes, so many dreams blazed in the girls' shining eyes!

"*Oi!*" said Marzhana. "There goes Kalimat!"

And she nodded toward a pale, haggard figure trudging along, bent almost double under the weight of her water jug.

"*Akh, akh,*" sighed the girls. "It's her. Ever since she dropped out and got married, pretty much everything has gone wrong. Poor Kalimat! She spends all her time hauling water and firewood, or sitting locked up at home!"

"Hi, Kalimat,' Marzhana greeted her compassionately. "How are things?"

"Fine," answered the unfortunate Kalimat, mournfully.

"Is your husband treating you badly? Do you regret dropping out?"

"What else could I do?" answered Kalimat. "My parents told me to, so I got married."

"Kalimat, why do you go around in those long scarfs and *chokhto*? Just tie on a cotton kerchief, or, even better, let your braids wave free in the breeze!"

"I can't," sighed Kalimat and plodded onward on her dreary way to her dismal home.

Silent and gloomy was the village. Its huts cringed together like starving children. Darkest despotism, cruelty, and misfortune wafted from its old towers, ancient mosques and *madrasas*. Only with difficulty did the sun's rays penetrate the fissures in the stone doorways, feeling their way along the village's zigzagging rises and slopes. But youth shone through the girls' eyelashes. Instead of shapeless silk dresses and baggy *shalwar* trousers, instead of *chokhto* left over from the old regime, they sported short school dresses, and instead of soft leather *chuviaks*, chic factory-made shoes glistened on their feet.

Now Marzhana was home. She said good-bye to her friends and flitted into the *saklya*. Her mother pounced.

"Where have you been? Your father has been asking about

you all afternoon. He wants to arrange a marriage for you to Nasyr."

Tears glistened in Marzhana's blue eyes.

Shamil flipped through several pages, glanced at his wristwatch, and resumed his reading.

How long had the mountains gone without rain! Driver Mukhtar slammed his tractor's door with a confident thud and looked down the cascade of narrow terraces to the foothills, so far down that the mountain river's meager channel could barely be seen between the banks. The stream's gentle curving bends reminded him somehow of Marzhana…

Shamil skipped several paragraphs.

A crowd of men, having donned black burkas, set off in a ramshackle procession around the village, brandishing the sacred rags that the first Islamic missionaries had supposedly been wearing when they arrived in the village. In the lead walked the elders; next came the younger men; in the rear trotted the boys, who had been taught to chant the prayers obediently and keep their heads bowed. Nasyr's father Ali chanted the verses with great energy, jutting his shaggy reddish beard forward. This was the same pious Ali who, they said, had secreted away who knows how many *sahks* of flour from the kolkhoz!

"What's going on here?" shouted Gadzhi, the kolkhoz

chairman. "Back to work, everyone! Reprimands for one and all! There's no rain; what's the point of asking Allah for it?"

But the villagers had lost all sense of reason. After noon only a few dozen people were left in the village. The women had abandoned their plows, shut the unmilked cows in their barns, and rushed to the top of the craggy cliff, which loomed above the fleeting clouds.

"Mama, don't go, you'll be ashamed later," said Marzhana to her mother, fiddling with her silky braid.

"There's no rain, Marzhana! I'm going into the mountains with the women," answered her mother. "We're going to pray. That's always helped in the past!"

"How can it be!" sobbed Marzhana, blinking back the tears that glistened in her long eyelashes. "First you say I have to marry Nasyr, then you bring shame upon the entire village with your prayers. Papa is out walking around waving some rag in the air, the men are planning to spend the whole night chanting prayers, and you're off to the mountain! That's not what the Soviet regime had in mind when they liberated you!"

"Silence! Enough, you brat!" snapped Marzhana's mother. "The chairman's put ideas into your head! He's corrupting the youth! You clean up in here, I'm in a hurry."

The women, including the elderly ones, gathered in a tight crowd and headed off toward the top of one of the escarpments, which they considered to be holy. And while the men appealed to their Allah, the women flattered their older, pagan deities, whose names are now nearly forgotten in Dagestan, and pleaded with them for rain.

"Mukhtar, this madness must stop! Nothing is getting done!

I'm going to dock them the entire week if they're not careful!" exclaimed the chairman, a fine figure of a man, as he measured the planked floor of the bright kolkhoz office with his canvas tarpaulin boots.

"Yes of course, Gadzhi, let's disperse the crowd! I'll persuade the young shepherds not to listen to their elders! We have no rain, but that's no tragedy. Comrade Lysenko in Moscow says that soon they're going to have new varieties of barley that can be planted anywhere—here, or even above the Arctic Circle!"

Raisa Petrovna came running from the school.

"Comrades, the old men have even dragged the children out of class to pray! How can that be?"

"Calm yourself, Raisa Petrovna,' strong-shouldered Mukhtar reassured her. 'I'll take care of it."

He put on his jacket and strode forth.

"What a fine young man!" clucked the chairman.

"Yes, someone like that would be a perfect fiancé for Marzhana," mused Raisa Petrovna. "Oi, there will be no happiness for her with Nasyr."

Shamil skipped another fifty pages.

The men of the mountain village piled into the community center and took their seats, ready to hear what the chairman had to say. The old men's watery eyes looked around suspiciously. They squinted malevolently at the red poster hanging above the stage, whose bold letters issued a summons to the mountain people: "Onto the plains, with property and livestock!" Next to the poster stood a crowd of children in scarlet Pioneer neckerchiefs, a regiment of future workers arrayed against the inert, dying hulk of the past. In their hands glittered garlands of electric lights; their faces were illuminated with innocent joy. The mountains, too, were illuminated, and without a single prayer or silly all-night vigil! Next to them Raisa Petrovna stood proudly in a crepe de chine dress. When she saw Marzhana making her way forward from the back rows, Raisa Petrovna waved to her.

"Comrades," Chairman Gadzhi stepped forward with his hands folded behind his back. "This is no ordinary gathering. We are here to discuss a most urgent matter. For centuries you have lived on these barren mountaintops without the slightest glimpse of the bright world beyond. At any moment a light could flash from the signal tower, and you would grab a bundle of dry mountain *kolbasa*, or, if you couldn't afford *kolbasa*, a bag of coarse-grained flour, and off you would gallop on a sortie. For centuries your homes have been built all clustered tightly together for protection like feudal fortresses and your wives have been poised to abandon the hearth at any minute and to take the attacking enemy by hook or by crook. Your forefathers lived on war alone, engaged in constant clashes with their neighbors or with tsarist occupiers. All day long they clung to the *godekan*, in a state of continual alert. Now we live in the indestructible and free Land of the Soviets! No longer do we clutch with desperate hands onto the embrasures and narrow ledges of these dark cliffs. No longer are we dependent on the word of some mullah or capricious cleric! No longer are we oppressed by khans and *shamkhals*. We have thrown off the fetters of millennial *adats* that stifled us! Just look around you, look at our youth! Our young shepherds and kolkhoz workers are dressed in bright shirts and modern trousers; they no longer have to carry sharpened daggers, to be ready at any moment to wreak revenge in blood. Look at these young pioneers!"

"Get to the point, Chairman!" shouted Nasyr, smirking cockily at his confederates.

"Here's the point. We have a great joy to share with you, comrades! Our torments have ended! Recall how, not so long ago, we used to haul earth by the jugful to the terraces of our meager fields. Recall the desolation of the winter, when the snows closed us off from the world, and the shepherds descended to their winter pastures. Am I wrong?"

"You're right!" exclaimed the beautiful Raisa Petvrovna.

"And now we can say good-bye to all that! The Kutan lands have already been prepared for us; we can be on the road by tomorrow."

"On the road where?" Old Kebed, leaning on his knotty cane, frowned.

"To the plains!" the chairman exclaimed joyfully.

"To the plains!" laughed Raisa Petrovna.

But the hall was silent. The faces of the villagers expressed dull obstinacy, nothing more. Only cheerful Mukhtar stirred in his seat, and Marzhana gazed dreamily at the ceiling. Would they really go? Would it really come to pass that instead of the many-tiered stone village, blending into the surrounding mountainside, instead of narrow covered passageways and blind alleyways of stone, she would see broad streets lined with spacious brick houses with sharp-peaked roofs, and would breathe in the fresh fragrance of a new, free life? Would it really come to pass! How she had dreamed of this day! She gazed at Mukhtar with eyes aflame.

"No, we cannot abandon our homes and our land," answered Kebed.

"We will not abandon them under any circumstances," voices rose on all sides. Loudest of all was the voice of Ali, Nasyr's red-bearded father. "You mean to destroy us! All the people who moved from here onto the plains died of malaria!"

"Let Gadzhi Muradovich speak! Give Gadzhi Muradovich the floor!" begged Raisa Petrovna.

At last the room fell silent and everyone looked at the bald chairman, who stood with his plump fingers pressed firmly onto the polished tabletop.

"All of you, everyone here, has been duped," he said sternly, swallowing the endings of his words. "Where did you get this unverified information? Instead of spreading panic among the people, you need to sort things out with the ringleaders, the slanderers and plotters. And you, Ali, don't try to change the subject; we know that you still have rams that you have not turned in. Turn them over to the kolkhoz by tomorrow, or we will take them from you by force!"

"But I was planning to invite you over and serve you those rams," Ali objected, smirking, "at my son's wedding. He's marrying Osman's daughter, Marzhana."

Everyone looked at Marzhana. The girl's lips quivered, and she dashed out of the club. Raisa Petrovna rushed out after her.

"Don't run away, Marzhana! Don't go!" shouted the young teacher. They ran until they could run no more; finally they stopped, breathless, at the spring.

"*Akh*, Raisa Petrovna!" exclaimed Marzhana, and she burst out sobbing on her teacher's shoulder. The black and chestnut plaits intertwined like streams from two waterfalls.

"I know that you love Mukhtar," said Raisa Petrovna, stroking her student on the back. "You don't have to marry Nasyr if you don't want to."

"I don't!" whispered Marzhana. "I'll jump off the bridge before I marry him."

"Good for you," Raisa Petrovna praised her. "I can see how disrespectfully the men here treat you; I can see how hard it is for you women in the mountains, how you have to haul water on your own backs. Don't repeat poor Kalimat's mistake; learn to stand up for yourself…"

Shamil sighed, glanced again at his watch, and flipped to the last pages:

The great bulging red sun rose on the horizon; the summer air filled with the chirping of birds. Marzhana leaned joyfully out of the window and gathered in the first hints of the new morning. Behind her now was her hard life in the dismal mountains; behind, too, crude Nasyr with his idle, insolent sneer; behind her now, the gossip of the village, the disapproval of her relatives. Ah, how shrilly they had laughed as they shouted to one another from the rooftops: "Osman's daughter has been seen with Mukhtar." So what if she had? Marzhana had sought him out on her own initiative. She herself had lain down in the mown grass next to the tractor and announced: "It is not the mullah who will join us in marriage, but he who is dearer than any mullah, dearer than any father." And she had showed the stunned Mukhtar a postcard with a photo of Lenin on it, smiling benevolently out at them.

And now, greeting the fresh steppe dawn, she could not even remember how Nasyr had threatened to kill her; how her former girlfriends had shunned her, turning away when they met on the street; how her father had dressed in mourning and announced that his daughter was dead to him; how her mother had sobbed in silence. Now everything would be different. She had broken away from the age-old mountains and ravines and had strode forth, forward to meet the sea breeze, forward to meet the laughing tractor driver Mukhtar.

Yesterday Marzhana had prepared balloons and banners, and had cleaned the glass of the precious framed portraits of the working people's leaders. "*Akh*, today I will march in the parade," Marzhana laughed to herself, "and Mukhtar will embrace me, and Chairman Gadzhi will smile at me!" A new village had come into being on the plain, new homes glittered in the southern sun. Only the most stubborn and lazy people were still clinging to the smoke-blackened pillars of their old *saklyas*, unwilling to part with their gloomy nests above the clouds. Marzhana's mother and father had closed themselves inside their home and refused come out; Nasyr's father Ali had greedily clung to his hoarded wealth; the old women had wailed and lamented.

And then the young Komsomol shepherds found a supply of gunpowder somewhere and used it to destroy all of the ancestral towers. The ancient, resilient walls did not give in easily to these firebrands; they refused to fall at first. Then, finally, sending joyful echoes across the cliffs, the stones tumbled in a great landslide down the mountain. The old village was no more. Old man Kebed no longer had anywhere to hide with his quackery and his superstitious books. The malicious gossip at the *godekan* fell silent. The *zurna* no longer played on the town square. Marzhana's fellow villagers settled into a new life on the broad steppe, where the livestock graze free, where a Pioneer reveille rings across the plain.

In the parade Marzhana walked hand in hand with Mukhtar and Raisa Petrovna; behind them, heaving grouchy sighs to the tune of the "Internationale," trudged the old men.

"Well, Marzhana," Chairman Gadzhi patted her on the cheek, "how was the move?"

"It worked out fine, Uncle Gadzhi!" answered Marzhana and pressed closer to the beaming Mukhtar.

"I proved it to myself, and I will prove it to everyone, that rye does not grow on stone," said the chairman. And his words went deep into Marzhana's soul, and she would remember them her whole life: not in the mountains, not in the old ways, is happiness to be found, but in the new and joyous morning of freedom.

8

Shamil tossed the book onto the sofa and, after a brief stop in the bathroom, set off on foot to Madina's. She lived close by, in a nine-story prefab apartment building with a jumble of homemade verandas clinging to the sides, the ones on the upper stories propped atop the ones below. In the dark entryway Shamil nearly overturned an aluminum bucket full of dirty water. Almost all the doors off the stairway were wide open or half-open because of the stifling heat, releasing to the outside world the sounds of talking and shouting, as well as the hum of televisions. One fleshy woman in a fleece robe was swabbing the landing in front of her apartment, and through its open door Shamil caught a glimpse of a long, narrow hallway with shiny gold-streaked wallpaper.

Madina was standing on her threshold. She was wearing a long patterned skirt and a colorful print blouse with sleeves that went all the way down to her wrists.

"Won't you be hot?" asked Shamil in surprise. Madina was silent, sullen. Her expression betrayed a vague, ominous tension.

"Why so grouchy?" asked Shamil, trying to make light of it.

She slammed the door behind her and started down the stairs.

"What have you heard out on the streets?" Her cork soles tapped down the stairs as she answered his question with one of her own.

"You know, don't you? Such an *aria-urai*! I stumbled on two different demonstrations going on at the same time." Shamil had a thought. "Hey, is your phone working?"

"No. They say almost all of the services have been disconnected. Some glitch in the system. Or maybe someone shut them down on purpose."

They came out into the courtyard, cluttered with garages, but still spacious. A bench nearby was occupied by a number of young people from the building; he greeted them, clasping hands. Then he caught up to Madina and started babbling the first thing that came into his head, just to break the silence:

"Listen, I wanted to come by car, but Magomed took it. It's all right—I'm thinking of getting an Audi. I can order this one Omargadzhi told me about, from Stavropol, only slightly used."

Madina was barely listening. She glanced at Shamil only once, to point out the glass door of a bakery to him. A sign over it read WINDOW TO PARIS. They entered an empty, cool little room, lined with shelves of cakes and pastries.

"Let's go to a regular restaurant," Shamil suggested.

"No," Madina said bluntly, sitting at a table directly under a humming air conditioner. She frowned, and her hands fiddled with a napkin she had picked up somewhere. A young waitress appeared behind the counter and sauntered lazily over to their table with a menu.

Madina was Shamil's third cousin. Their great grandparents had been brothers who lived in the large mountain town of Cher, on one of the branches of the Great Silk Road. Cher was divided into quarters, each with several *tukhums*, each of these centered around its own mosque. One *tukhum* was military; another was made up of farmers and herdsmen. There was a *tukhum* of weavers who made cotton textiles and hempen cloth; one *tukhum* comprised merchants and boot makers of Jewish ancestry; and there was a *tukhum* of stonemasons and former slaves, descendants of Georgians who had been taken into captivity long ago. Their great-grandfathers had belonged to the agricultural *tukhum* known as Khikhulal, which was very distinguished, and which had occupied a place high up the mountain, overlooking a steep precipice.

At one point after the death of their parents, the brothers quarreled. Madina's great-grandfather Zakir had decided to marry a beautiful girl from a noble family, who was expected to have a substantial dowry. In those days dowries consisted of land—that is, the most valuable commodity in the mountains. But if a girl married into a different free community, khanate, or kingdom, she would receive nothing at all. When he learned that his younger brother's intended bride would come from another community, and so would not have a dowry, Shamil's great-grandfather Zapir was livid. He forbade Zakir to appear in his house with his new wife: "You can plow on her forehead," he raged, "and reap her eyebrows!"

So Zakir took his wife, a horse, and several friends, and set out to conquer an adjoining territory, one with fertile fields and pastures belonging to alien tribes. Numerous raids on settlements there resulted in a formal complaint in court, with all the local authorities and clerics presiding. They presented Zakir with a copy of the Koran and compelled him to swear that the land that he was attempting to occupy, and on which he was now standing, had belonged to his ancestors. "If you can swear to this, then the land is yours," they declared, smiling craftily.

Everyone was convinced that this would send the alien occupier slinking home with his tail between his legs. But Zakir had planned a clever ruse; beforehand he had gone to his own village of Cher and had smeared his boots with mud from there, so that, upon his return to the enemy village, he would be able to swear, with a clean conscience, that he was indeed standing on the land of his ancestors.

Thus Zapir remained in Cher, and Zakir settled beyond the

next mountain. He named his land Ebekh, which means "nearby, neighboring."

Shamil was getting annoyed. "What's the matter with you? Look at me!"

"Why do you keep asking me the same thing?" Madina objected. "There's nothing wrong with me. Instead tell me what's going on with you."

"That's what I'm doing, Omargadzhi is promising to set me up with a job in the court or maybe Uncle Alikhan will offer me a new job…"

"I didn't expect that from you," interjected Madina.

"What?" Shamil was taken aback.

"So you want to work for thieves?"

Shamil said nothing, trying to understand.

"I didn't think that you would be crawling on your hands and knees to beg to work for thieves."

Shamil paled. "When did I ever crawl on my hands and knees?"

"I know what you're hoping for. To be just like Uncle Alikhan. Or Uncle Kurban, who works for the police. To live off the suffering of the *umma*, to cheat your own people. Who do you think you are? Are you even a Muslim?"

Shamil was stunned; he couldn't muster a reply.

"Why don't you say something?" Madina was incensed. "It's because of people like you I can't live an honest life according to the Prophet's will. I can't even dress the way I want. And I'm not talking about our parents—they were brainwashed long ago, but you're young, you need to do everything you can to resist the *munafiqs* and all those *kufr* keepers. *Subhanallah*, now everything will be different. All the traitors will be punished. Before it's too late, before your own brothers catch up to you…"

"What do you mean?" Shamil interrupted, flushing. "Have you lost your mind? Who do you think you're yelling at here? Who's going to let you put on the veil?"

"The way things are now, wives don't have to ask their husbands' permission before they decide to go on jihad. And children don't have to ask their parents," continued Madina, sounding more and more as though this performance had been rehearsed in advance.

She looked completely calm again. Shamil jumped out of his seat and clattered the chair back into place.

"Fine, now I know you've lost your mind! *Abdal!* Yell at your teachers, if you like, but don't try that with me," he rasped, not even able to hear the words coming out of his mouth anymore. "Who do you think you are, anyway, to judge me? I have never stolen so much as a kopeck in my life!"

Shamil cleared his throat and ran out of the bakery, bumping into the back of his chair as he went, and not sparing a look for the waitress, who had come out from behind the counter again. A minute later he realized that this outburst had probably been uncalled for. He should have behaved with more dignity: taken the bitch home and *then* broken off all contact. And of course warned her parents, if they hadn't figured it out already. With this in mind, he quietly returned to the Window to Paris and peeked in through the shop window. Madina was still sitting at the table. Chuckling to herself. A chill ran down Shamil's spine, and he slipped away.

First he returned to Madina's apartment building. He went up to the bench where the neighbors were still sitting, and questioned them in detail about her: how she dressed, where she went; with whom she associated. They warmed to this subject immediately, spitting out sunflower husks as they spoke. It turned out that over the past six months Madina had stopped hanging out with her old friends in the courtyard; a couple of times someone had dropped her off at home after nine in the evening, and one of the guys on the bench had even seen her out somewhere in a hijab. Shamil was shocked despite himself. He went back out onto the street and walked and walked, suppressing the waves of rage and pain washing over him, trying to get a grip on himself. He decided to go to Nariman's to work out and burn off some energy.

Dusk crept over the city. People gathered on the street in small, restless clusters. Shamil walked with his eyes down, avoiding the crowds. Occasionally, music could be heard in the shops; TV newscasts hummed in the background; babies cried. At one intersection a large crowd had gathered around a sharp-eyed young guy in a striped shirt. The guy was brandishing a cellphone and shouting:

"There's not enough to go around! Stay in line, *le!*"

Beyond that point the street had been closed off. Police vehicles were blocking it, and flustered faces under visored caps peered out of their windows. Shamil decided to detour through a bare little square where an old marble statue of some shackled revolutionary gleamed in the setting sun amid a meager planting of dog rose bushes. A small crowd had formed around the statue, men of indeterminate age, many of them potbellied.

A few of the older men stood apart from the others, while a number of the younger attendees were circulating through the crowd, asking an endless stream of questions wherever they went. Two of the potbellied men were holding up a large oil-painted portrait of the red-bearded Imam Shamil in a white Circassian coat.

"The people who want to divide Russia from the Caucasus are spreading panic!" a blond man was shouting, waving his hands in the air.

"It's all because of the new people who have come into power in Moscow. But we must maintain our friendship!"

Questions from the crowd: "Who's building the Wall? Why don't we know anything?"

"Unfortunately, I don't have any information—all I know for certain is that Russian troops have been withdrawn from Botlikh and Kaspiisk, though that could simply be for maneuvers."

"It's all because we, the children of Dagestan, have renounced our Imam!" rasped a man with a huge head. "We haven't taken to heart the lessons he taught us. There's not a single monument to Shamil in Dagestan!"

"Not a single one!"

"It's idolatry!" came a voice from the crowd. "It's forbidden in the hadiths!"

"In what hadiths?" the big-headed man spoke up again. "You're making it up! *Khapur-chapur!*"

A new voice came from the crowd gathered around the statue: "The hadiths have nothing to do with it!" A gray-haired, heavy-jawed man appeared from behind the dusk-grayed backs of the men, jabbering breathlessly: "That Imam Shamil of yours burned entire villages alive for not submitting to his will! He spared no one—not the old men, whom he murdered indiscriminately, and not the women either, if they refused to live by sharia law! His own allies from the mountains turned him over to the Russians because he tormented the people! That Imam of yours was worse than any *vakh*! Why did you bring his portrait out here, why are you working up the crowd? Especially with all the rumors going around…"

People hissed. Several onlookers who had been standing at the portrait went over to the gray-haired, big-jawed speaker.

"You see? Because of people like him, the Imam died in a foreign land!" exclaimed the square-headed man, pointing his finger at the one with gray hair. The crowd seethed, and the potbellied man shouted:

"Imam Shamil was no *vakh*, he was a Tariq sheikh and military commander—he was a friend of Kunt-Khadzhi! Under him everyone in Dagestan was literate, many even went on to higher education, and it was all thanks to the Imam, it was all because of him! He brought the people together. Don't you know there used to be a monument to him in Azerbaijan?"

"The Azeris took it down!" the large-headed man exclaimed hoarsely, with great emotion. "The Zakatal, Belokansk, Kakh regions of Azerbaijan are a part of our ancient Avar lands, but they're turning our brothers there into Azeris. Television, the newspapers, everything is only in Azeri, and all the political positions are held by Azeris. Whereas under Imam Shamil the Avars were united, together like a fist, see…"

"They were not united!" the gray-haired man shouted again, this time from the other side of the crowd, far from the statue. "His own Avar people betrayed him!"

"That's enough!" repeated the blond guy, turning first one way, then another. "Enough!"

Shamil continued on his way and soon came to the stadium. He walked a short distance along the adobe wall, then ducked into a nondescript doorway and descended a flight of stairs into a stuffy basement gym. Laughter came from below. Two men were wrestling by the workout machines. Nariman stood in red shorts with his back to the entrance, wiping his bare torso with a white rag and offering a loud, running commentary on the fight. When they saw Shamil, all three of them stopped what they were doing and greeted him enthusiastically.

"*Le*, Shamil, let's see your biceps—making any progress?" Arsen frowned and looked over at the sleeves of Shamil's T-shirt.

"Another centimeter!"

"Let's check!" Arsen bounded over.

"Hey, forget it, not now," Shamil waved him away and sat down on one of the leather benches. "What did you work on today?"

"We did some pull-ups," answered Nariman, "That's all. Why didn't you come to the mixed fight today?"

"Today was such a mess, I didn't have time."

"Nariman really clobbered Karim in mixed," Arsen began, breathless. "He pinned him for five points! Take a look! Gadzhik, come over here, let's show him!"

He waved to Gadzhik, who had already positioned himself on the weight bench. Gadzhik sprang over and they started wrestling again.

Nariman stood admiring them. "Mike Tyson, I'm telling you! Arsenchik, you're just like Tyson!"

"Where is everyone?" asked Shamil, glancing around the gym.

"Someone blew up a store down the street—they went out to take a look."

"The one that was selling vodka?"

"Yes, Salman's, that's the one. Are you going to work out?"

Shamil scratched his head. "I didn't bring a change of clothes."

"There's no one here—just take off your shirt."

"Look, see what I did with my leg?" shouted little Arsen, crawling on his knees along the floor and seizing his opponent.

"*Le*, you wild Indian, you're doing it wrong!" shouted Nariman, and joined in the fray.

Shamil pulled off his T-shirt and went over to the combined weight bench...

9

As he lay looking up at the whitewashed gym ceiling, Shamil recalled something strange that had happened to him a few years ago. He couldn't say now exactly at what point the catamarans with the tourists had disappeared from view—whether it had been at the mouth of the Ansandiril-Tlar, beyond the turn of the turbulent Gakko, at the Dzhurmut rapids, in the shallows and overflows of the Motmota, or in the "black holes" of the Kila. But he did know that it had been at one of the places where these tributaries flow into the foaming Andiika. Shamil and his friend Arip, who was now living in Moscow, had been hiking. They had started off following the path of the river. The tourists had sped away in their four-man rafts, oars churning the water.

The grassy banks rushed along the swift-flowing Koisu, clothing themselves in hornbeam and pine, detouring into gloomy gorges, plunging into canyons of dizzying depth, disappearing under houses perched on pilings over the river, with Akhvakh and Chamalal women peering inquisitively out their windows.

Evergreen rhododendrons whispered tales of the Caucasian island's subtropical past, when it had been surrounded on all sides by an ancient sea; of the climate's sudden change; of the mountains' majestic birth; of the tiny people who had taken shelter in their folds, artifacts themselves, endemic, like the flora that surrounded them.

Who were they, these peoples who settled the mountains ten, a hundred, five hundred thousand years ago? Who had dwelt in the riverside settlement of Velikent; who had sculpted ceramic vessels at the Chokhsk anchorage, hunted bezoar goats and inscribed calendars onto the cliffsides? Fragrant medicinal plants with their roots clinging to the steep scree teased the nostrils with strange odors, bitter and sweet at the same time. The horizon vanished beyond the semicircular arches of the mountains, echoing their feminine curves.

Arip stopped by the pockmarked walls of an eight-story signal tower that rose above the channel of the raging river, and waved to Shamil:

"Where there's one tower, there's bound to be another one nearby."

Shamil made his way over to him, trampling the coarse stalks of chicory in bloom under his sneakers, then tipped his head back and looked up. Silhouettes of elemental stone loomed above the rocky peak of the next mountain.

"What village is that?" asked Shamil, pointing up.

"It's just the way the cliffs crumbled. There's no village up there," answered Arip, though without much conviction.

"Let's check," suggested Shamil, and they started climbing the slope.

Within minutes they were both convinced that they had only imagined the signs of civilization, but some force drew them higher and higher, above the churning river, up toward the cone-shaped stone peaks. Shamil climbed, bracing himself with his palms against the warm earth, overgrown with melliferous vegetation, sensing with his entire body the invisible trembling of the air, fraught with the buzzing of honeybees and the fluttering of brightly colored butterflies.

"How long have we been climbing?" asked Shamil.

"Forty minutes," answered Arip.

"Impossible—we've been at it at least two hours!" Shamil flopped down on the grass.

Arip sat next to him and looked over at the thickly forested slope of the mountain opposite them. Far below, the river gurgled invisibly. They were almost at the crest. Beyond they could see what looked like ruins, blending in with the craggy precipice.

"We're almost there," Arip noted, with relief. "You were right."

"We'll be there in no time—let's just take a short rest here and then we can go the rest of the way," said Shamil, letting his eyelids droop. A feeling of drowsiness, which he had begun to feel at the beginning of the climb, now spread through his entire body, leaving his limbs limp. He tried feebly to resist, then succumbed, giving himself over to sweet sleep.

Arip lay back on his back and also surrendered to the clinging drowsiness. Across his stomach, flashing its iridescent blue-green torso, scurried a huge beetle. Arip tried to lift his hand to brush it off, but sleep preempted the gesture.

Before long, in a matter of minutes, they were awake again.

"There's the path, do you see it?" Arip said, pointing. "How could we have missed it?"

They got back up and began climbing toward the structure, which peeked out from just beyond the crest. Soon they realized that what from below had appeared to be ruins was actually a solid, fortified wall looming over the abyss. The path approached from the side and led into a narrow arched passageway between the façades of two residential towers, which had been constructed of neatly matched rough stones assembled without mortar. On the brown polished surface of the towers' sides large petroglyphs spiraled in double loops.

Arip and Shamil exchanged rapt glances and followed the path up a covered street. The village's buildings clustered together in the traditional way, linked by stone bridges; their flat roofs doubled as courtyards, and the houses, which on one side appeared to be modestly immured in the mountain, but from the other had mutated magically into hulking five-story monsters.

They came out onto a square with an ornate structure built over a spring, which by all appearances served as a *godekan*. There wasn't a soul around; the cascade of dwellings, each resting on the one below, gave no sign of human habitation. Still, there was an unmistakable smell of hearths and cooking smoke. From above, mighty timber-framed windows with disks and spirals carved into their shutters looked down on them. Many of the buildings had wooden double doors that were also adorned with spirals, crosses, triangles, and stars.

"Why don't we just have a look in one of the houses?" proposed Shamil, but Arip didn't reply.

Then, in a dark archway ahead, they saw a tall, nondescript man of around fifty wearing a light-colored homespun shirt belted with a silver strap over wide trousers. There was nothing at all unusual about him save for the leather bag that he was holding. The bag was open at the top, and was packed tightly to the brim with wool. The stranger smiled and greeted them in the traditional Avar way, with a rhetorical question, which might be translated as "Are you ready?"

Arip and Shamil went up to the man and shook hands with him. They were eager to learn the name of the village and to find out where everyone had gone. The man gave a knowing smile and answered their questions with proverbs: "He who took the path did not return—but he who took the road, did." "A dog who has once eaten a bone in Keleb will not stay in Gidatl." Shamil couldn't make sense of anything else he said; his dialect was saturated with archaisms. Besides, his mouth hardly moved as he spoke; he didn't address them so much as mumble quietly and rapidly to himself. In his pronunciation the village's name sounded like "Rokhel-Meer," the Mountain of Celebrations.

The Rokhel-Meerite must have given them his name, but if so, he had garbled it along with everything else, and it was awkward to ask him to repeat it. The man led them to his house, which was marked with petroglyphs like all the others. In the spacious, dark interior, Shamil could make out a wooden structural wall with a long bench running along it, carved with elaborate geometrical designs. Tinned copper, clay, wooden, and metal vessels were arranged on the walls, as in a museum, and fragrant bunches of dried herbs, sheep's tail, and dry-cured meat hung on poles attached to the ceiling.

After some hesitation the guests accepted their host's invitation to sit on a large oaken bench in front of a hearth in the floor in the center of the room. Over the hearth a soot-blackened brass kettle hung on a chain, swaying slightly. The mysterious man said that his wife was away, and served his guests himself. He took a carved wooden ladle out of a cupboard and scooped servings of bouillon into bowls for them. Then he brought out some meat with garlic sauce and *khinkal* that his wife had prepared before she left, and set the dishes directly on the floor before them.

Shamil looked around the room, seeking a table, with no success. Arip seemed surprised as well, and at a loss as to how to proceed. He slipped one of the dumplings onto a wooden fork, looked closely at their host, and again began to pelt him with questions. But the man still only answered in riddles: "The tongue has no bones, but breaks many bones." After the meal, Shamil began to doze off, and the man suggested that they take a nap before meeting the rest of the villagers, who were expected to return by dawn. Meanwhile dusk was setting in; by the time the three of them had settled themselves on bedding laid out on the floor, a crisp, thick darkness had turned the room completely black. Shamil heard the sound of cows lowing in their sheds, and thought, "They're back from pasture, but there's no one here to milk them…"

Then his thoughts became jumbled inside his head, and he fell asleep again, for the second time that day.

When he woke, he saw that he was lying on the buzzing, sunny mountainside, the same place where he and Arip had fallen asleep, just below the settlement.

Had he dreamed it all?

Shamil poked the sleeping Arip, and when he saw his startled face, burst out laughing.

"You too, Arip? We fell asleep!"

"*Le*, he must have carried us back out here," mumbled Arip, shaking the beetle off his T-shirt.

"Who?"

"The old man from the village. He made up a place for us to sleep, and then in the middle of the night he picked us up and carried us outside. That's not the kind of hospitality you expect in the mountains."

Shamil frowned. "So you also remember how we went up into to the village, and how big and well fortified it was?"

"Yes, we went up into the village, and there was no one there, and we went into someone's house."

"Wait, he invited us, what was his name...he wasn't an old man, around fifty or so..."

"No one invited us. We went into some house on our own. It was empty, but there was a fire smoldering in the hearth. The hearth was old-fashioned, not modern. And then that...what was his name... showed up."

Shamil and Arip looked at each other in silence.

"Let's check," began Shamil, but he broke off before finishing his thought. The imposing crest of the mountain, which had served as the village's primary defense, was completely bare. No towers—no ruins, even.

"Well, I guess we did fall asleep!" he exclaimed, looping around the mountainside, looking up.

Panting, they climbed to the peak, but there was no sign of any settlement. Arip got out his cellphone and showed Shamil the date and time.

"If we slept, then we slept out here all night and all morning too, and didn't even feel the cold."

They remained silent on the way back until they saw the river and the bend beyond which the rafts with the tourists had disappeared. Then they walked a couple more kilometers and finally reached the road.

Shamil had forgotten this incident and had recalled it only now, in the gym. Even more than it had at the time, the entire episode now felt like nothing more than a dream.

10

It was late when they finished their workout and went outside; night had fallen. Nariman got out the car's key remote and clicked open the lock. A black Priora parked by the stadium flickered its headlights and beeped three times. Shamil got in front, and little Arsen sat in the back seat.

"Arsenchik, how are things at the uni?" asked Shamil, watching the darkness speed by in the tinted side mirror.

"Greased the skids as usual. Really warmed up the profs. Basically used up all my money, so by the time I went in for the last exam, I was completely broke...Didn't feel like coughing up any more cash. I thought, my dad and Isaev, my prof, are best buddies—they'll work it out without any capital exchanging hands. But Isaev turned out to be a real jerk. Can't get anything done without throwing some kopecks around."

"What about the ladies, any luck on that front?"

"There's this one piece…" Arsen noted with some satisfaction.

Nariman slapped the wheel and guffawed: "You're lying! No chance! Nothing's shaking at all. One time he picked up this slut in Reduktorny," he said, then turned to Shamil to explain:

"Our genius here managed to get her phone number; she lured him to cafés a couple of times, really ran up a tab, then she replaced her SIM card, and that was the last he saw of her!"

"Bullshit." Arsen was flustered, "Want me to call her right now?"

"Go ahead!" Nariman laughed and jerked the wheel back and forth, swerving all over the road. The car began to shake.

"What the hell?" yelped Shamil.

"They're putting up a shopping center; it's a big deal, will have an escalator and everything. It's Crazy Maga's thing."

"Maga the deputy?"

"Who else?"

Nariman lowered the window, poked his head out, and yelled to someone at the top of his voice: "Le, saul, Rashik, Rashik! What's up?! What's with the suit? Hey, how about you lend me your tie?"

Shamil tried to see who was being addressed, but Nariman had already left his target behind.

"So what's going on with you and your girl?" he asked Shamil, with a sly look.

"It's over."

"On account of the wedding?"

"I got tired of her," answered Shamil, leaning back. "I can give you her address, she lives near the Central Mall."

"I'm on to her, the guys briefed me. Anyway, she's with Gazik now."

"Is she putting out?" asked Shamil indifferently.

"And how! Gazik's already shot an entire series of dirty videos with her on his cell."

"So have you heard about the Wall?"

"What Wall?" asked Arsen.

"A wall, as in an actual wall. Border troops are building it in Stavropol, supposedly, to cut us off from Russia."

Nariman guffawed again. "What, Shoma, are you out of your mind?"

"I'm telling you, that's the word on the street," said Shamil.

"Wait, Nariman, stop!" Arsen hissed suddenly. He rolled down his window and leaned out excitedly.

"What's up?"

"Look, over by the movie theater."

Shamil lowered his window too, and saw the silhouettes of two women moving briskly along the dimly lit avenue. A large crowd trailed behind them, picking up loiterers along the way. Cars honked and braked. Nariman wheeled around and joined the procession.

"Hey, girls, hop in, we'll give you a lift!" came from all sides.

One of the girls was very tall, with a mass of curly yellow hair. She wore a kind of sarafan that was waving in the breeze. The other was a short brunette in tight jeans with a famous brand name embroidered in rhinestones on the back pocket. They walked without looking around, clicking their heels loudly on the sidewalk. Nariman and Arsen joined the chase, beeping enthusiastically and calling out invitations to the girls.

Shamil observed these goings on complacently.

Soon some of the drivers gave up; the crowd of pedestrians

following the girls thinned out, but the two of them kept creeping along the avenue, which led inexorably into unilluminated wasteland.

"I like the one with the curly hair," said Nariman. He fumbled around in his CDs and put on a popular foreign song.

"They've stopped!" shouted Arsen.

The girls had indeed stopped and were standing on the side of the street, shifting helplessly from one foot to another.

"There's some mud over there," noted Shamil, trying to see the sidewalk in the darkness.

Nariman poked his head out the window: "Honestly, girls, we're not going to do anything, we'll just take you home," he reassured them. "Someone's going to pick you up no matter what, you know."

"No they're not!" shouted the brunette.

"I'll be right back," whispered Nariman to his passengers. He got out of the car and walked up to the girls.

"I bet he'll talk them into it," snickered Arsen from the back seat.

They could see Nariman talking and gesticulating; the girls kept turning away. Finally he held out his hand to the one with the curly hair, and she took it after another moment's hesitation. He led her across the mud, skipping over the deeper puddles, then went back to the brunette and helped her over to where her friend was waiting.

"Shamil, turn the music down, what's he saying?" said Arsen.

Shamil ignored him. "What difference does it make?" he asked listlessly.

Nariman was pointing to the car and talking energetically, explaining something to the girls, who were laughing now. Finally the three of them headed toward the Priora.

"Nariman, what a player," whistled Arsen, impressed.

While everyone got settled in the car, Shamil turned down the music and adjusted the front mirror so he could get a better look at the girls.

The tall one's curly hair was bleached, and her features seemed just a bit too large for her face. The brunette was nice looking, but too young.

"Let's get acquainted: I'm Shamil, this is Nariman, and this is Arsen," he began.

"We've already met Nariman," giggled the girls.

"What're your names?" asked Arsen ingratiatingly.

The girls exchanged glances and the curly haired one paused, then answered, "I'm Amina, and she's Zaira."

"What's your ethnicity?" asked Shamil.

"We're Avars."

"Where are you from?" asked Shamil.

"Soviet District."

"Both of you?"

The girls giggled again.

"*Mar'arul mats' l'alebish?*"* Shamil asked.

"We don't," answered Zaira, "All I know is '*Kvanaze rach'a.*'"†

"*Le*, you're a sly one, Shamil," Arsen broke in, "you won't let anyone get a word in edgewise."

"I'm just curious. It's almost midnight, and here are these beautiful girls out on the streets all by themselves. Where were you headed?" grinned Shamil.

"We were at the movies," Amina said, adjusting her hair as she justified herself. "We didn't realize that the movie was going to go on so long. It started at 7:30 and lasted four hours, what a nightmare."

"We followed you all the way from the theater," Nariman pointed out.

"Why?"

"Well, we took a real liking to you."

---

*   Do you speak Avar? (AVAR)

†   Go have something to eat. (AVAR)

"To tell the truth, there's only one thing we didn't like." Shamil said, smirking.

The girls were clearly curious. "What's that?"

"You got in the car with us."

"Cut it out, Shoma!" Nariman waved his hand in Shamil's face.

The girls snorted: "It never changes; you're all the same! We're bad if we don't get in, but if we do, we're even worse."

"He was just joking," Arsen said, hoping to calm them down. "How about we take you to Tarki-Tau?"

"No, take us right home, please," Amina said firmly. "To Uzbek Gorodok."

"Sure, no problem," Nariman smiled. "But tell us about yourselves in the meantime. Where do you go to school, what do you do? You first, Amina."

"I'm from Khas."

"You go to school around here, is that it?"

"I'm not going to tell you."

"What the hell?" Nariman was getting irritated. "We're having a perfectly pleasant, normal conversation here."

"She goes to Pedagogical," Zaira gave the game away. "Anyway, we're almost home. Why aren't you saying anything?"

"Where should we stop?" asked Nariman.

The girls whispered to each other and finally pointed to a corner of a five-story brick building looming up at the end of an alley.

Nariman didn't believe them. "Is this really where you live? Seems to me we got here a little too fast."

"Yes, of course, thank you very much."

They stopped, but no one was ready to call it a night.

"Looks like they're not waiting up for you," noted Shamil, "or else you wouldn't be out so late."

"It's not actually where we live. It's our aunt's apartment. We're staying at her place while she's in the hospital," said Zaira.

"So let's drive around some, we're not weirdos or anything," said Nariman.

"We'll just go downtown, do some donuts," added Arsen.

The girls held another whispered consultation, then Amina said, "All right, but just a quick trip."

They wheeled around, merged onto the avenue, and sped back the way they'd come, toward the streetlights and sparse neon signs.

"Narik, take it up to two hundred, I'll take a picture with my phone," Arsen suggested gleefully.

Nariman floored it, as if he'd been waiting for the invitation. The girls squealed.

"Too fast!"

Someone turned the music up. Tires squealing, they turned onto the main street and sped toward the center of town, dodging and weaving around the other cars on the road. The speedometer needle strained and hovered at maximum. More squealing. Arsen rolled down his window, and the girls' hair whipped him in the face. Shamil languidly watched the streets as they looped around to the pulsing rhythm of the song, the whistling of the wind, and the joyful cries of his fellow passengers.

"I'm going to take the picture!" howled Arsen, holding his phone in his outstretched hand.

"Hey, are you getting any service on that?" the girls asked him.

"No one's got any these days," answered Arsen, and then, shoving his entire torso out the window, he roared:

"*Ai saul!*"

Someone on the street yelled back.

"Let's hit the square!" proposed Nariman. He was really getting into it.

"What do you mean? It's closed off," said Shamil.

"I've got a pass," bragged Nariman.

"Wow, you can get onto the square?" simpered the girls.

"Just turn down the music some," Shamil said blandly.

A grim-looking sergeant inspected the ID that Nariman held out the window, scrutinized his face, and, to Shamil's surprise, lifted the barrier. The Priora shrieked and leaped onto the broad, completely empty square. The girls gasped. Arsen laughed. Nariman grinned proudly, braked in the middle of the square and started wheeling the car around its axis. The girls shrieked again.

"*Ai,* I'm going to throw up!" fake-groaned Amina.

Judging from what Shamil saw in the mirror, both of them were actually ecstatic.

"Nariman, back up and wheel around again," suggested Arsen, bouncing on his seat.

Nariman obediently performed the maneuver, skidding across the pavement.

"Now it's off to the Padishakh!" shouted Arsen.

"What do you say, Shamil?" asked Nariman.

"To the club? Right, let's go," Shamil said, and they sped off.

II

It was a boisterous night in the Padishakh. On a stage in the outdoor seating area a girl with rainbow-dyed, shag-cut hair, wearing a provocative silvery jumpsuit, was performing a suggestive dance.

Spotlights strafed the crowd, catching the dancers' euphoric faces, their undulating backs and upraised hands.

"It's Sabina Gadzhieva!" shouted Zaira, gaping and pointing at the stage.

The crowd roared, and a man in dark glasses and a grotesque fur vest, with a red bandanna around his head, leaped onstage and stood next to the performer.

"*Yoi*, Makhachkala, welcome Sabina Gadzhieva!" bellowed the man.

"And Maga-Do-o-o-odo!" added Sabina Gadzhieva, dragging out the sounds.

The techno gave way to a throbbing drumbeat, and the man in the bandanna launched into a rap recitative.

"What an assclown!" smirked Shamil, squinting and casting a contemptuous glance over Maga-Dodo.

But Nariman's and Arsen's thoughts were elsewhere. They energetically scanned the lively covered galleries around the open-air bar, looking for a place to sit down with the girls.

"So Shoma, are you going to try your luck with the blonde—Amina?" Nariman inquired, half whispering.

"Nah, do whatever you want, but look…the other one is a little unripe. She's still in high school or something, near as I can tell."

"We're good, Arsen will figure it out. Right, we're off to find a table."

They started jostling their way through the crowd, drawing the excited girls after them. Meanwhile, Sabina Gadzhieva gyrated and sang along with the rapper in a hoarse, passionate voice:

> *Your lips kiss,*
> *Your hands caress.*
> *But your heart is stone,*
> *Don't leave me alone.*

See me dance,
Give me a chance.
Don't hate, don't hit,
You Yank or Brit.

Don't leave me alone.

The people on the dance floor howled along while the man in the bandanna continued his unintelligible rapping. And only then, for some reason, did Shamil recall giving his pistol to Amina before they'd entered the club, and watching her hide it in her cute little clutch. Nariman and Arsen had done the same, on the assumption that the girls wouldn't be searched. Their calculations were correct; they'd managed to get the weapons through. Now Shamil wanted his gun back. He started squeezing through the crowd after his companions. There weren't that many girls on the dance floor, but they were pretty. One of them in profile looked like Madina, and he half-intentionally bumped into her with his shoulder. A stocky, hulking guy appeared out of nowhere and gave Shamil the evil eye, but he had already stepped off the dance floor and made his way to the bar.

"*Salam*, let me have one of those cocktails," Shamil said to the lanky bartender, and again, from a distance now, observed the dancers and Sabina Gadzhieva. The star was grinding against the rapper, all but melting in his arms. Her silvery jumpsuit radiated multicolored sparks in the glow of the spotlights and her thick lips were parted in a broad, sultry smile.

Shamil got his cocktail and started squeezing between the tables in the gallery, jostling others like himself, young men with time on their hands, looking for something. Finally he located Arsen and Zaira, who had perched at a corner table on the balcony from where they could see the whole dance hall.

"What's going on?" Arsen asked.

"Nothing, I just wanted to get my piece."

"Amina left her purse here, I'll get it for you," said Zaira, reaching into her friend's beribboned clutch.

"Leave it where it is, Shamil, they'll be able to see it under your T-shirt. You can get it back later," said Arsen.

"No, I'm out of here—I'm not feeling it," objected Shamil, and clanking his cocktail glass down on the table, he slipped his pistol inconspicuously into its holster.

"Maybe we can go together?" Zaira asked anxiously.

"What are you so nervous about?" Arsen tried to calm her down. "Look at your friend, she's really feeling it!"

Shamil glanced down at the dance floor and sure enough, there was Amina, undulating under the brilliant spotlights in a cloud of wild yellow curls, the folds of her sarafan billowing around her, much like Nariman, orbiting her in ever-narrowing circles.

Arsen stood up, put his arm around Shamil's shoulders, and whispered:

"Brother, this chick is being a bad sport—she's a real grouch."

"Better leave her alone. She looks underage."

"Why did she put on such a show, then? Why can't she just have a normal conversation with me?"

"Can we get some food here? I'm starving."

"*Le*, go order something; I'm going to drag her downstairs. I promise, I'm not going to leave her like this. There's no point in her playing naïve."

Arsen turned to Zaira and started sweet-talking her.

"I don't want to," whined Zaira.

"You're so pretty, how can such a pretty girl not want to dance?" chirped Arsen.

Zaira said nothing and hung her head.

Shamil meanwhile ordered lamb shish kebab and a marinated seafood salad. He let his eyes wander idly over the stage, which was temporarily vacant, and the hall, which had been plunged into semi-darkness. The sound of a saxophone playing a slow tune was drifting in from somewhere. Shamil tried in vain to spot Nariman and Amina. When his food arrived, Arsen and Zaira were also nowhere to be seen.

A heavily perfumed girl paraded past, teetering on spike heels. With some surprise Shamil recognized her as the sister of one of his friends, and felt for his phone so he could share the information. Then he remembered that his phone wasn't working, and anyway was on the sofa at home where he had tossed it. "Maybe everything's all right now—no Wall, network's back up. Maybe it was all just some kind of trick?" he thought.

When his order came, Shamil made short work of the meat and soaked up the last of the gravy with a piece of lavash. He began to feel drowsy. He paid, picked up the purses that the girls had left behind, heavy with the weapons, and headed for the balcony.

The balcony looked out onto the dark nighttime sea, whose usual rumbling was drowned in the loud music. A salty breeze blew from the shore, dispelling the heavy languor that had come over Shamil. He lingered there, leaning on the metal railings and listening to the unintelligible voices of the men smoking outside until Nariman, looking concerned, stepped out onto the balcony and beckoned to him.

"I've been looking for you everywhere, where have you been? Little Miss Prissy, Zaira I mean, Arsen was pressuring her to stay, and she made a scene."

"Where is she now?"

"She took off somewhere, the little bitch. Ruined my night. I was making real progress with Amina, and then Arsenchik shows up, and he's like, the chick gave me the slip."

"I have her purse, how far could she get? All the guys will be hitting on her."

"Maybe she went to security."

"What, is she out of her mind?" Shamil was beginning to lose his temper.

They walked along the gallery, peering into people's faces as they passed. On the dance floor a plump woman in a sparkly bra and a rhinestone-embroidered skirt was undulating her belly to an Arabic song. Crumpled banknotes poked out of her cleavage. Finally they heard Arsen's voice:

"*Le*! Here she is!"

Arsen was over by the exit, glaring at Zaira who was standing there in stubborn silence, staring down at the floor. Amina stood beside her, alarmed, stroking her arm and trying to get her to talk:

"What happened, tell me? What's going on?"

"Enough, we're on our way, we'll take them home," announced Shamil, and they left the club.

"Take us home, please—but swear by Allah that you really will!" said Zaira abruptly.

Nariman gave a loud laugh. "Just look at her. Now she wants us to swear."

"Zaira, they're just normal guys," mumbled Amina, "We were just dancing…"

"Shall we go to the beach and smoke some hash?" Nariman proposed quietly to Shamil.

"No, some other time, I'm going to bed." Shamil turned away.

Nariman shushed him, then muttered, "All right, we'll drop you off, then we can go get wasted."

Zaira overheard him. "Take us home first," she commanded.

"What's with all the complaining? Just listen to her: 'bitch, bitch, bitch'!" said Arsen. "Amina, why is your friend such a spoilsport?"

"She just got a little spooked, she's fine," simpered Amina. She had calmed down and was getting her second wind.

They sped along the empty streets, braking once to look at a crowd that had gathered and to ask some of the gawkers what was going on. It was just an ordinary fender bender. In spite of the late hour, a lot of men were still loitering around the streets. Amina was finding everything amusing; she looked out the car window as they went, attracting whistles and hoots from the sidewalk, and kept asking Nariman to play some song that only she knew. Zaira pouted and stared grimly at the road.

"I guarantee, I've seen her somewhere before," said Arsen suddenly, casting a hostile look at Zaira.

"Where?" everyone asked.

"Right, like I'd really tell you all that."

"You're lying," blurted Zaira.

Amina laughed. "You're so funny, Arsen."

"Where did you see me?" asked, Zaira, increasingly alarmed.

"I'll tell you guys later." Arsen nodded to his friends.

Shamil noticed that they had reached his neighborhood, so he asked Nariman to stop. Zaira got very nervous when she saw that he was getting out.

"Don't worry, they'll take you home," Shamil reassured her, though he wasn't really at all certain.

"Don't get lost!" shouted Nariman after him.

The Priora roared off and disappeared, beeping a farewell.

The elevator wasn't working. Shamil went up the stairs to the apartment, exhausted. "I got up too early today," he told himself. When he got to his room he saw that his mother had already made his bed.

He shed his pants and T-shirt, collapsed on the mattress, and immediately fell asleep.

PART II

I

In the morning the city came to life. Workers in dusty overalls walked briskly along the pitted streets to their worksites; women's voices rang out as they darted through the courtyards with their milk jugs; joggers appeared on the streets in gaudy shorts, and old men trotted down toward the sea. Shamil awoke with a hangover. He stumbled around the empty apartment for a while, then, feeling a sudden burst of energy, he grabbed his swim trunks and set off toward the beach. Along the way he glanced into courtyards and observed clusters of children wielding rubber hoses, rinsing the lather out of freshly washed carpets.

He stopped at a booth to buy a hot crusty loaf of bread that had just been delivered from the bakery. The booth was outside a beauty salon. As he paid for the bread, he glanced into the salon window and recognized his neighbor's daughter Kamilla. She was sitting in one of the salon chairs as the hairdresser worked on her thick hair; she didn't see Shamil. He went on his way, breaking off and eating pieces of the bread one by one, his unshaven cheeks moving rhythmically as he chewed.

Kamilla went on telling the hairdresser about the Khanmagomedovs' wedding.

"*Ua*, a million just for the dress!" gushed the hairdresser, as she liberated Kamilla's curls from the velvet-flocked rollers.

"I saw it, Elmira showed it to me herself. It's got real pearls, you can tell immediately, and the lace is all handmade."

"*Mashalla, mashalla*," whispered the hairdresser, enthralled, expertly working her fingers through Kamilla's hair. "My neighbor chose something simple. Mermaid style, but plain, no spangles, no nothing. She looked pathetic, really, just drab, and later everyone said that she had gotten married on the cheap."

"We don't know what it cost, it might have been more expensive than it looked."

"But it wasn't! Some people I know went to the shop and found out exactly how much it cost. You can't keep something like that secret from us. Now, how about we add a little gold glitter?"

"No, I don't like it."

"Yesterday, you know, I was doing a manicure. A really smart lady, has a good job. Anyway, she was complaining that her daughter is basically clueless, a hick."

Kamilla laughed: "What do you mean?"

"She goes, my daughter's as strong as any guy in the neighborhood, she wears her sweat suit everywhere. And when she's late for the transport van, she just sprints after it and catches up!"

"Are you kidding?"

"I swear it's true. So, anyway, one morning this girl is on her way to school, and the van passes her. She starts running after it. She runs and runs..."

"And she caught it?"

"No, the van got to the corner and then someone blew it up!" For some reason the hairdresser gave a throaty laugh.

"When did they ever bomb a van around here? We've never had anything like that."

"Don't you remember, it was during *Uraza Bairam*. The whole town was celebrating, there were dance performances, they'd set up tables of food on Lenin Square. And the guys with the beards, you know, got upset that people were drinking, so they blew up the van."

"Oh, I remember now. But it wasn't the beards who did it. There was just some guy driving along, and he was juggling a live grenade, trying to impress his friends, and he dropped it by mistake—what an asshole!"

"No, that was a different time. And it wasn't some guy juggling, it was a drunk soldier driving along holding the grenade in his hands, and he dropped it. A girl was sitting there, she was from Kizilyurt, she kneeled down and shielded the grenade with her body, so nobody else would get hurt. At first the cops couldn't figure it out, they thought that she was a suicide bomber, but eventually they figured out that she was actually a hero…"

"Wow…"

"Anyway, so I was on the van yesterday. It was completely packed, people had to stand. And a woman stops in the aisle with her feet stretched out like this," the hairdresser spread her hands way out. "She looks around, and there's nowhere to sit. 'Just scoot over a little,' she says to me. Everyone laughs. I had to give her my place and stand the whole rest of the way."

Kamilla smirked: "Have you seen the sign they've put up in the vans? 'Can't get through? Just stop trying.'"

The hairdresser nodded: "And there's another one: 'Ride without a ticket, get thrown in the thicket.' Har-de-har. And, hey, I've even seen one that says, 'Keep your hands off the driver.'"

"'Slam the door, get a free handicapped sticker—after we cripple you.—The Mgt.'"

"But tell me more about the wedding—what else are they going to have?"

"Well, last night they had the bride's party at Elmira's."

"Why didn't you go?"

"I say let the other girls go…why would I? I was invited to the groom's party, anyway. They say Omarbekov is coming from Moscow with his son the oligarch. Everyone who's anyone is going to be there."

"Listen, is it true what they're saying that they've canceled the flights to Moscow?" The hairdresser asked.

"I've heard the same rumors, but I don't believe it…my uncle flew there just a couple of days ago."

"Today my sister-in-law's brother's wife couldn't get a flight out, and there's another rumor about clashes in Moscow between Dagestanis and the locals. That's why our phones can't get any signal."

"What do our cellphones have to do with it? Our men are always causing trouble wherever they are. My brother is always heading out to some street fight…"

"Cut it out! Our guys never start anything so long as no one tries to lay a hand on them. And they can smell fear, you know? If someone's scared, they'll beat him to a pulp." The hairdresser set the rollers aside, sprayed something on Kamilla's hair, then squeezed a drop of white gel from a chic little bottle and worked it lightly through. "Just look at these curls!"

"Thank you, Rakhmat, it's perfect!"

Kamilla admired herself in the mirror: big curls, shiny with gel, framed her plump cheeks and cascaded onto the shoulders of her short dress, which was studded all over with sparkling gemstones. Matching stones gleamed on her high-heeled sandals.

"Shall we leave your bangs?" asked the hairdresser.

"Yes, let's keep them," answered Kamilla. She took one more look in the mirror, and, liking what she saw, she got up from the chair and reached for her name-brand knock-off clutch. "I'm already late."

"Why so early? Usually they don't start until after lunch."

"It's at eleven today, and they're being really strict about permits. I can't get there after Elmira—I'm going straight to the banquet hall from here."

Kamilla went outside and, seeing a van with a ROUTE NO. 5 sign on the front windshield, signaled to it to stop, and got in. There were several passengers, two young men sitting with their legs out, blocking the aisle, a woman in a summer hat with a red flower on the brim, a fat woman in a leopard-print housecoat, and a girl in a light-blue dress.

Kamilla shut the rusty door, which had another one of those jokey signs on the panel above it—"For hitting your head"—and sat on a seat with tattered upholstery. In spite of the van's decrepit, neglected-looking appearance, it was equipped with an up-to-date audio system with huge speakers. A hand-printed sign above them read: "Discount for girls in hijab." A prison chanson was playing.

Unfortunately, she hadn't gotten the driver she preferred, the blue-eyed master of the "7G," a dead ringer for Leonardo DiCaprio. One time he hadn't even charged her. A single incident marred this generally positive picture, however: she'd been riding back from the university; when they passed DiCaprio's van by the shopping center, she saw some guy reach into the driver's side window, grab him by the hair, and beat his head against the steering wheel. It was horrible!

The Gazelle raced on, weaving from side to side and rounding the turns with its brakes squealing. At the clogged intersections the driver pressed his hand to his heart in an appeal to other drivers to let him through, managing along the way to reach out through his window and shake hands with them as they passed, and to carry on a shouted conversation with the passengers over the blaring music.

The passengers would ask him to stop somewhere—"here," or "there," or "over there by the woman in the green skirt," or "wherever you can"—and proudly refused to accept change back from him when they paid their fares.

Kamilla got out near the park, which was named after some German who had designed it years ago. She'd only gone a few steps when she heard taunts and wolf whistles behind her.

"Hey, baby, where'd you leave your skirt? Hey, can I use your phone?"

Kamilla walked on without slowing down or looking around, trying to act normal. The guys who sold CDs on the street had already set up their noisy canopies; behind money-changing tables, proprietors waved wads of cash in the air, and children carrying gym bags darted in and around the crowd.

She passed a courtyard with trellised grapevines, under which a man sat reading a newspaper, with his bare feet propped on a chair in front of him; she then turned into an alley. There, matrons sat on benches exchanging whispered gossip, and food stands filled the air with a commotion of appetizing smells and sounds. A crowd of teenaged boys rushed past Kamilla, splashing her with water from a spray bottle. She drew herself up to her full height, planted her sturdy, high-heeled feet wide, and inspected her dress with horror.

"It'll dry in the sun, dear!" the chuckling women on the benches reassured her.

"Hey, I'll dry it for you personally! Give me your number. Hey, baby! How about you take us with you!" men shouted insolently.

Kamilla continued on and soon came to a splendid white building. On its flat roof stood a big helicopter with gleaming tinted windows; around it guards armed with machine-guns had taken up positions lying along the edge of the roof where they could look down onto the street from different angles. The building had been tightly cordoned off. A crowd had gathered and was gaping at the row of Land Cruisers and Porsche Cayennes parked outside. With dignity Kamilla made her way through the jabbering throng, adjusting her shimmering dress and hair as she went, and extracting from her clutch the gold-embossed invitation with its dancing figure on the cover and a crest in the form of an eagle.

A mustached policeman winked at her: "Give me a call later."

At last Kamilla made it through into the cool lobby and lunged for the ladies' room, so she could put herself back in order. Singing could already be heard from the second floor.

2

In the huge banquet hall, a flurry of thousand-ruble and hundred-dollar bills swarmed in the air above the dancers like snowflakes. In front of the elaborately decorated head table, a troupe of drummers was entertaining the newlyweds, juggling their drumsticks in the air, springing from one foot to the other in their soft-leather boots, and jumping agilely onto one another's strong shoulders to form a lively human pyramid.

Steam rose from the boiled beef and *khinkal*, forming a warm cloud that softened the tipsy guests' exuberant faces. The bridegroom's father circulated around the hall with a twisted ram's horn goblet, clinking glasses with all the guests as they arrived. Long, ardent speeches alternated with a deafening lezginka or a stirring Caucasian song.

Men kept coming up to Kamilla and asking her to dance; after twelve dances she lost count. A wallflower sitting opposite turned periodically to her neighbor and hissed: "Some people make a point of sitting at the end so they'll get invited first."

Kamilla didn't particularly take to the women seated at her table, who had the look of poor relations in their tiger-print scarves and tight skirts. They displayed an unabashed curiosity, and every once in a while one of them would blurt out something like "Look, Crazy Maga is on the move!"

Crazy Maga was indeed in constant motion. He strode around the hall, embracing businessmen and athletes as he went, poking them in the sides with his hairy fists. Occasionally he would drag some random girl out from behind a table and launch into a frenzied dance around her, tossing up handfuls of banknotes that rained down on her head. Then he would stop abruptly, kiss this latest partner on the crown of the head, and set off to the *tamada*'s table.

"Five minutes!" gasped the relatives in the tiger prints. "He danced with her five whole minutes! It's scandalous!"

Five minutes was of course too much. Indecent, even.

The singer Sabina Gadzhieva appeared in a latex dress, heavily made up, her voice hoarse. Kamilla managed to get up close and even to clasp her hand at one point in a round dance. Anticipating the bride's entrance, a relay dance began, with the dancers passing the traditional wedding baton from hand to hand until finally one of the more mature female guests, dressed to the nines, would invite the groom to dance, after which the groom was to invite the bride.

With the milky folds of the bride's hand-worked lace dress at its center, a crowd of hands, feet, and heads whirled in a mad dance. They began tossing the groom into the air. Two young men performed somersaults in unison.

At the height of the festivities someone beckoned Khanmagomedov the elder to one side. Kamilla overheard an insistent whisper:

"Khalilbek is calling, it's urgent. And take Alikhan with you…"

Elmira in her lacy dress didn't even look at Kamilla.

"She's become one of them, the show-off," thought Kamilla resentfully.

The tiger-print women kept on whispering. One of them, jingling massive earrings in her big ears, was sharing her wisdom: "I can tell who's who on sight. When people start looking for a bride, I'm the one they ask. Want to know my method? I go to some house where there's an unmarried daughter, right? Before I go I get my shoes really dirty. If I'm going with my husband, I get his shoes dirty too. We sit there a while, chatter and whatnot, then, when it's time to go, I take a good look at our shoes. The right sort of girl will have washed and dried them, and left them in the entryway all polished and ready. But if our shoes are still dirty, then I don't leave it at that, I'll let everyone know what a slob she is."

"*Vababai*, Kalimat, you're a crafty one!"

"There's more: when I'm at someone's house I always go to the bathroom and look into the john to see whether it's clean. If it's dirty, I go and find the cleaning supplies and wash it myself without saying anything. With my own two hands. Give them something to think about."

"And you're right, too, Kalimat. Girls have gotten so lazy these days."

"They've gotten so high-and-mighty, let me tell you!" exclaimed Kalimat, giving her earrings a shake. "But it's not like our *dzhigits* are any better. My friend's son got married. A decent guy, but then he started going to religious lectures somewhere, and got a little big for his britches. He won't even let his wife go to class. Or she'll have to study for an exam, and he'll bring friends home late at night and make her stop what she's doing and cook *khinkal* for them. She's a handful herself, though—she finally packed up and went home to her mother."

"What about the guy?"

"*U-u-u*, he dug in his heels. 'I don't need my wife to be educated,' he says. Says, she doesn't need that stuff she's studying. Arabic is another thing. I'd get that!'"

"*Ua*, those kids have basically lost their minds."

"It's all for show. Anyway, his parents knocked some sense into him—served him right, the dimwit!"

Kamilla let the conversation wash over her, catching scraps of words here and there through the din. The microphone went to some tall man from the neighboring republic, who began with wishes for the couple's happiness and then skipped to the vexed topic of the Wall, pointing out the need to seek diplomatic paths and not to fall for any provocations. Then, claiming urgent business and mentioning Khalilbek's name, the man made a quick exit. Crazy Maga and the other dignitaries had also vanished. Bowls of black caviar and an entire baked sturgeon languished on their abandoned table, forlorn as orphans.

"Some of our esteemed guests and hosts have a small, terribly pressing meeting they have to go to—we all know, of course, that in the republic we have not only joy, not only weddings, but also many worries," the *tamada* announced, speaking slowly, and looking around him.

Kamilla decided to go down and take a look in the mirror; she felt that her carefully sprayed hair might have begun to droop. At the exit stood a man in a black T-shirt, letting no one through.

"I need to go to the restroom," declared Kamilla.

"Not right now, just hold on a little bit," said the man, without a trace of a smile.

Nothing had changed in the hall. Some breathless guy darted up to her with a flower and an invitation to dance, but this time Kamilla turned him down, claiming a sore foot. The man was offended, of course, but she didn't like his looks, and anyway, she wasn't in the mood.

"Father of the groom, come forward!" someone at the microphone shouted cheerfully, emphasizing every word.

"Just wait, they'll be back in a minute—they're out serving the People," explained the *tamada*.

The crowd responded with a restless though good-natured rumble of indignation.

"A fine time they've come up with for a meeting!" someone grumbled.

Kamilla got tired of eavesdropping and started watching the dancers. She spotted the son of her university's rector, a complete womanizer. They said he'd seduced some girl, made her strip down to her underwear, and then dumped her out of his car, right on the street. Poor thing! Kamilla also saw the groom's great-grandmother, an ancient woman, famous for her perfect memory and her love of tea. During the war, when everyone was starving, she had sold her cow to buy more tea. Marya Vasilyevna was here too, gliding majestically across the hall. And over there...

Kamilla tuned in again to the women's conversation.

"Yes," Kalimat was saying, "I just heard that those bearded lunatics have herded up all the *khakims* and taken them off somewhere."

"Khalilbek, too? and Alikhan? and Crazy Maga? Khanmagomedov, too?" they clucked. "But why?"

"Maybe to shoot them. Or load them on a boat and send them off to Tyulen Island. Allah only knows why."

"*Vababai*, Kalimat, don't talk that way!" exclaimed one of the women, and set off toward the exit, taking delicate, mincing steps.

Kamilla got up cautiously and followed her out. The man in the black T-shirt was gone. She proceeded downstairs unhindered and was about to go into the ladies' room, then changed her mind and headed outside. There was no one at the outside door either—no gawkers, no policemen, no one. Kamilla walked around outside the building, but there wasn't a soul anywhere. She heard the sounds of a lezginka through an open window, and someone whistled and shouted, "Hey, good-looking!"

"That's strange," thought Kamilla and, as though recalling something important, hastened back into the foyer. She had to check her hair.

3

Makhmud Tagirovich ran along the dislodged slabs of pavement in his Lak sandals, favoring his right foot a bit. Signs leaped past: "Cement milling;" "Limousine Rental for Matchmaking;" "Air Conditioners, Humidifiers, Dehumidifiers;" "Amelia's Facials;" "Cinder block removal;" "Fine Couture;" "Glass and Aluminum Design."

Exhausted, he leaned against a gray spackled wall, on which someone had scrawled in chalk: CHAT 647987669. A gust of wind then whisked Makhmud Tagirovich's straw hat off his head and bore it off in the direction of an industrial complex. Some passerby tried to snag it with two fingers, but after alighting briefly on the ground, the hat was immediately swept off to one side and barely escaped being crushed under the wheels of passing cars.

Makhmud Tagirovich stood panting, trying to catch his breath. Anticipating how upset his wife would be, he headed to a little square where some of the trees had been cut down, figuring he could spend some time there pondering his great epic poem. (In fact his novel was his life's work, but he'd gotten blocked and had turned to verse as an outlet for his creative energy.) The poem was dedicated to his wife, of course, and told the story of her early years in her mountain village.

According to his outline, the "Childhood" stanzas would flow smoothly into "Youth," at which point the heroine would meet this same Makhmud Tagirovich. Then there would be a travelogue of the wedding cortege's journey to Makhachkala, with a detailed listing and description of all the stops along the way. In the finale, the happy bride and groom would gaze up at the starlit sky and whisper:

> Together forever, wife and man
> Nature bound us, and Dagestan.

After some hesitation, Makhmud Tagirovich replaced the word "Nature" with "Allah."

He settled down on a tree stump amid a tangle of prickly black-berry bushes and took his graph-paper notebook out of his briefcase. Hastily leafing through the first few yellow-streaked pages, he started reading, mumbling contentedly to himself:

> The straw, a vivid fiery sheaf,
> On bended backs the women bear;
> Manured roadway, carved relief
> On dung-adobe walls, and there
> An unrepeatable design;
> The local scamps abuse, malign
> The village fool; they mock, deride:
> "*Abdal, abdal!*" they cry, then hide
> Beneath the leaves of roadside trees

To dodge the vengeful stones he hurls,
Which fall like hail that stings and whirls
And rends their shady canopies.
All this your mind preserves, and more:
Dreams, images, and village lore!

In olden days, timid and shy,
You'd visit gray-haired matrons there;
And then their muddied boots you'd spy
And gaze with eyes of dull despair.
So much of it you could not bear:
The women's greased and plaited hair,
Their nosy questions and the speck
Of slobber where they kissed your neck.
A crowd of frisky naiads throng;
They shout, they praise, they draw you in;
They whirl you round, they make a din;
And then they carry you along.
To your soft cheek they all are drawn,
Each wanting it to touch their own.

With hasty steps you'd rock the floor,
And bring to each new guest a treat;
You'd greet them warmly at the door.
And when your father shared a sweet,
You'd take it from his calloused hand.
The touch, the feel, the taste was grand;
And at those times, in home's warm nest,
You felt that you were truly blessed.

But learned, noisy guests would flaunt
Their learning, overwhelm your head,
Would puzzle you and young Akhmed,
With musty erudition they would daunt;
And then they'd sit you down to chess
And teach you both what moves were best.

Before your childish, fresh young eyes
The road's long dusty path unfurled;
Above, the eagles in the skies,
Below, the hens in their cooped world;
The men stroll homeward from the club;
Tobacco smoke, manure, a rough…

Makhmud Tagirovich extracted a crumpled handkerchief from his
pants pocket and blew his nose with a satisfying honk.

Tobacco smoke, manure, a rough
Young ruffian jostles you, and you're
Entrapped, his reckless eyes a lure;
His gang of leering, laughing toughs
Observe your grimaces, your fumbles,
Your hand takes up a stone, it trembles;
They block the road, they fix their eyes.
Miraculously the rock you throw
Glances across his egglike brow;

The village aunties' bossy cacklings,
The strands of hair across your cheek,

The road's dry dust gets on your stockings
As down the village streets you streak
And enter gardens, newly seeded,
Their shade, the rows all neatly weeded;
To roosters' raucous cries you run,
To fading rays of melting sun;
The beehives on the woodshed walls
And someone's shouted call, "*Chchit!*"
The cat, disgruntled, flees from it;
The hinny trudges by, hee-haws,
And where this childless creature strode,
The ram casts pearls across the road.

In morning often you would tread
Your father's porch, outside its door,
And in the winding streets ahead
You'd hear the bustling village roar.
With languid, idle eyes you'd seek
The sun's bright ray beyond the peak;
Neglected, your *buruti* tipped;
And down the water spilled and dripped.
You pushed the prickly, restless broom,
And with a growing sense of dread
In fear of blows you bend your head,
Your mother's slaps and pinches loom.
And fearing that you'll hear the cry:
"*Azbar bak'ararbi, yasai?*"‡

---

‡   Have you cleaned the courtyard, wench?

The heroine then runs to the *godekan* to look for her father, and ultimately finds him. (Makhmud Tagirovich skipped ahead a few pages:)

The brow's sharp wrinkle comes in sight
The shoelaces, the lofty gaze,
The trouser leg, and what a fright:
The craggy profile of his face,
The prickly stubble on his cheeks,
His mouth's abyss, the words he speaks,
The mop of locks with which he's crowned,
Behold, behold, your father's found.
The people were alarmed by talk,
Of toppled mansions, riots, coups,
Of evil, kolkhozes—strange news;
The men locked shoulders, set to walk;
Axes in hand, the boughs they chopped,
And Marlboros from fingers dropped.

The dusty trucks roared as they sped;
Women made spindles wind, unwind
Great strands of endless flaxen thread,
When all around was dark and blind.
The truck dripped gas, a hulking brute;
Its honk shattered the air, fell mute.
Its lights shone in the darkened night
Like wolves' eyes gleaming at the sight,
As they roam on the wooded slopes.
And then Volgas and jeeps appeared,
And from inside them strangers peered.

The people stirred and felt new hopes.
The dignitaries sought to meet
The locals, shake their hands, and greet.

Makhmud Tagirovich was somewhat disturbed that his wife's childhood, which had unfolded in the '60s, had unexpectedly become
overgrown with regalia from the post-perestroika period. But he cast
aside his doubts and chalked it up to poetic license. Anyway, a can-
didate for deputy comes to campaign in the village. That kind of
thing was still happening in the '90s. In the poem, the description of
political disputes was weak, but Makhmud Tagirovich was quite proud
of the rhymes that he had come up with at the end of the stanza:
"The cow, a roan, went mincing past, and left a gift upon the path."
The poet followed that up with some lyrical passages:

But off the noisy cohort rushed,
As Grandpa stood and watched and waved;
And to the escort loudly gushed
And like a moonstruck child behaved.
Up mountain slopes, you and your dad
After the mule, the hike you had;
How you and he enjoyed those times,
Makhmud Tagirovich's rhymes,
The house's whimsical casement,
The drowsy zigzags on it carved,
Ravines below, arches above;
The clouds, a graying regiment;
Under the cow a future bull
He drinks and drinks until he's full.

In the garden stones were knocked
To call the swarm back to the hive;
Two gaudy, valiant roosters squawked,
Engaged in fierce mad feathered strife.
As one must fall so fell the foe,
The bloodied loser brought down low,
Amusing idlers gathered round.
Above, along the paths are bound
The mountain girls, to beg the sky;
For a rich harvest supplicate,
Summon their gods, and tell their fate,
A pagan chant they sing and cry.
The men their sacred din intone
And "God is one" in chorus drone.

But then Makhmud Tagirovich's reading was interrupted by the crackle of shots being fired, followed by the sound of automobiles honking. The poet pushed through the bushes, scratching his hands on their branches along the way, and peered out onto the street. Two schoolchildren with satchels were looking out from behind an electric pole, and in front of them on the pavement a man in a police uniform lay dead. A crowd was gathering. Gawkers emerged from their cars, waving cellphones, and within minutes a dense traffic jam had formed.

The poetic mood was ruined. Makhmud Tagirovich stowed the notebook in his briefcase, felt around on his head for the missing hat, and strode off in the opposite direction. He tried to eradicate the scene with the dead policeman from his mind, and to direct his thoughts to his upcoming conversation with Pakhriman, the Lak.

The two friends got together for lunch at Pakhriman's on Thursdays.

They would eat *kurze* with sorrel, or *chudu* with cottage cheese, would play backgammon and would get into passionate arguments. During their last conversation Pakhriman had been trying to convince him that the Surkhay-khan who had defeated Nader Shah in 1741 was a Lak, and Makhmud Tagirovich had gotten upset. Citing an Arabic epic poem for evidence, he'd insisted that Surkhay-khan had been a Turkish agent, and that his wife had been in Nader Shah's harem. The argument almost led to blows, but at the decisive moment Pakhriman's wife had brought in a bottle of Kizlyar Madeira, and the evening ended peacefully.

But Mahmud Tagirovich realized that it was still a long time until Thursday, and he turned into his yard. His house stood behind a tangle of grapevines facing one of the main streets. Makhmud Tagirovich climbed the old wooden stairs, got out his keychain with its charm in the shape of two mountain ridges, and opened the door. With a thrill of terror he realized that his wife was still home.

"Makhmud!" she called from inside.

"Yes, Farida," he replied, again reaching up to his unhatted head.

"Makhmud," she whined, coming out of the living room and wrapping her feather-light golden shawl around her, "Marat is having more trouble at the university. You work there, why can't you do anything for your own grandson?"

"What can I…" he began.

"What can you do?" his wife spread her hands wide. "Allah sees that you haven't lifted a finger to help either your son or your grandsons! Take Abdullaev, you must have seen how much he did; he set his children up for life! And Omarov? His wife wears five kilograms of gold on each hand!"

She sank onto an armchair and buried her face in her hands.

"Farida…" Makhmud Tagirovich tried again.

"And look at your brother." She heaved in her chair. "He's ten years younger than you, he doesn't have your education, and he's going to be factory director. You need to take a page from his book."

"I have a good job." Makhmud Tagirovich was starting to get angry.

"And what's it gotten you? Everyone there thinks you're an idiot, I'll tell you straight out," Farida said, vicious now. "Normal people make money and they help their relatives out. You've had so many opportunities, and I've given you such good advice, but do you ever listen?"

"Farida, what's all this *ai-ui*?" Makhmud Tagirovich was squirming.

"I haven't even gotten started." His wife continued, wagging her finger. "I've got plenty more to say. What are you up to, going to Pakhriman's again?"

"I go where I want to," sniffed Makhmud Tagirovich.

"So go, have a good time, do your scribbling while your wife toils away," she said, glancing at his briefcase and gathering up her purse.

Taking advantage of the pause, Makhmud Tagirovich ducked into his room and lurked there until he heard the door slam.

4

Makhmud Tagirovich liked to remind his grandchildren that his own grandfather, who came from a family of Khunzakh khans, had in his childhood by some miracle escaped death at the hands of Imam Shamil. He was taken prisoner, ransomed, and after undergoing a multitude of adventures and peregrinations, had ended up in Petersburg high society, where he had even served as an officer guarding the imperial quarters. Makhmud Tagirovich's uncles, and there were eight of them, had perished in various distant parts of the crumbling empire, and beyond its borders as well.

One of them had given his life on the battlefield in the Russo-Japanese War, another during the First World War, and another at the hands of hostile Bolsheviks during the Civil War, but all of them had earned medals for valor in battle. Makhmud Tagirovich's father was the youngest, so they spirited him away to a distant Khunzakh village. There he stayed until 1931, when he left to enroll in the newly opened Makhachkala Pedagogical Institute. Though he was expelled shortly thereafter for being the son of a White general.

Returning to his quiet village, he spent his youth copying out the Koran and working on translations, until one day, overcome by a wave of Red Romanticism, he hammered out a poem of repentance, in Avar, in which he renounced his unfortunate past.

In mannered lines, abounding in Arabisms, the poet elaborately recounted the sad fates of the simple Khunzakh people, who had bent their backs for centuries on end under the yoke of the treacherous khans and their plotting wives. A recurrent figure in the poem was a famous epic hero from free Gidatl who had led the khan's young sons with him into the fire.

The poem was well received; it circulated widely, and Makhmud Tagirovich's father was summoned to Khunzakh and given a position there as a schoolteacher. Within two years he had managed to become the son-in-law of the collective farm's chief agronomist. Shortly thereafter he was named director of the school, and then, after serving in the Great Patriotic War, joined the Ministry of Education in Makhachkala. By that point Makhmud Tagirovich's father had left his poetic endeavors behind him.

Makhmud Tagirovich himself was a late baby; by the time he was born his three elder sisters were already in high school. He grew up in a private apartment in the city, with local celebrities always visiting, including poets in *kirza* boots bearing *pandurs*. Before long his father became bored with his mother, who yielded her place to various enchantresses from the nomenklatura. When Makhmud Tagirovich was eight, his mother died in Khunzakh under mysterious circumstances after celebrating the fiftieth anniversary of the Soviet Socialist Republic of Dagestan. It was said that she had eaten too much greasy meat with *khinkal*, had washed them down with ice water, and had died from a swollen intestine.

Within a year Makhmud was blessed with a stepmother, the daughter of the Oblast Committee Secretary, and his sixty-year-old father came into possession of a personal car and, soon afterward, a new baby. Left to his own devices, Makhmud Tagirovich quickly developed a taste for alcohol and for writing in his diary. He stocked up on notebooks in which he copied down quotations from Marx, Engels, Saint-Simon, Gorky, and Gamzatov, as well as jotting observations from his own life experience.

Alone now in the house, he took a stack of these notebooks out of the cupboard, picked one of the thicker ones, opened it to the middle and began to read greedily:

16 MAY 1980

For some reason I woke up today not in my bedroom, but in the living room. I recalled that last night after seeing my parents off to Czechoslovakia, I immediately called Rustam and Volodya and invited them over. Rustam arrived first with some dry wine and a bottle of vodka, and I got out some cognac. We needed to warm up before our expedition to Irka's and Vadik's, who celebrated their three-year anniversary (of living together) the day before yesterday.

Turns out, Tonya had also been invited to the party; I'd met her in April on the trip to Baku. Rustam started in immediately on how he'd hooked up with her while his plump little Nadya was away in Saratov. "Tonya isn't my type, though," he told me. "Tonya is for guys like you, Makhmud. Intellectual conversations give me a stomach ache."

I was flattered by Rustam's allusion to my intellectual superiority, though at the same time I felt guilty about being so vain. We had almost finished the booze by the time Volodya showed up. He was feeling blue. I proposed taking the tape recorder and some cassettes and going directly to Irka's and Vadik's.

So we left. We flagged down a ride at the Komsomolets Movie Theater and headed to Kirov Street. And at that point I realized that I'd completely forgotten to bring a gift. But it was too late, so I figured that if it came up I'd just give them money or drop hints about a surprise still in the works.

Ira met us wearing an apron. Vadik had gone to the neighbors to borrow a corkscrew. The table was already set, and they'd put out a lot of appetizers. Various people I'd never met began to show up. As it turned out, they were relatives of Ira's from Piatigorsk. Volodya immediately ducked into a corner and started to leaf through a photo album, but I made a point of mingling. One of the guests from Piatigorsk, who was much older than everyone else, said that my name was very Dagestani. I told him that it had been the name of a great Avar poet from Kakhabroso. Then Ira came out and started pressing me to recite something from Makhmud in Avar. I wasn't about to play coy, but I announced that I would wait until everyone was there. Meaning, Tonya.

Finally she arrived. You couldn't call her beautiful, but she has a nice, pretty face. She went out onto the balcony first thing, probably to have a smoke. Later, when we sat down at the table, Tonya sat right across from me and asked, "So, Makhmud, are you going to be gallant and serve me some wine?"

"Don't forget you already have a suitor—he's on your right," said Rustam, sitting down on her right there and then.

That bugged me, but I didn't say anything, just proposed a toast to Ira and Vadik:

"Today someone mentioned my namesake, the poet Makhmud from Kakhabroso. Maybe some of you here don't know his story. He was the son of a coal miner who didn't approve of his son's poetic inclinations. But Makhmud couldn't help writing, because he was in love with the beautiful Mui. And she loved him too. But Mui's people, who were rich and of high birth, refused to let her marry the poor Makhmud.

"Meanwhile his fame thundered across all the towns and villages of Avaria; wherever he went, crowds would gather to hear him. The future last imam of Chechnya and Dagestan, the counterrevolutionary Nazhmudin Gotsinsky, was enraged that Makhmud wouldn't write poems to order.

"'Why won't you write about our spiritual leaders?' he asked Makhmud.

"'Because I'm not in love with them,' answered Makhmud.

"Then Gotsinsky commanded that Makhmud be given a hundred lashes with the knout, and Makhmud went lame in the right foot. After the whipping he was forced to go live in the Transcaucasus, but when he finally came back to his motherland, he was welcomed like royalty, because everyone loved him; they knew his poetry by heart.

"But Mui was already married by then. So they found a new woman for the disconsolate Makhmud, a woman who liked to sing, and he married her, but before long he left her and went away to work in Baku. There he learned that Mui's husband had died, and the flame of hope was kindled in him. The poet, plotting beforehand with his beloved, planned to abduct her so they could elope, but Mui backed out at the last moment, afraid that her relatives would murder Makhmud in revenge.

"To drown his sorrows, the poet enlisted in the Dagestan cavalry. One day, somewhere in the Carpathian Mountains, he was pursuing an Austrian soldier. The terrified Austrian tried to take shelter in a church, and Makhmud burst inside after him. There he found himself standing in front of Michelangelo's *Madonna with Child*, and was struck with the Virgin Mary's likeness to his beloved Mui. 'I lost my mind,' he later said, 'I stood there in front of the painting and couldn't keep silent. I asked some people there, "Who is that woman on the wall? Why does everyone have her portrait in their house?"'

"'It's Mariam, who, though a virgin, gave birth to the Prophet Jesus.'"

"Well, that's a translation, of course. Anyway, the thunderstruck Makhmud went on to pen a long narrative poem, *Mariam*. Of course he never saw his own Mariam-Mui again, she died while he was away at war.

"Makhmud himself didn't have long to live. He was felled by jealous rivals, who shot him in the back of the head after the last in a series of brilliant victories at poetry competitions.

"They say that at the exact moment he was shot, Makhmud was reciting a poem about his own death: 'A mind of gold in a silver skull; I did not suspect that I would die in vain.' That's my own translation, by the way. But we are now near the end of my toast. Dear Irina and Vadim, cherish and preserve what was not given to Mui and Makhmud: keep your dear one at your side…"

While I was pronouncing this long toast, everyone was silent. I think I made an impression. They began to shout: "Makhmud! You need to be the *tamada* at weddings!" And Tonya's fiery eyes burned into me. I joked, laughed, I was on top of the world, but I also didn't neglect to drink. Volodya and I managed to down a half-liter of vodka in only thirty minutes.

We went into the next room to dance. I danced with Tonya, then with some little old lady, and then with Tonya again. She was clearly interested. She asked me to recite from Makhmud in Avar. I was already tipsy, but my recitation was brilliant, and everyone applauded. Even Rustam and Volodya were amazed.

Tonya asked about my career plans. I answered that I wanted to go into industry, to work for the greater good of communism, and to eradicate the flaws that so abounded around us. Then, after I told her the story I've already described above, about taxi drivers who double as pushers and capitalist landladies making money off other people's misfortunes, Tonya told me that she sometimes felt like eradicating herself, that that would be even simpler. She often had thoughts of suicide, she said. I scolded her a bit, saying that this was a sign of weakness.

Later, while everyone was dancing, I downed a couple more shots on my way to the john. Had some greens from the hors d'oeuvre table. By that point Volodya could barely talk, and was having trouble keeping vertical.

It was already past nine when the party started to break up. We said our good-byes and left, caught a ride, and came home to my place to keep things going. As if just to spite us, all the stores in the neighborhood were closed.

Makhmud Tagirovich scratched at the yellow wart on his right cheek, put aside the notebook, shook his head, and looked outside onto the balcony. On the street, shouts could be heard, and a siren wailed. Always something. Makhmud sighed, went back into his room, and shut the PVC door tight to keep out the noise. It was quiet. Felt good.

5

Makhmud Tagirovich's wife worked for a government agency. Here is what her working day was like: she and her colleagues would arrive around ten in the morning. They would chatter, put on their makeup, primp. Eleven was teatime. The women brought in candy and baked goods, and served them to the men.

At noon they went to their desks. The younger employees went online, and the older ones gossiped. At one they prepared for lunch. They got out thermoses of soup, cellophane-wrapped cold cuts, pies, fresh vegetables. They locked the office from inside and set everything out on the table with elaborate care. The entire department ate together; over lunch they discussed the latest news, taking their time. Then they cleared the table, put the lunch things away. Occasionally in the afternoon they would have to take care of some people who stopped by with official business, but for the most part they just sat around talking among themselves. Around five they had tea again, after which they went home for the day.

Farida arrived later than usual, after lunch. It was noisy in the office. No one was at their desk; everyone was upset. At that time of the day Roza always took up her position at the window, got out a bottle of nail polish, and touched up her toenails, but today she looked a bit disheveled, and was standing in the middle of the room, shouting:

"Let's try calling him at home again!"

It turned out that none of their superiors had showed up to work. Not the director, not his deputy. Rumor had it that none of the other government offices and agencies were open either. After the Khanmagomedovs' wedding yesterday, all the decision-makers had disappeared.

Roza was yelling something about how they'd all been shot by the "goddamned beards."

Faizulla Gadzhievich, a thin, hoarse-voiced man, claimed that that was all nonsense, and kept repeating, over and over, "I'm sure it's just that they've had to call an urgent meeting."

Zarema Elmurazovna stood with her fists pressed against her quivering, full bosom, exclaiming, "My daughter told me that they loaded everyone on a motorboat and hauled them off to Tyulen Island."

"But why?" asked Faizulla Gadzhievich.

"So they'll die of starvation out there!"

An anxious-looking, cow-eyed young man appeared in the doorway: "Has Uncle Alikhan showed up yet?"

"Now where exactly would he come from, Shamil?" lamented Zarema Elmurazovna.

"He might still come. They can't all have been devoured by the *shaitan*," mumbled Faizulla Gadzhievich.

Stricken, Farida sank back onto her chair: "So should we just go home, or what?"

"No, let's have some tea," proposed Roza.

The young man, which is to say Shamil, declined their invitation and left. The last couple of days had gone by in a kind of strange, blind fog. He had gone from one house to another, from one set of relatives to another. He had helped them haul their belongings around town, bumped along in stuffy vans, had called at various offices. He had even made a quick run to the airport, only to find it deserted, with its windows blocked with plywood and the entrance locked and dead-bolted. The ticket counters were closed; all the planes had flown off to Moscow, and it was highly unlikely they would ever come back.

His mother spent days in a mute stupor. Then she admitted that someone had been sending threats to her school's director, and that final exams had been canceled. She started packing for the village.

The Internet had been down for days, and Shamil spent practically every night in front of the TV, mindlessly flipping though the channels. It was impossible to make sense of anything on the news. Some stations simply continued their normal programming, making no mention of the crisis; on others he occasionally heard the dry phrase "Operation Expulsion;" finally he came upon some reports from the Stavropol border. They showed guard towers, armed soldiers, barbed wire, women screaming incoherently, and nothing more.

Shamil clicked over to Channel One for the nth time. A heavily made-up, disingenuous-looking face appeared on the screen, with multicolored curls flowing every which way down her cheeks. The singer Sabina Gadzhieva jerked her neck desperately from side to side, as though she wanted her head to fly off, and jammed a microphone close to her gaping lips, which were generously smeared with wine-colored lipstick. Shamil cursed, glanced out of the room, and felt his way to the veranda. His mother's voice called to him in the darkness. She seemed to be standing in the doorway to her bedroom, fully dressed. Though it was hard to tell.

"What's all this about you and Madina?" she asked.

"We have to call it off," Shamil flapped his hand at her, and offered no further elaboration.

His mother reached out and touched his head gently. Shamil backed away from her and went back to his room. Nothing would surprise him. He grabbed the remote and again went through all the available channels. He came across an explicit, adults-only cartoon, a tedious action movie, and a stultifying women's talk show. Finally he gave up, turned off the TV, and flopped down on the couch, which had been his father's.

Dreams came not right away, but in phases. First Shamil heard ragged noises and sounds, then images appeared, lurching before his eyes like a video shot by a drunkard. He was back home in the village, in Ebekh. A crowd had gathered, mostly Shamil's relatives, on a road that was still damp from a recent rain. They were shouting and laughing, pointing at him.

Then Madina's mother arrived in a formal fringed scarf; she was still a beautiful woman. She squeezed her way through the crowd, took Shamil by the hand, and led him off down the road. The crowd followed, tiptoeing, whistling greedily, and cracking jokes about Shamil's boots. Shamil looked down and saw that he was wearing a pair of ridiculous white numbers with metallic clasps.

They passed several houses and then made their way, slipping and sliding through thick, almost impassible mud, to some place that used to be a club. From there, skipping from stone to stone, they passed abandoned houses, decrepit and overrun by weeds. Shamil's white boots turned black from the mud. Ducking, still gripping Shamil's hand in hers, Madina's mother led him through a beautifully chiseled stone arch into a dark passageway. Watery cow manure squelched under his feet. To his right a young bull bellowed, then fell silent.

The crowd had settled down and was now only whispering its jokes, as though sensing the gravity of the moment. "How are they all going to get in here?" wondered Shamil, taking care to step in his never-to-be mother-in-law's footsteps. At last, a strip of daylight gleamed through a crack in the wall, and soon they emerged from the dark passage and found themselves on the other side of the abandoned building. It looked out over the edge of a terrifying abyss, with the mother-of-pearl thread of a river glinting far below.

Madina's mother turned her laughing, youthful face toward him, and gave him a playful slap on the shoulder. The crowd tumbled out through the narrow archway and gradually filled the tiny scrap of land at the edge of the ravine. "We can't be in Ebekh," thought Shamil, disoriented. "There's no ravine there." The patch of ground at the cliff edge was overgrown with weeds, and the people in the crowd that had gathered there were beating on calfskin drums and laughing. Old Mukhuk was dancing with precise steps, at the head of an entire line of laughing women. "Patti, raise your hand up higher, you look like a sick heron, and Zahra, you're lurching like a chicken," he kidded the other dancers.

Shamil stood with the toe of his boot braced against a large stone at the cliff edge, afraid he might lose his balance and tumble into the ravine. At this point the crowd began to poke and pinch him, tousle his hair, and whirl him around in circles. He had almost managed to free himself from the frenzied mob when with an ecstatic whoop Madina's mother threw herself off the cliff and plunged into the abyss. Then the others hurled themselves down after her, beating on their drums and urging Shamil to join them as they passed. From below there came the sound of women's joyful shrieks and men's laughter.

Shamil couldn't move, couldn't look over the cliff edge, couldn't think. He stood for a moment, then turned and rushed back the way he had come, but the archway was gone; there was only a blank wall, warmed by the sun. He pulled off his boots, which were plastered with mud and manure, and tossed them into the abyss. There came a great crashing sound, and a fine hail of pellets, the size of sugar lumps, rained down onto the earth. Shamil woke up.

He fell asleep and awoke several more times until he finally woke up for good. His mother had slipped a note under the door. She wrote that she was going to the gas station with one of his cousins, Mashidat, and after that they would go to their home village, and that he should come too, whenever he was ready. Shamil cursorily washed his face and hands and, unshaven, headed off to Mashidat's place.

6

At Mashidat's door he ran into Asya, her daughter, who had been at the family apartment the day he'd had his fateful conversation with Madina. Asya looked bedraggled, diffident. It turns out that her parents had left early that morning, and Shamil's mother had gone with them. Asya had refused to leave, had insisted on staying behind in the city with her brother.

She caught Shamil up on the news, and they walked side by side along the uneven, muddy road, barely making progress, as though their feet were sinking into deep sand. To their right was a fence running alongside the road with a kindergarten behind it. When he saw that the metal bars of the fence had been bent, leaving an opening, Shamil ducked through. Asya followed.

He kept running into her, Asya, on the streets. He had even begun to suspect that she was seeking him out, and he'd had the urge to poke fun at her, taunt her, hurt her feelings, so that she would back off. But, honestly, it just kept slipping his mind.

Now he took a closer look at her. She was pale and had clearly not put any attention into grooming herself, though she was pretty in a childlike sort of way. Dark blue circles were coming out under her eyes, however, casting an anxious, wasted pall over her young face.

"They've come clean about the Wall," she said abruptly.

"Who has?"

"It was on TV today, on the local news."

"I spent all last night flipping the channels, I didn't see a thing!" Shamil snapped.

They came up to a creaking iron wheel, the skeleton of a merry-go-round. Asya sat on it and adjusted her hair.

"I want to get out of here," she said, and strands of hair streaked across her lips.

"Where would you go?"

"Moscow, maybe."

Shamil chuckled. "What do you suppose you'd do there? Just smell the roses?"

"No, I wouldn't stay anyway, I'd leave there too," she said solemnly, without looking at Shamil.

"Are you off your rocker, or what?"

"Of course I am," she blurted. "I can't dance, I never know what to wear, I don't know what to say to people, I don't know how to smile. Of course I'm off my rocker. There's only one option for me: the Buinaksk psych ward."

Shamil gave a nervous laugh. "You've got a point there. It's not going to be easy for you to find a husband."

"I don't need one anyway," snapped Asya.

"You should have gone with your parents, then…"

"I have to finish my coursework."

"I have a feeling there won't be any more courses," said Shamil. "We're done for."

They sat without talking, just watched the squeaking iron wheel as it turned.

"Madina got married, she did a *nikiakh*," said Asya abruptly.

Shamil tensed up. "How do you know?"

"She didn't even tell her parents," continued Asya. "You can guess who she married. A zealot and murderer just like all the others. And they were always holding her up to me as an example, Madina this, Madina that…"

"Who told you that?" roared Shamil.

Asya shuddered and stammered: "Everyone's talking about it, Mama told me. And your mother knows about it too. Everyone knows. Go ask them yourself."

She tucked her light-colored hair back behind her ears and looked into Shamil's eyes. Hers were red.

"It was all over with me and Madina anyway," said Shamil for some reason. "Where were you going just now?"

Asya blushed. "Me? Just to a friend's."

Well, that can't be true, thought Shamil: she doesn't have any friends. "I'll go with you."

But Asya looked quite frightened now; she hopped down off of the wheel, quickly said good-bye, and darted out of the playground.

Shamil stroked his unshaven chin and stood there another minute. Then he headed off toward Madina's house. This time the bench at the entrance was empty, and the steps up to her floor gave out a hollow, dull echo. Madina's mother, wearing a striped velour house-coat, opened the door and recoiled. Then she collected herself and politely invited Shamil in. The apartment was bustling with activity;

someone was dashing from one room to the other. Though Shamil couldn't see who it was, he felt, and knew, that it was Madina.

Her father came out. He was wearing a faded shirt and looked even older and grayer than before. After saying their *salams* they went into the spacious formal room with its crystal chandelier and portraits of their ancestors lining the walls. The TV was blaring. Some religious program.

"They say we've been walled off," rasped Madina's father, gesturing vaguely in the direction of the TV. "Next they'll be taking over and dividing everything up."

He cleared his throat.

"Is it true that Madina has had a secret religious marriage?" Shamil got straight to the point.

"It's a great dishonor for our family, Shamil," Madina's father began quietly, without looking at him. "We will return all your gifts, but we ask you not to break ties with us, you are near and dear to us, and..."

He cleared his throat again.

"How did it happen?"

Madina's mother appeared in the doorway, having changed into a long frilly dress.

"Here's what I can tell you," she began. She came over, sat down next to him, and placed her palm on his wrist. "You can see what things are like these days. It happened so fast—before we knew what was going on, they had stuffed her head with all kinds of *khapur-chapur*. The boy is one of ours, you know, he was in her class, then dropped out, they say his brother is one of those men hiding out in the woods..."

"He's all right, though—he hasn't killed anyone!" interjected Madina's father.

"He's all right, but he's in a tough spot because of his brother... anyway, Madina got carried away..." her mother hesitated and wiped away a tear, "and I noticed that she was reading these new books, all of a sudden…she got all serious, stopped going to weddings. She didn't go to Bashir's wedding either, remember? Then she was trying to tell me how to pray properly, and was also trying to indoctrinate her father…We told her, *va-a-a-a*, Madina, if you say one more word to us about religion, we're going to stop letting you leave the house. So we thought she'd given it up…"

"She always used to obey her father, always, she had *iakh'namus*."

"Maybe we can start over, Shamil?" Madina's mother asked then, plaintively. "Nothing happened between them, they went to the mosque out of sheer stupidity, and it can be undone, you know."

Shamil frowned. "What do you mean, nothing happened? You know what she told me? She said that I work for thieves, and all kinds of other insulting stuff. Why should I put up with that? Who does she think I am? Why should I crawl out of here like a whipped dog?"

He was becoming incoherent. The floorboards creaked and Madina was there, pale, wearing a beige hijab.

"Mama, why are you disgracing yourself, selling me to a *murtad*?" she asked in a grim, hard voice. "I already have a husband."

"You don't have a husband, *k'akh'ba*!" roared her father "These religious marriages have no weight without the parents' approval!"

"And what if my parents live in *kufr*? If they're infidels? In that case the law permits me to turn to more appropriate guardians. I'm sorry to make things so inconvenient for you all, but how much longer can I go on hiding? Shamil, you have to listen—not to me…I'm a woman and must not try to teach a man…*Inshallah*, but perhaps others can remove the scales from your eyes."

"Shamil, please don't tell anyone about all this," intervened her mother, "or they'll inform the officials about those connections she has, take down her name."

"They will not, *Mama*," objected Madina. "Now those *murtads*, *subhanallah*, are afraid even to show themselves on the street, Allah has heard our prayers at last. And our brothers aren't terrorists, they are Muslims who want to live like Muslims. And soon everyone will live that same way."

Shamil was aghast. He looked at Madina's father, who was uncharacteristically silent. He sat hunched over, crushed, with his eyes fixed on the folds in his trousers.

"I understand," said Shamil, not sure why, and made his way in silence to the door.

In the corridor Madina's mother could no longer restrain herself, and burst into uncontrollable sobs.

"*Vai*, Shamil, we're ruined, disgraced. There's nothing we can do with her—they're out of their minds."

Shamil ignored her and walked out the door. He felt so bad for them, he couldn't face them another moment. He felt worse for them than he did for himself, in fact. He couldn't grasp how this catastrophe had come about. As recently as a few days ago, he hadn't suspected a thing. They hadn't been seeing each other much, it's true, but it would have been improper for Madina and himself to get together more often. And she hadn't given Shamil a single hint before that last conversation of theirs...

He imagined what people would say. They would be so eager to spread the terrible news; gray-haired Nurizhat, licking her lips, would pick over both families' bones—Shamil's as well as Madina's. He blamed himself; why hadn't he tried to find out whom she was associating with? Chances are it had been some relative of hers who'd done the damage—someone who attends a particular mosque, someone who recognizes no governmental authority, including his village chief—only his mullah. Shamil began to sort back through the men in his own family who had begun to observe the strictest religious rituals, who had begun condemning alcohol, who'd shown an aversion to sheikhs, *ustads*, and miracles. All of them were disaffected with the powers that be, of course, and with the officials who had subjected them to such cruel interrogations. But all of them had also claimed to be nonviolent, and to only want to be left in peace.

Here Shamil recalled that something had been said about the rise of the *Salafis*. But of course now, with the Wall, a lot could change.

He was still in the courtyard of Madina's building when he heard someone shouting his name. Her father had come out of the house and was hurrying to catch up with Shamil. As he walked, he took out a pack of cigarettes and some matches.

"I didn't want to talk in there," he said without preamble. "Here's what I think, Shamil. They're taking over, no doubt about it. And you know, sometimes I think to myself, maybe they're not so bad..."

He stopped, seemingly lost for words. Shamil recoiled: "Now don't you go losing your mind too. They're flat-out insane!"

"What about my nephew? He's not at all crazy, just a normal guy. He might have gotten a little carried away, sure, but he's no criminal. Last Friday, he and the others were in the mosque, and all of them got dragged out and beaten in the street. They hadn't done a thing. And it's not the first time..."

"They must have done *something*."

"But they didn't," repeated Madina's father, curtly, flicking away some ash. "All they want is to live according to the Koran, and that's their right."

"They're not the only ones with rights—other folks have rights too."

"But they happen to think that those other folks are living in sin."

"You've been listening to your daughter too much. I'm sorry to have to be the one to tell you, but you should have given her some good knocks on the head instead of lapping up her nonsense. They've ruined her life."

"Calm down, Shamil. Have *sabur*." Madina's father lifted his hands into the air and declaimed:

Try to tempt her, try in vain!
My guilt, my shame, eternal pain—
"Forget me for all time, forever
Will I forget you? Never..."

Shamil's non-father-in-law's voice had become shrill.

Shamil couldn't understand the point of this little performance—neither could he understand the rest of their conversation, for that matter. They shook hands sadly, and Shamil headed off to find Uncle Alikhan at work. Madina's father remained standing in the yard, holding his half-smoked cigarette.

At the office Shamil learned that neither Alikhan nor any of the other higher-ups had showed up to work. Shamil remembered the closed airport, the eerie absence of airplanes. Could they have skipped town?

He sat down on the low cement wall outside the building and surveyed the street. There were practically no women out; now and then, excited children ran past. Clusters of men were standing around on the sidewalks arguing energetically. Cars hurtled by along the rough, pitted streets like metal meteors.

Shamil closed his eyes and remembered his trip to the goldsmiths' settlement. Maybe he should go to his family's village, get as far away as he could from these problems, from all this confusion, from the evil thoughts that were plaguing him. Then some increased activity among the various clusters of men caught his eye. They had gradually abandoned their individual conversations and had started moving, in groups of two or three, toward the square. Shamil stood up listlessly and followed.

7

Seeing a group of men and women on the square holding big posters with photographs on them, Shamil thought, "Not again," and decided not to stick around. But something held him back; this was different from the usual demonstrations. There were more posters than before, and the people holding them seemed more aggressive. An unruly crowd had gathered around the poster-bearers, everyone was nodding, waving their hands, yelling. The women, practically all of them veiled, were holding photographs of naively smiling young men and shouting: "Bring back our brother!" or "Bring back our son!" There wasn't a single policeman in sight, which was especially strange.

A man in a warm-up jacket, gesticulating, was talking into several video cameras: "My cousin's name was Nazhib Isaev. He was killed in March of this year, right in front of my eyes. We were walking down Lenin Street toward the computer center, and suddenly this blue sedan with tinted windows pulls up next to us. Some guys in ordinary sweat suits get out and head our way, and as they're walking they pull on masks and just start shooting, basically."

"What were they shooting at?"

"Straight at us! So Nazhib jumps one way, and I jump the other. And he just falls over, basically. And with me right there watching, they shoot Nazhib in the head, to finish him off. And then they toss something down next to him…"

"What was it?"

"An automatic rifle, this and that, 'evidence' to make him look guilty. Then they went into the store there, got a bag, came back, collected the empty shells in it, and took off…and that was it."

Shamil walked on. In another group a man in a light linen jacket was giving a speech: "Murad was abducted this past winter when he was on his way home from the gym. They dragged him into a car and took him who knows where. They were wearing Special Forces uniforms. His parents have been trying to get him back for over six months…"

As Shamil listened to the scraps of stories and the coughs of the onlookers, a strange sense of boredom came over him, and yet wouldn't let him leave. He walked between the groups, looking into the flushed faces of the yelling women, at the high chain-link fence in front of the moribund government building, at his own polished shoes, at the empty faces on all the posters.

Then he noticed Velikhanov, his former colleague from the committee and an old friend of the family, a tall man with graying temples. Velikhanov was explaining something insistently to a few old men in short straw hats who looked a lot like the ones Shamil had encountered in the seaside park after the Kumyk demonstration.

"Hey, Shamil, I've just been going over everything for these guys. Look what's happening over here!" drawled Velikhanov, shaking Shamil's hand. "I've always said that we need to take more advantage of young people. Remember that rally we organized in Mashuk? *Vakh*, so many people, it was great! We sang the national anthem, organized competitions, Tutkin himself came! This here is nothing, by comparison."

The old men grumbled.

"Shamil! It's a total breakdown in logic! And all because they wouldn't let Alikhan and me organize any educational activities back when the time was right. And we already had this plan to invite guys here from other regions, to take them up into the mountains, to the reservoirs and waterfalls, to show them our trades, our traditional arts, our circuses, carpets..." Velikhanov lost his train of thought. "What else? Shamil?"

Shamil smiled. "Yes, sure, we could've taken them up there..."

"But no! All of those so-called journalists! Look at them over there, circling like vultures with their cameras. Just getting in the way! A handful of hired stooges show up—" He nodded toward the random groups of shouting people. "—and they're already putting it on TV: 'People are being kidnapped and murdered here, right on the streets! People are being murdered right in front of our eyes!' The press can't find anything better to cover! Let them come to my village, I'll show them what they should be putting on TV. There's a guy in my village who makes inlaid furniture with his own hands. Or look, they can film my mother, see how she spends her days. Why is it that they're only interested in slobbering over filthy stories like this?"

"Who is it that's walling us off, anyway?" asked one of the old men. "Who's destroying the country?"

"So called 'journalists,' like them!" Velikhanov shot back angrily, jabbing his index finger into the stuffy air. "The crooks!"

Shamil turned away for a moment and caught sight of Madina's beige hijab. She was standing half turned away from him, as though taking refuge among the shoulders of her new girlfriends. Some bearded guy was standing to her right and shouting.

"What's he yelling about?" asked Shamil.

"Why waste your time with them?" snorted Velikhanov. "They're all suffering and oppressed, they're being dragged around various dark cellars by the police, they're not being allowed to pray, they're being maimed by hot irons, their chests are being branded with crosses, their beards are being plucked out with tweezers, you name it!"

The bearded man was indeed yelling something to that effect, but all Shamil could make out were fragments: "*Alhamdulillah*, praise be to Allah, the infidels have retreated...The cowardly *murtads*...without a functioning government...freedom of the Caucasian Emirate... everyone opposed to filth, injustice, moneygrubbing, everyone... *Allahu akbar*...soon those in hiding will no longer have to hide—now, *inshallah*, people will no longer be persecuted for their religion..."

At some point while Shamil was listening, Velikhanov and the old men vanished into the crowd. Shamil's head was filled with memories. Here he is, a little boy in his cotton underwear on the shore with his father and Velikhanov, untangling fishing nets. Velikhanov is putting worms on hooks. They are alone on the salty shore. Tethered to an iron stake, slippery boats bobble on the water. Velikhanov is telling some joke that Shamil doesn't understand; his father laughs, baring his silver crowns. Shamil reaches with his white palm for the jar of worms...

Then he pictured Velikhanov's sons. The first was named Peak, in honor of Ismoil Somoni Peak, which had been renamed Communism Peak under the Soviets; the second was named Mig, maybe to sound good together with his brother's name, or maybe in honor of the Mig jet fighter. Mig Velikhanov later worked at the torpedo production facility in Kaspiisk, had helped develop submarine weapons, and most recently, as far as Shamil could tell, was continuing his work in Petersburg. Gentle, kindhearted Peak had spent his whole life working at the Derbent cognac distillery and had never married.

Shamil brought himself back to the present day and dully surveyed the restless heads of the crowd until his glance snagged on a couple of his cousins. They were happy to see him, and the three of them launched into an animated conversation. They were all on edge, ready for something to happen, though they had no idea what. They talked excitedly for a half hour or so, then Shamil suggested that they go see Aunt Ashura, who lived nearby. For some reason they thought that there, in her small, one-story house behind its wooden gate, everything would become clear.

Her yard was bustling with activity as usual. Chubby Khabibula was adjusting something on the dairy separator; Aunt Ashura's sons, who already had families of their own, were in the barn, tossing their babies up and down in the air—there were always a lot of children running around here—and talking with the women as they worked.

They ladled out some *kharcho* for Shamil and his cousins, showed them the new exterior doors that they had just installed, and argued about what they should do with the old ones. Someone suggested they sand and paint them and use them for repairs in the addition. Aunt Ashura, on the other hand, was leaning toward keeping them in the barn for the time being, and then giving them to one of their Kutan relatives, maybe Khabibula. Aunt Ashura's younger son stubbornly insisted that they just throw the doors away.

Someone asked Shamil about his mother. Uninhibited, sharp-tongued Aunt Ashura placed her hands on her hips and snorted when she heard that Patimat had gone back to the village, as if to say, how can that be, here her son's in trouble, and what does Patya do? Instead of heading for the hills as though nothing's wrong, she should have been giving Madina's family an earful. The Zakir branch of the family were always up to something like this...

Turned out not everyone there knew that Madina had become a devout Muslim and secretly gotten married. They were indignant when it all came out. Aunt Ashura's son let slip that Madina's husband was a distant relative of theirs named Otsok in honor of a distant ancestor. Recently Otsok had taken a more traditional Islamic name, Al-Jabbar, which means "redemptive force."

The moment they started talking about "the former Otsok" and about what Madina had done, Aunt Ashura lost all sense of restraint and began to grumble and rant...She couldn't understand Madina's parents' attitude; they were pandering to their daughter, maybe were even in cahoots with her. This Al-Jabbar guy had been providing food to the militants hiding in the woods, and had been spreading some particularly nasty gossip about Sheikh Gazi-Abbas. Madina would meet a miserable end, she said—like an accursed serpent.

Aunt Ashura's daughter, sucking on a caramel, put aside her glass of tea and brought up the instructive example of her neighbor's daughter, who had died last year after some kind of special operation against insurgents:

"He was talking with her on the phone while she was sitting right there in a building under siege. He told her that Allah wouldn't forgive her for abandoning her children like a dog. He asked her to reconsider, to come outside. But she just bombarded him with quotes from the Koran. Ultimately he told her she wouldn't be alive for long in any case, and after her death he wouldn't even open the gate for mourners, much less let them into the house, and he wouldn't recite a single *sura* in her memory. And he didn't. She died, and they didn't receive any guests or read a single prayer. As though she had never existed."

"What a nightmare," said the listeners, then went back to their routines. Aunt Ashura's son, smiling, hauled some mechanical contraption out of the shed and started lubricating it. The daughters got into a spat about apricots, about where in the country they ripened soonest, about which ones were cultivated in one settlement and which in another.

Shamil left Aunt Ashura's yard in a brighter mood. He decided to go home on foot. He walked faster than usual, thinking about his friend Arip, who would be back from Moscow any day now. The trains were unpredictable, but Arip usually came by bus anyway. Shamil decided to take a cold shower, then go work out. After that he'd go to a café with his friends…

"*Salam aleikum!*" someone called to him from the sidewalk.

A disheveled, unshaven man staggered up to him. He looked about fifty, though it was hard to tell.

"*Vaaleikum salam,*" answered Shamil, with a grin.

"Got a couple of rubles on you, brother?" asked the man, slurring. "To dry out?"

"To create a bright, good, eternal future," the man said, enunciating with difficulty.

Shamil scooped up whatever change was in his pocket and dropped it into the drunk's dirty, calloused palm.

"*Barkala,*" mumbled the man. "Call me Vitalik. And think, up there in the Kremlin, they're just sitting around, those…" Vitalik cursed.

Shamil made a fist and shook it in the air in a joking sign of solidarity, and then hurried on his way.

8

On the landing of their floor, which reeked of chlorine and wet rags, Shamil ran into Kamilla. She looked into his eyes and smiled, primping her curled hair.

"What's the news, Kamilla?" he asked, stealing a look at her breasts.

"Well, I went to the Khanmagomedovs' wedding," she announced with some pride. "They brought out new food every half hour."

Shamil started. "Listen," he said, "they say that our *khakims* were there. Where did they go afterward?"

Kamilla shrugged.

"Most likely to someone's villa at the shore—they're probably still there now."

"Why did they leave in such a rush?"

"How should I know? Supposedly some guy named Khalilbek took them there."

"Khalilbek, Khalilbek," thought Shamil. "Sounds familiar."

Kamilla went over and lingered in the doorway of her apartment. She seemed to be in no hurry to say good-bye.

"Shamil, you said that you're going to get a car soon?"

"I was planning to buy one. What, you want to go for a spin?"

Kamilla laughed: "You could take me and my friend to the beach."

They heard steps behind them. Someone was coming up the stairs. Kamilla cast a worried glance down the stairwell. It wasn't her mother. She relaxed.

"Well then?" she playfully tapped the toe of her right shoe on the cement floor.

"No problem," answered Shamil, beaming. "Are you going to invite me in for tea?"

Kamilla made a show of being offended: "Some nerve. First take me to the shore, and then we'll talk about tea."

The footsteps died away, but a moment later there was a rustling sound from below. Shamil, who had already sidled closer to Kamilla, glanced down the stairwell and was surprised to see Asya.

"Asya, what are you doing here?" he called down.

She briskly climbed the stairs, stopped in front of them, and held out a blue plastic bag.

"Your mother forgot this this over at our place. We still have some of your stuff too."

"What stuff?" snorted Shamil, looking into the bag.

"You can see next time you come over," answered Asya, and she ran down the stairs without looking back.

"Who's that girl?" asked Kamilla disdainfully, with an insinuating look.

"Just a cousin," Shamil said dismissively, and reached playfully toward Kamilla's perfumed hair to give it a tug. She turned away, lightly opened the imitation-leather upholstered door to her place, and, grinning broadly, waved him away.

"My phone's not working, I'll come over later and ring your bell," said Shamil, imagining what her skin might feel like.

At home he opened the bag and found some brightly colored, neatly folded pieces of cloth with a couple of large sheets of paper inside, folded in half. On the front was written in an unsteady hand, "To Shamil from Asya. Secret."

Shamil felt a combination of curiosity and distaste. "What, a love letter?" he wondered. He didn't like that they were related. It complicated matters, would prevent him from taking full advantage of the situation.

He paced around the apartment, opened some kitchen cupboards, then returned to the letter. He read it in one sitting:

TO SHAMIL FROM ASYA. SECRET.
I think we should run away to Georgia right away. If there's a Wall up north, if they've disbanded the patrols, that means the border

troops to the south also won't put up much of a fight. We can go to Kidero, my brother has friends there, and from there we can cross the mountain using local guides. Believe me, it will be a lot more interesting with me than with Madina.

You'll ask, "Why Georgia?" And I'll answer, "Because if Russia has closed itself off from us, that means that no one will be expecting us to show up there." Things here are just going to get worse and worse, though my brother says that we need to take things into our own hands, to join up with the Chechens, the Adygs, to start the factories and canneries goings again…Haha.

When he got to the "haha," Shamil couldn't help but smile. He tossed the letter aside, went into the kitchen, opened the refrigerator, and got out a bottle of sparkling, ice-cold water. He drank straight from the bottle, splashing some on the floor. Then he wiped his lips with his hands, put Asya out of his mind, and started to get ready for the gym.

9

Shamil had gotten no more than five steps out of his building when he heard someone shout his name. He turned and saw a young man, tanned, with thin cheekbones like a woman's and a mop of red-blond hair. It was Arip. They embraced and clapped each other on the back. Arip snorted. "We're in deep trouble, brother. I barely made it back yesterday—I got no signal, my parents are all upset. The bus was stuffy and hot, and it stank. They held us up for two hours at the border, by the Wall."

"What's going on there?" Shamil was burning with curiosity.

"The window was filthy, I couldn't see very well. They made us stay on the bus. Looked sort of like hills. And towers, barbed wire. The bus was completely packed. There was this one guy, an engineer, he was sitting next to me, he'd planned to fly in, but there weren't any flights. Now, he says, the idiots are going to be overjoyed, they've closed off the Dags and their kind. What they don't understand, he says, is that they're really just trying to hide from themselves."

"What's it like in Moscow?"

"Anyone with any brains is scared, Shamil, and fools are celebrating. They think that they've solved all their problems, that by stopping the subsidies they're saving money. But have we ever seen any of those subsidies here? My village did everything on its own, installed plumbing, built a gym—and they did it at their own expense, with their own hands. All they got from the central government was excuses, and not a single kopeck…"

They came out onto an intersection. The wind hurled dust into their faces, whirled plastic bags up off the street in little tornados, and moaned through the cracks of the apartment buildings around them. As if on cue, with a squeal of brakes, a police sedan rounded the corner, and several men in half-unbuttoned uniform shirts leaped out. Tearing off their caps as they ran, they plunged into the jungle of houses by the street. Their car sat orphaned on the curb with its four doors hanging open. Shamil and Arip silently continued on their way, heading toward the city center.

The streets were strangely empty; the only person they saw was a small boy who darted past, his face smeared with ice cream. Arip, who was able to multiply three-digit numbers in his head; Arip, a champion athlete in the traditional sport of stone-throwing; Arip, who could recite by heart endless one-liners from Soviet films; he seemed overwhelmed now, depressed.

"So are we going hiking this year?" Shamil's question was out of place; he just wanted to change the subject.

"What? Where?" asked Arip indifferently.

"We were planning on a trip, remember? Before you went away to university. We can wander around, do some climbing, visit abandoned mountain villages…we could even go rafting on the Andiika. Or did you lose interest in all that while you were in Moscow? Hey, remember that time we fell asleep on that mountain?"

"What mountain?"

"You don't remember? We dreamed about a village, both of us had the same dream. This strange man served us *khinkal*."

"News to me…"

They came upon a little mosque, nestled under some willow trees. Men in skullcaps had gathered around the fountain for ritual washing.

"That's strange, it's not time to pray," said Shamil.

"*Le*, let's see what's going on."

"I was on my way to the gym, actually. It's no big deal, maybe this mosque has its own way of doing things…"

One of the men in the yard noticed their hesitation. He came over and invited them in.

Shamil hesitated, Arip insisted, and ultimately they accepted. They were given something to put on their heads, took off their shoes, and entered a small room. The floor was spread with carpets and the space was divided up with cupolas and elaborately decorated columns, which gave it the sense of being a grander room than it actually was. Two men sat on carpets next to the *mikhrab*, arguing quietly. One of them was in full ritual garb, a shirt with a tall collar and something like a turban; the other, who had a semicircular, close-trimmed black beard, wore an ordinary checkered shirt. Between them on the floor

ALISA GANIEVA

several books lay open, some with ornamental ligatured Arabic script, others in Cyrillic.

The listeners sat on the carpets, some cross-legged, others reclining on the floor. Shamil and Arip found a place in back, close to the door.

"The hadith of the Prophet, *salallakhu alaikha vassalam*, given by the Imam Muslim, says that it is prayer, *namaz*, that distinguishes man from *kafir*. He who does not perform *namaz*, though he may consider himself a Muslim, is an apostate," said the man with the clipped beard.

"Wait, wait, give me a chance to respond," the man in the turban interrupted gently. "He who does not perform the *namaz* is close to renunciation of faith. Close to renunciation, but no more. According to the words of the Prophet, *salallakhu alaikha vassalam*, spoken by Imam Akhmad ibn Khanbal, he who does not perform the *namaz* five times a day, if he is forgiven by Allah, will not enter paradise among the first. If Allah does not forgive him, then first he will be punished in hell and only then afterward will he be admitted to heaven. As for true nonbelievers, Allah will never forgive them, according to *ayat* thirty-four from the *sura* 'Muhammad.' From this it can be concluded that those who do not perform *namaz* are not nonbelievers; they are only close to apostasy."

"That's not at all what Imam Akhmad said!"

"You are referring to an earlier opinion, which he later renounced. He who recognizes the need to pray, but does not pray, is a sinner, but only he who denies that need is an infidel."

"All right. Let me ask you a question: why do you Sufis say that twitching your finger while during the reading of the *Tashshakhud* is a sign of *Wahhabism*?"

"Because this business of twitching one's finger is simply for show."

"That's what the late Khanafites believed, and in this they were

168

even contradicting their own *mazkhab*, but the messenger of Allah said: 'Verily, the index finger in prayer acts more powerfully against the *shaitan* than iron.' Some believe that you should move your finger, others say that you must not. Both of these views are correct, *inshallah!*"

"In the hadiths of Imam Muslim the word *ishara* is used, which means 'to indicate, to give a sign,' but not 'to twitch.'"

"No, you can also define *ishar* as 'twitch' or 'move.'"

The crowd rumbled. The bearded man continued: "So you're defending those who don't perform the *namaz,* but you're getting all worked up about something as simple as finger twitching! Don't you realize that the first thing the Prophet, *salallakhu alaikha vassalam,* commanded, is *tawhid*, monotheism, the second is *namaz*, third comes fasting, and then the *hajj*, and on down? You are justifying those who do not perform *namaz*, while accusing those who are opposed to innovations like *Mavlid* of not loving the Prophet, *salallakhu alaikha vassalam*... that is, you are recommending *takfir* for them. How can that be?"

"*Mavlid* is a painful issue for us in Dagestan. And we truly do not understand those who have so little love for the Prophet that they do not celebrate on the day of his birth, who do not praise Allah on any and every joyful occasion in their lives!"

"The only argument that any of you can make in favor of *Mavlid* is that it's good and joyful and supposedly filled with love for the Prophet, *salallakhu alaikha vassalam*. But if it's so good, then why is it that no one ever observed *Mavlid* during his own time, nor during the days of his followers, nor of the famous Imam scholars? We can hardly have achieved a higher knowledge of sharia than the generation of the Prophet, *salallakhu alaikha vassalam*, but *Mavlid* came into being much later, two hundred years after the death of the Imam Shafii. The first *Mavlid* was held by the Fatimids, who, in the words of Khafiz ibn

Kasir, Allah have mercy on him, entered into a conspiracy with the Crusaders, took money from them, and were notorious for all sorts of treachery! So it is indeed a dangerous innovation!"

"You want to justify your own lack of love for the Prophet, *salallakhu alaikha vassalam*, in any way you like," retorted the man in the turban. "You even believe that his parents are in hell, that his relatives were ordinary people, and so forth. Yet, if you truly loved the Prophet, *salallakhu alaikha vassalam*, then you would go to the *ziarat*."

"Going to the *ziarat* and bowing down to graves is polytheism, and the first and most important rule that the Prophet, *salallakhu alaikha vassalam*, commanded us to obey is *tawhid*. But here you are openly spreading idolatry, exalting your sheikhs like gods. And I won't even bring up the kissing of hands!"

"According to the authentic hadiths of the Prophet, *salallakhu alaikha vassalam*, based on the example of the righteous men who were his companions, the kissing of hands among scholars and parents is permitted by sharia. Ibn Abidin said that there is no prohibition against kissing the hands of *alims* and devout people to receive *barakat*. It is *sunna*. Abu Daud quotes the words of *Umma* Aban, who said that the delegation of Abdulkais kissed the Prophet, *salallakhu alaikha vassalam*, on both hand and foot…"

Shamil looked around. New people had come in and were sitting behind them, listening.

"How much longer are we going to sit around for this?" he whispered to Arip.

"Give it another minute," answered Arip, who was listening intently to the dispute. "Maybe they'll explain what is going on…"

"Don't you see, it's just dueling quotations…" Shamil began to argue, but people started hissing at him, and he let it drop.

"You must hold to the path and understanding of *As-Salaf-As-Salih*, and then people will have more *iman*, there'll be more justice, life will get better…you'll feel it yourselves," continued the bearded man in the checkered shirt. "What's most important now is that the faction of *iblis* is collapsing, all those people clogging up the government offices, people willing to sell their eternal salvation for fifteen thousand rubles a month. Believe me, punishment awaits these *munafiqs* beyond the grave, so don't allow yourselves to be intoxicated by this worldliness…"

"By saying such things you yourselves are sowing *fitna*, discord among the Dagestanis, you're encouraging slaughter of the youth…" the man in the turban interrupted.

"We're not the ones causing all the trouble, it's those Sufi snitches, aiding the *kafirs* and other foes of Islam. As if you didn't know who's pushing our youth into jihad! I'm no supporter of such slaughter, I am for gradual reforms and for keeping to the true religion. But I also understand the men hiding in the forests. If a single good, observant man tries to struggle against police corruption and inefficiency— those guardians of *kufr*—what happens to this just man? He gets fired! He ends up without a job, so out he goes into the forests like the rest. Even the police are going into the forests! But now it will stop, *inshallah*, the *kafirs* have come to recognize their ideological defeat, they've panicked and have closed themselves off from us…"

"I'm leaving," said Shamil and began to make his way carefully to the exit. Arip came out after him.

"What's the matter, Shoma?" he asked, taking off his skullcap and giving it back to the attendant.

"They're just harping on the same old thing. I've had it up to here." Shamil slashed the side of his hand across his neck.

"Maybe there'll be some real change? We could have a new state, one that'll care about truth, justice, and morality more than cash…"

"You really believe that?"

"Well at least we'll be free of all that mindless propaganda, those vapid TV serials, degenerate reality shows, and the action movies with their piles of corpses. Maybe our brains will finally get purified."

"Arip, the brainwashing will go on as always, just in a different way. Now when you go to the beach you'll have to wear long pants, even in the water. Now there won't be music or dancing at weddings! You of all people ought to know better. Don't go around talking bullshit!" Shamil fumed.

"Calm down, will you," Arip retreated. "I was joking, just messing with you."

"Let me tell you, I'm sick and tired of that kind of joke," Shamil shot back. He spread his arms wide and stretched, glad to be back out in the open air.

They went on their way, but Arip and Shamil hadn't gotten very far before they heard noises under the willows in the courtyard behind them.

Someone shouted, "So now who's acting like a swine?"

They ran back. The men in the mosque had poured out into the yard. In the crowd a man of forty in a green embroidered skullcap was yelling at a strapping, red-cheeked, unshaven youth in a cheap T-shirt with a picture of an upraised index finger on the front.

"Don't you try to teach me about *shirk*, I know perfectly well what *shirk* is!" His words shot out like bullets. "Who do you think you are, *astauperulla*, accusing us of polytheism! Take a look at yourselves, you *haram* mongers!"

"Heathens! *Kafirs*! For sale to the highest bidder!" the kid shot back. His friends hooted approvingly. "Traitors to the faith! You dance around like monkeys now, but you'll burn in hell with the *murtads* and *dzhakhils*! How much did they pay you?"

"*Astauperulla*, here's the lost sheep bleating about money! How much did the businessmen pay *you*? Go ahead, tell us! And who slipped those flash drives to them? Who's threatening to blow up the cellphone tower? Who's out there terrorizing the shop owners? You think it's us? You *Wahhabi* asses!" spat the man in the skullcap.

The crowd jerked and swayed; the young guy and his friends lurched at their adversary, elbowing their way through the crowd. Someone's jacket flapped open and slapped Shamil across the chest, and somewhere a man howled: "Stop it! *Le-e-e!*"

The mullah rushed out and appealed for calm, but no one heard him, they were already lashing out right and left with their fists, not caring whom they hit. A couple of shots rang out behind Shamil's ear, and the brawlers scattered. As he made his way out of the tangle of human flesh, Shamil noticed a plump body lying at the side of the street.

He turned toward the crowd and shouted, "Hey, stop! You hit someone!"

Arip gave up trying to pull an enraged guy with a beard off a thin, fidgety fellow holding a string of beads, and ran over to the prone body at Shamil's feet.

"The police won't come, they're hiding inside," muttered the man who'd been yelling at the kid in the finger shirt. He'd lost his skullcap in the brawl and was clutching at his cheek.

The body on the road lay with fleshy arms spread wide, motionless eyes rolled back, and a blank smile. A yellow wart was visible on the deceased's plump cheek.

10

The moment Makhmud Tagirovich finished his poem, he took it straight to an editor he knew…though the poem itself was less important to him than the thick manuscript, printed on an inkjet printer and tucked into an old folder with white cord ties: this was the novel that Makhmud had begun long ago, about the lives of the mountain peoples before the October Revolution.

Freed from his burden, the proud author strode briskly along the ravaged, deserted streets thinking about how the editor, and then all of Dagestan, would react to the gift he had bestowed upon them. He had begun the narrative back during his student years, jotting down accounts of his escapades in cheap notebooks with their state-decreed prices printed on their cardboard covers. Years ago, however, his labors had been cut short by his scrawny, malicious stepmother:

"Haha, Makhmud, so you want to become a poet like your father? Times have changed! Write or don't, no one cares, you're not going to get a car out of it. There are plenty of others out there besides you," she hissed, having stumbled upon his heap of muddled pages.

"It's not poetry, it's about our homeland," said Makhmud, wondering what any of this had to do with a car.

But the evil seed had been planted. Makhmud Tagirovich set aside his literary labors and, not knowing what to do with himself, took up drinking again. And every once in a while his stepmother would whisper to her husband, as he sat engrossed in the newspapers, "Your Makhmud will come to a bad end, he doesn't know the first thing about life! Since he doesn't have to earn a living, he's decided he's a writer out of sheer boredom…"

But Makhmud Tagirovich had already forgotten about his plan to write a prose paean to his native land, and instead became infected with the perestroika bacillus. He lost his faith in a bright future and neatly tore out of his diaries the pages that contained naïve slogans and praise for the Party.

Instead of an ardent desire to serve mankind, Makhmud Tagirovich came up with a new goal: to rebuild and reform the country through perestroika. He read articles on the subject in national and local newspapers and journals, taking meticulous notes. He spent sleepless nights writing letters in longhand on lined notebook pages, and in the morning sent them to editorial offices, dense passages of text punctuated by exclamation points and question marks. He wrote, and he waited for the time when the malodorous weeds of falsehood would be uprooted from Soviet life, and when the flowers of justice would bloom at last.

His early marriage to the daughter of the cannery director and the birth of his son again aroused the passion for writing in him: a sense of his new grandeur and responsibility as the helmsman and provider for a family. In this new iteration his novel was no longer simply a reconstruction of life before the Soviets, but a family saga with dozens of characters, whose names, features, and actions slithered away through Makhmud Tagirovich's hands like lizards. Introducing some character, he would take up his or her entire family history and, against the author's own will, would find himself making lateral leaps over to brothers, sisters, and cousins. From there it was a mere skip and a jump to third cousins, cousins twice and thrice removed, and beyond. All connected by a single umbilical cord. The manuscript expanded and swelled from one month to the next.

Meanwhile, the times were uncertain. His father, who had entered doddering old age, quailed and grumbled about glasnost, which frightened him; Makhmud's stepmother and his wife Farida were going loopy over imported goods; his half-brother, now a teenager, ran around to various house concerts, where intellectuals, drunks, and the offspring of the elite would gather to listen to rock music; while his son cycled through various unsavory illnesses and soiled his diapers.

Finally the moment came. Price controls were released, speculators flooded the streets, and all bank accounts were rendered unto dust. Makhmud Tagirovich's father, having lost all of the wealth he had accumulated during his years in the ministry and in retirement, was felled by a stroke. His stepmother collected all of the ebony cigarette holders, precious ivory-handled Dagestani daggers, gold-embossed pistols, silver trays and tea sets, gold-encrusted wooden canes and pipes, thick-piled carpets, and ceramic pitchers—basically, all the things that grateful subordinates had bestowed upon her husband over the years—and in no time sold the whole lot to an American who was passing through. She used the money to buy her son-by-blood a house of his own with a big garden.

Her son graduated with an economics degree and plunged head over heels into the free market. He rushed around carrying big wads of cash and vouchers, drumming up business. He bought things, then sold them, talked himself hoarse making deals, stepped on people's toes, went to Moscow on long business trips, and hid in his own garden from the people who were out to get him. In the process he messily but inexorably accumulated a fortune.

Makhmud Tagirovich, who by then was teaching Dagestani history in one of the city's universities, followed his half-brother's example and hurled himself into the fray. He established open stock societies, created fictitious accounts under the names of his entire extended family, closed deals, went around telling everyone about his hopes and dreams, and inevitably, lost money. Farida tormented him with accusations: her husband was ruined yet again, and meanwhile word had it that his brother's storeroom was completely overgrown with "greenery."

Farida suffered from both sides. Her own brother had privatized the cannery inherited from their father, taking a majority stake, which sent Farida into an abyss of abject spite.

Basically, the world was coming apart at the seams. Other people were raking in money hand over fist, but Makhmud Tagirovich lost out wherever he went; every enterprise ended in failure. He retreated into his study and puttered around with his novel. At one point he tried to establish a Dagestani historical research society, but was unable to pay the rent. Late one winter night a gang of masked strangers showed up on his doorstep, dragged him out of his house, shook him by his plump shoulders, beat him on the back of the head with a boathook, stuffed him into a culvert, and just left him there.

They found Makhmud Tagirovich in the morning, frozen to the bone but still clinging to his presence of mind. His brother later used his special contacts to ferret out the culprits, and took revenge in some covert way that he wouldn't talk about. And Farida had to reconcile herself to the fact that after Makhmud Tagirovich's night in the culvert, he was unable to father any more children.

Several times she thought of running home to her mother, but each time her imagination depicted the scene in horrible detail: her sister-in-law, draped in sables, pursing her lips in contempt and pity for her, a hapless divorcée. So Farida stayed.

His novel took on new twists and turns, but Makhmud Tagirovich could never manage to get the ending right: he couldn't marshal all his characters and herd them into his triumphant culminating scene.

And at home it was one thing after another. His son's teachers were demanding money and gifts, and Farida was constantly feuding with Makhmud Tagirovich's stepmother.

"That she-reptile's son has five buildings in Pervukha, Makhmud," she would whine in the evenings, "but she insists on living with us, and she won't even sign over your father's apartment!"

Ultimately Farida won out, and the stepmother was banished. But her place was filled in due time by their son's young wife, a woman with an inflexible character and an enterprising spirit. She opened up a storefront where she sold cheap Turkish clothing, and Makhmud Tagirovich's son took on the role of courier, errand boy, and shop assistant.

Farida grumbled under her breath. "I didn't go to the trouble of getting my son an education so that he could run around delivering bags of garbage."

But she couldn't bring herself to say anything out loud. By then Makhmud Tagirovich had sunk into torpor. He gave up his efforts to establish companies and foundations in support of a Dagestani renaissance, resumed his teaching position, and began putting on weight. He spent a lot of time with Pakhriman and other men his age, discussing politics, sports, and historical events, but never told them about his novel. He hadn't come up with the ending yet, so he turned back to his poem.

A few days ago, though, Makhmud Tagirovich got a flash of inspiration: his great epic should culminate in a triumphant encomium in praise of Dagestan. The only thing that united all his heroes, after all, was their love for their native mountains. Once he had made his decision, Makhmud Tagirovich could neither sleep nor eat. He ignored everything around him—his panicked wife, the alarming Wall rumors, the explosions and unrest—and to all the admonitions directed at him about this or that, he responded only by saying: "Everything will be fine, our region is invincible."

And so the novel was completed, the manuscript printed out and delivered, and Makhmud Tagirovich strode out to commemorate his great triumph. He would buy some Kizlyar dessert wine, and he and Pakhriman would celebrate together.

Oddly, several of the wine stores were closed, and the doors of the cognac shop were bolted shut. Makhmud Tagirovich wandered the neighborhood, disoriented. The area had changed in some ineffable way, and everywhere he went, the stores were closed.

"Excuse me, why isn't anything open?" he asked a pockmarked, tanned passerby.

The man grinned in surprise. "Don't you know? The owners are hiding from the beards!"

Makhmud Tagirovich, somewhat alarmed, but still in the throes of his creative euphoria, strode on. Then he heard noises nearby, voices and the sound of fists hitting skin. He ran around a corner and came upon the courtyard of a mosque. A crowd of men had gotten into a brawl there and several men in turbans were trying to break it up. Makhmud Tagirovich gave a bewildered smile and started toward them to help, but then he felt a sharp jolt and an unbearable burning in his chest.

The street tipped sharply downward, and the enormous white sky descended, crowding out consciousness.

PART III

I

Chaos set in. Every day generated new alliances and organizations. They would exist briefly, then disintegrate, join with others, or evolve and develop new profiles and goals. The police, in civilian clothing, went into hiding in their families' basements. Some, the most visible and high-ranking among them, were ferreted out and killed. Clashes between various groups flared up on the street; on every corner terms of abuse intermingled in a cacophony with appeals to the holy *ayats*, and on Thursdays, instead of the usual backgammon, Pakhriman drank in solitude.

At different ends of the various towns and villages, and even in the capital, bodies of murdered prostitutes began to turn up in rented apartments, and the proprietors of certain underground establishments hastily grew beards and swore that they were on the front lines of the struggle against fornication.

Dark shapes scurried around at night, proclaiming monotheism and setting fire to theaters, concert halls, and restaurants. Monuments and busts lay beneath their pedestals with their ears and noses knocked off.

Khabibula rushed to his *kutan*, where his wife Salimat was straining whey from fresh cottage cheese, and told her that Makhachkala's most prominent monument to Lenin had fallen and crumbled into dust. His lips trembled with emotion, and Salimat did some mental calculations of the potential losses to their farm. The port was almost completely abandoned; on the few scattered ships that hadn't been evacuated to Astrakhan, the masts creaked forlornly, and the decks crawled with vagabonds and the mentally ill who had strayed out from the city. At night, people in full battle gear broke into houses and dragged away squealing fortune-tellers with gold rings on their fingers, their faces distorted in terror. Their bodies littered the courtyards of the city.

It wasn't clear who was in charge. Threatening slogans scrawled across the collapsing fences and walls of abandoned construction sites gave the city an oppressive feel. "Women who do not cover their *avrat* will be, *inshallah*, killed!" Many girls, terrified, began wearing hijabs, but even this disguise didn't always save them. In Aunt Ashura's courtyard, terrible rumors were going around about the brutal execution of the singer Sabina Gadzhieva.

According to one version of the story, she had put on dark glasses and draped herself in long scarves, and had tried to slip out of town. But her pursuers chased her down, blocked her car, and hurled cobblestones and bricks at it. Another version had it that she and her lover had been tracked down on the Stavropol border, at which point their car had been blown up with a grenade. Aunt Ashura's sons swore that all the murders of singers and prostitutes were the work of one gang that was trying to seize the reins of power. There were still other rumors that Sabina had in fact somehow managed to escape.

The streets clattered and rumbled. Former tradeswomen from the bazaar loaded themselves down with kettles and blankets and sought new places of refuge. Children burned dumpsters and shot bottle rockets, and the republic's chief emir, a man with a long scar running across his face, occupied a prominent place on the TV screens of Dagestan.

In universities, in the civil courts and ministries that had been abandoned in the panic, *mujahideen* who had emerged from their forest hiding places greeted one another with their index fingers, laughing joyfully: "*Assalam aleikum.*" "*Vaaleikum salam.*"

Heavily loaded tractor-trailers left for the south or tried to break through to the north. Marya Vasilyevna bounced up and down in the back of a long-haul trailer, wedged between oaken tables and heavy suitcases, which were covered with stickers left over from the Soviet days and packed full of donated goods. Inside Marya Vasilyevna's bra, against her soft breasts nestled wads of moist rubles that she had miraculously obtained by selling her apartment, and her thin lips rehearsed lines for an anticipated conversation with the as-yet invisible guardians of the Wall: "In Christ's name, let me through, I'm one of you, I've spent my whole life slaving away for this non-Russian rabble!"

The school where Marya Vasilyevna and Shamil's mother worked had been converted into the party headquarters of the Caucasian Emirate. The director and twenty-five of his colleagues, so Aunt Ashura had been told, had been hanged on the main avenue of the city—on old linden trees that had for some unknown reason survived the axe—for being infidels, and especially for not allowing girls in hijabs into class.

Black Prioras rattled through the towns and villages and cities, scattering leaflets along the dusty asphalt roads. The leaflets hissed out a call to recognize Madjlis-ul-Shura, the emirs and *qadis* of the great Muslim Emirate. A nasal voice from the television issued loud, intoxicating appeals: "We, *mashalla*, have expelled the *kafirs* from our lands, and now the time has come to consolidate our power, to do away with the aiders and abettors of evil, with those who robbed and cheated, who pandered to Moscow! And then, *inshallah*, the Caucasus will no longer be *Dar-al-harb*, a war-torn territory: it will become *Dar-ul-Salam*—a territory of peace! When sharia is established in our land, peace and justice will come to our homes, and the borders, *inshallah*, will expand to the original boundaries of the Islamic world!"

"There's no way that lunatics and murderers can come to power," Velikhanov kept repeating to his family, waving his yellowish palms in the air. "They'll have their little celebration, and then we'll sweep them away!"

"We who? You stay indoors!" groaned his wife, collapsing on the sofa under the carpet with the portrait of Imam Shamil that hung on the wall.

Finally, black flags rose and fluttered in the air over the government building. They depicted sabers under the words, in Arabic script, "I testify that there is no God but Allah, and I testify that Muhammad is Allah's Prophet." Then, according to rumors that were flying around in the mountains, the foothills, and plains, the members of the Dagestan *dzhamaat* had given a ceremonial welcome to the Chechen chief of jihad. Several thousand young men who had not yet shed blood had sworn loyalty to him, publicly reciting the *bay'ah* oath of allegiance.

The *qadi* of the phantom state emerged from the shadows and established a field tribunal to try people who had rejected the main dogmas of *Salafi*, who had shown their devotion to this or that incorrect religious school or scholar, or who had introduced pernicious innovations, told harmful allegories, or performed demonic Sufi dances.

Girls stashed CDs of popular songs deep under their mattresses, and in hushed whispers exchanged terrible stories about a certain Najiba from Leninkent who had been shot by her own cousin, and all because she had refused to cover her hair; and about Marina from Buinaksk who had been sealed in a cement-filled drum for hanging posters of handsome young musicians on her bedroom walls.

Kamilla couldn't help gloating, even as she recalled with nostalgia the poignant image of flat-chested Elmira in her sumptuous wedding dress. She suspected that if the Khanmagomedovs hadn't managed to get away in their helicopter, they would have long ago been rotting in the ground. Though it was impossible to be sure of anything. The editorial boards of the newspapers were lying low, the kiosks had fallen silent, and instead of the former chaos of multiple dailies and weeklies there was only one paper of record, with, on its cover, the ubiquitous *shahada*, with sabers instead of a masthead and logo.

The phone and Internet situation was peculiar. The Web would occasionally flicker to life, at which point the smart phones that had been lying dormant in pockets offered peeks out into the world: fitful, intermittent glimpses of a colorful news ribbon, or of social network pages teeming with complaints, appeals, arguments, and counterarguments.

But having barely stirred into life, virtual reality would again fade from view, sending distraught users back to their radios, where through the jamming they could occasionally catch foreign broadcasts in the various national languages of Dagestan. The voices sounded alternatively jubilant and congratulatory; they shared dreams, conferred blessings, and cursed, in the end completely baffling their listeners.

The most widespread and effective news medium was word of mouth. Rumors flew, mutating as they went, communicating mysterious tidings about mad cows in Botlikh, or apricots in Gergebil that all had suddenly withered and died, about an uprising in Mamedkala and Magarmkent, and about a counterattack by the *mujahideen*, who'd routed separatist Southern Dagestan.

"We have no nations, we have Allah!" proclaimed the chorus of voices on TV. "Chechens and Kabardins, Balkhars and Ingushes, Karachaves and Dagestanis will forget all borders, renounce their individual pre-Islamic *dzhakhil* customs, and rise up as one united Islamic front under the banner of *tawhid!*"

But other rumors circulated as well—about forces that were rallying in the mountains around the Tariqat sheikhs, about a covert plot against the *Salafi* government, about nationalist fronts preparing a surprise attack, and even about a new movement of militant atheists with a mixed program, not liberal exactly, but not communist either.

The people wandering the streets of the capital would occasionally stumble upon the city's own decaying flesh. Water seethed up from under the manhole covers; electric wires arced and frayed, flared up and then went dead. Old women scurried around the streets, hunched under propane tanks, and people searching for food hastened to stand guard at the doorways of depleted stores that stood forlorn, devoid of their stocks.

The scariest rumors were about sabotage at the hydroelectric stations in the mountains. Destroying the gigantic arch dam of the Chirkeisk Hydroelectric Plant would not only cut off electric power to the entire Emirate, but also would send the white waters of the Sulak River rushing down the mountainside, inundating the Caspian lowlands, and even Makhachkala itself.

Farida was deep in mourning. Meanwhile, her daughter-in-law, with minimal reflection, shed her brightly colored sweaters, donned a blacker-than-black niqab, hoisted the black flag of the newly fledged Emirate over her sales booth, and stationed her docile husband behind the cash register.

"These days women are forbidden to go out to work," she explained to Farida, "so let them think that my husband is running everything."

Farida's sister-in-law, her rich brother's wife, came running to her in tears, wailing. "Khasan went to divvy up the factory with them so that they wouldn't close it! First they'll bankrupt him, and then they'll kill him!"

Farida remained silent. She sat with her eyes fixed on the wall, where the man with the yellow wart smiled down from his photo, and pondered the question of rice. She wanted to cook some *plov* in the iron kettle, but there hadn't been any food deliveries, and it was impossible to get rice anywhere.

"Soon they'll change the money too, and they'll put the Saudi king on the new bills," continued her brother's wife. "And you've seen how many Palestinians, Jordanians, and Arabs there are around. Before you know it they'll only be using Arabic in the schools. In fact there won't be any schools at all, just *madrasas*. That's what Khasan says."

Sure enough, olive-skinned foreigners had showed up on the streets, armed to the teeth, and they would go up to women who were out walking by themselves or without veils, and harass them. One of them even became the *naib* to the Emirate chief, and urged him to intensify reprisals against recalcitrant *murtads*. Some of the young men who had become enamored of *Salafi* considered this *naib* to be the Messiah, the descendent of the Prophet, who would purge Islam of its monstrous admixtures once and for all, and the *mujahid* veterans had to punch their young comrades in the backs of their heads and admonish them: "Rid your brains of this Shiite plague! Don't you dare place the *naib* above the emir, and the Messiah above the Prophet!"

But this Messiah, calling himself Mahdi, showed up anyway. First in Kumukh, then in Levashi, and then even in Kurush, two thousand five hundred sixty meters above sea level. The story went that, at the height of the fighting, one of the inhabitants of Kurush descended to the new Kurush settlement on the plain. Several villages in the Dokuzparinsk region had been relocated there after their lands had been turned over to Azerbaijan in 1952. After going around with his followers to the households and *tukhums* of the Kurushets, Ikhirts, Matsints, Smugults, Lekhints, Khiulints, and Fiits, this morose man proclaimed himself to be the famous Mahdi, about whom the hadiths had prophesied.

"His origin is in the Arabic tribe of Koreishites, like all Kurushets, meaning that he's the descendent of the Prophet, *salallakhu alaikha vassalam*," reasoned his followers. "Plus he was born in 1979, that is, in the 1400th year, *khidra*, which was predicted by the scholar Badiuzzaman Said Nursi. He is the first true *Mahdi*, destined to become your ruler and to restore the purity and strength of Islam!"

Many who were already in the habit of believing fervently in the stories they'd heard of children born with the name of Allah inscribed on their backs, and of beehives on which citations from the Koran appeared spontaneously, put their faith in this one true Mahdi, and began to organize processions in honor of the new Messiah, and to sing hymns to him. His uncle's house in New Kurush became a destination for pilgrimages, and was adorned with flowers and green cloth, and a gleaming half-moon appeared on the roof.

When news of Mahdi spread through the Emirate, and gifts and tributes began to pour into New Kurush from neighboring Chechnya, the Madzhlis-ul-Shura deliberative assembly sounded the alarm. The uncle's house was cordoned off and mined on all four sides, though Mahdi himself managed to abscond southward with all the gifts he'd been given.

The unrest continued. Posters bearing the inscription "Let us burn everything that is written from left to right!" appeared on the streets of Makhachkala.

"That's strange," mused the people, "since it turns out we'd have to burn these posters too!"

They were right; it didn't make sense. The government had decided to transliterate all the *vilayats* into Arabic script, but it was hard to do this all at once. Plus, the *mujahideen* themselves didn't know Arabic— nor, in fact, their own disappearing native languages, and were forced to communicate with one another in Russian.

Nevertheless, not only archives and music collections, but libraries as well, went up in flames. Then, literally the next day, the order was rescinded. The conflagrations ceased, and Russian translations of the Koran were saved. It had been decided that it might be better to proceed gradually.

After she moved out of her parents' home to her husband's, Madina began visiting the wives and widows of the *mujahideen*. All of them were excited about the unexpected victory and dreamed aloud of a time when nonbelievers would finally be reeducated or just disappear, when the true Emirate would begin, and there would ensue a life of freedom and bounty, as had happened in Saudi Arabia.

"Our husbands did not die in vain!" a Muslim woman would say, puffed up with pride. "They are all looking down at us from Paradise, rejoicing that we lived to see the blessed day!"

"Hold your tongue, Zariat," another would scoff. "When your Usman, may Allah receive his *shahada*, was killed, you were at home with him, and when the *murtad* dogs called, you went out to them. They say that you betrayed several of our brothers."

"What are you talking about, *auzubillah*! Who are you to lecture me? My 'sister,' who talked to men in chat rooms, knowing that it was forbidden! My sister, who asked them not to murder her brother, a policeman and defender of *kufr*, who was unwilling to break ties with her *dzhakhil* parents! They would have kept on pressing you, and you would have left, would have gone back to your infidel family, to your cursed brother! *Subhanallah*, we opened your eyes and saved you from taking that terrible step! And Usman himself asked me to go outside and to convey his last words to the *umma*, to tell the story of his courage! While I was being congratulated, do you think I didn't feel like crying? Of course I did, but I smiled and rejoiced that Usman was in Paradise, and didn't feel sorry for myself, for that would have been pure selfishness and folly."

"But of course your parents didn't beat you for wearing the hijab! You weren't told, 'Better come home pregnant than in the hijab!' That's what it was like for me!"

They spent their evenings arguing like this and then they would read the hadiths and look after their children, and Madina sensed that, inside her womb, together with *iman* and the baby who had already begun to stir, faith was taking firm root, a faith in a happiness that was just about to begin.

2

"Come on, hurry up!" One of Arip's sisters shook him awake. "Have you heard what's going on? They want…"

There were rumors that the people who had been out at night setting fire to theaters and restaurants had now taken to burning museums as well. Arip jumped up and, cursing at the dead telephone connections, rushed toward the square, where the bronze Lenin still lay on its side, past the boarded-up doors of the boutiques, the tattered and torn flyers about cinderblocks for sale, jumping across gaping manholes and stinking piles of garbage…

At home Arip's father lay on his venerable bed, shoving away with his feeble, trembling hands a spoon that his mother was holding out to him.

"He's willing to die from hunger, anything but show how weak he is," Arip's sister kept complaining.

These battles went on constantly, several times a day. Their immense mother would crouch down next to the feeble body, which lay with its muscles clenched up from sheer stubbornness, snorting and cursing. Their father lashed out, refusing to be fed; he would grab the spoon away from his wife, but then immediately drop it onto the floor.

How on earth had these two gotten married? Studious Murad had spent his younger years and most of his thirties completely submerged in papers, temperature gauges, and calculations. No one in his family believed that he would ever give in and take a wife. Yet the miracle had come to pass, and he had married.

After the wedding, the new husband plunged into his research with renewed zeal. He would rush off in the morning to the Institute for High Temperatures and would return in the evening disheveled and rejuvenated.

"Just imagine, Khadizha, we've already constructed a building that runs year round on solar energy. Soon the Caspian region and the mountains will be full of photoelectric, thermodynamic, solar-biofuel, solar-wind plants with power output of…"

And Arip's father would launch into eloquent soliloquies about heliostats and heat exchangers, about automatic control systems and boiler batteries. His wife Khadizha would listen, rapt, flushed with excitement, as she furiously polished the blackened bottoms of their pots and pans until they gleamed.

Without waiting for his comely wife's reactions to his speeches, Murad would run into his study and hunch over his marvelous blueprints, which contained the germs of a magnificent future, enormous palaces saturated with the sun's light and energy. For hours on end he would pore over a map of Dagestani geothermal deposits, would calculate the number of solar days and the force of the wind, then rush back to the Institute, where other projects of stunning audacity were being developed, projects that would revolutionize agriculture, and even the defense industry.

While Murat was out developing his radical solar-energy projects, Khadizha was home mopping floors and polishing furniture. She bleached and starched linen, made stuffing, marinated, canned, and baked. Day in and day out, her large red hands chopped, rolled, kneaded, mixed, pressed, cleaned, tied, steamed, and grated, and her belly swelled and subsided, swelled and subsided. Every pregnancy produced a girl, and Khadizha sobbed bitterly. "When am I going to get a boy?"

Standing by and watching as his apartment, scorched with dreams of the sun and sterilized with Khadizha's rags, filled with noise, the shouts of Saida, Faida, Naida, Aida, Zabida, and Valida, Murad only smiled and chuckled.

"Maybe we have enough?" he would ask his wife. But Khadizha, smelling of fried onion and oiled skillets, refused to give up. She needed to give birth to a son.

And it came to pass. In the wake of Saida, Faida, Naida, Aida, Zabida, and Valida, Arip made his entrance in the world. He also fell into the solar trap. His father took him along on research expeditions and showed him mysterious vaults and gigantic basins illuminated and warmed at night by solar power that had been captured and stored over the course of the day.

When Murad came home in the evenings, he beheld his fresh and clean daughters, seated docilely in a row over their needlework, and the rooms all spotlessly cleaned and polished. He would go to his study, then burst back out, bug-eyed: "Not again, Khadizha!"

"What, Murad? It was such a mess in there, just terrible. I tossed out all those old scraps of paper that were stuck in between the pages, and put all the books neatly back on the shelves. If it weren't for me, your desk would have turned into a worm farm years ago!"

And Arip's father would groan and curse, and would start sorting through the books, which his wife had arranged by size and color, trying to find the places he had marked so carefully.

And then the solar dream popped like a soap bubble. The research was discontinued; the projects were frozen, or they simply vanished into thin air, and Arip's father turned pale and drooped, as though he had been punctured. His mother, though, began to expand outward, as though compensating for her husband's increasing incorporeity.

Every once in a while Murad seemed to jolt back to life. He would begin to scribble articles and appeals, alternatively pleading and demanding, dignified and aggrieved, but to no avail. The installations with their colossal arrays of lights went dark; the great basins, vaults, and marvelous edifices meekly effaced themselves from time and space.

His mother, to whom fertility had imparted an all-encompassing generosity, became even more confident and energetic after Arip's birth. She pickled, preserved, and ground with even greater fury, and Faida, Naida, Aida, Zabida, and Valida were easily and comfortably dispensed with, sent off to husbands with ample supplies of plump pillows, table settings, crystal vases, garlic presses, and thick carpets.

Arip's mother decided to keep the eldest, Saida, with her at home for companionship. Doomed to eternal spinsterhood, Saida soaked her mother's feet, prepared veal for her finicky father, whitewashed the ceilings, crocheted fringes on scarves, and tended countless nephews.

From childhood Arip had been in thrall to numbers. Like his father, he was infected with a utopian dream of the sun, and he contributed grandiose fantasies of his own to his father's grand plans. By middle school he devoured logic problems whole, was hacking into various networks, and had mastered the principles of analysis and econometrics.

His father bought his son the latest books on computer science; his mother stuffed him with meat dumplings. Saida smothered him with bitter kisses, which he tried to fend off as best he could, and Faida's, Naida's, Aida's, Zabida's, and Valida's husbands teased him, calling him a "little brainiac" and forcing him to do a hundred push-ups at a time.

Sometimes Arip allowed his mind to wander away from equations, and when he did, he succumbed to the cheap mysticism of numerology, trying to discern the secret digits of his own fate. He divided words up into their individual letters, assigning each one a number based on its order in the alphabet, and then divided and multiplied them in an infinite series of combinations.

He calculated that the Cyrillic letters in "Dagestan" add up to the number 69, which is a six reversed onto itself. Arip added the two individual digits together and got 15; then he did it again, and came up with 6. Thrilled with this result, he started in on his own name.

If his mountain tribe ancestors had been able to pronounce Fs, he reasoned, then Arip would have been Arif. "Arif," divided up into numbers, also yielded the mighty six, signifying equilibrium, harmony, the seal of Solomon, success, the Days of Creation, the hermaphroditic Number of the Universe…

Shamil dragged Arip out of the world of calculations into the world of street brawls, noisemakers, potatoes baked over a campfire behind the garage, and violent fights that drew blood. The next neighborhood over was under the control of the hulking Seryozha, whom the local kids called Serazh and idolized for his superhuman-seeming strength and courage. Serazh had grand plans to take over Shamil's and Arip's neighborhood as well. After a few dreadful melees, which attracted upwards of two hundred spectators among the local boys, a pact was concluded, and Serazh entered into peaceful collaboration with the enemy.

When they—and their biceps—matured, they started launching various "enterprises" together, offering protection for money, prying rails from abandoned railroad tracks, and even going to mixed dances.

Meanwhile, Serazh assembled a new gang of working-class Russian kids, whose grandmothers and grandfathers had fled the starving lower Volga region to fertile Dagestan back in the day. He would knock the vodka bottles out of their hands and offer moral instruction: "Take your example from the Dags. They don't drink, they work out, and all our guys do is hit the booze. There won't be anyone left bury our old people!"

Even as he cultivated alliances with Dagestanis, Serazh joined a fascist cell and promoted the idea of healing the Russian nation through imitation of the enemy; in the intervals between political education and physical training he made a decent income writing term papers and theses to order. Then, when Arip went to school in Moscow, Serazh would come, spend the night with him, and the next morning would set out in his homespun Russian shirt with its embroidered side collar to commune with the skinhead brotherhood that haunted the city's outer reaches.

It was from Serazh that Arip heard for the first time about the Wall, which, according to a bunch of barely literate, skinhead hoods, would rise up and save Russia. Back then, those stories seemed as though they couldn't be anything more than wild fantasies cooked up by restless thuglings who had too much time on their hands...Now, though, they had unexpectedly taken on flesh and clarity.

In Moscow State University's Department of Mathematics, Arip had to work like crazy to catch up with his classmates, geniuses who could recite pi to the thousandth digit from memory, who knew more about multivariable calculus, topology, and complex variables than about their own family trees. First in the university, and then at work, Arip circulated among savants and lunatics whose whole world was mathematics. He could never have imagined that the world would split in two, would ripple and burst, that the fantasies of Serazh's gang of morons would actually come to pass, and so quickly.

The streets of Moscow were filling up with bloodthirsty throngs of teenagers when blond Arip managed to get out of the city to the Dagestan buses and sped off, heading back to the world on the other side of the Wall, where nothing would ever be the same.

The square was just ahead. Arip made two more turns before realizing that he was too late. Before the entrance of the orphaned museum stood a black pile of shattered ceramic pottery. Men wandered around the square, averting their eyes, and one of them, when Arip asked, said quietly, "They came in the morning, at dawn, with excavators...said that it was idolatry."

Arip squatted down in front of this display of pulverized history, and something dull and heavy rose from deep inside him, constricting his throat from below.

He looked at the fragments of antique plates, ceramic flasks and lanterns, and grain-storage jugs with pictograms in relief, while from the direction of the newly arisen Madzhlis-ul-Shura, a row of olive-skinned emissaries advanced upon him, rattling their weapons.

"Get away! Get away, brother!" shouted one of the men who had been standing by, observing the scene, and Arip obeyed blindly.

With malevolent but vacant stares the emissaries watched as Arip walked away. Today the museum vaults and display cases had been plundered. Today the antique weapons and Kaitag embroidered textiles had been looted, along with the carved wooden boxes and carnelian-jet beads, nielloed gilded belts, and silver breastplates; knobbly, gem-encrusted bracelets and earrings with coiled serpents; *kukems* and *dumchi*, *chokhtos* and bronze pins. But the greatest loss were the bronze statu-ettes, cast millennia ago, of bare-breasted, full-buttocked nude female figures, laughing horsemen with dangling legs, dolls in adoring poses, ancient mountain men in tall turbans like crowns lifting horn goblets in the air, and homunculi, entirely naked, with protruding genitals. It had been decided by the emirs of the *vilayat* to melt down and recast the shameful figures into sculptures of Arabic script spelling out the name of Allah, in this way reinforcing the power of the one and only God.

Leaving behind the leering emissaries and morose, shadowy wit-nesses, Arip headed for the basement cafeteria where he had agreed to meet Shamil. The people on the streets were discussing the ravaged museum treasures. Old women shushed them from the corners; towns-people trudged along with backs hunched, biting their lips, while the triumphant *mujahideen,* descendants of those same laughing horsemen, rejoiced at the justice that they had wrought.

On the street that sloped down toward the sea and the ruins of the demolished railroad tracks, a giant bonfire raged, spewing flames to the sky.

"A fire! Let's hurry, Magashka, it's really burning over there!" teen-agers yelled, waving their hands wildly in the air.

In front of the next museum, objects lay in a giant heap—European plaster Madonnas and Graces, American Indians on horseback, Christian saints and Soviet propaganda ceramics depicting sailors, slogans, and banners—and a bonfire raged, devouring paintings of people and animals. They melted and fused in the heat. A Turk holding a hookah and a Virgin Mary ascending to heaven, the eternal bird Gamayun and a woman with a bottle, an Italian girl at the bath, a still life with a hare, mountain tribesmen in raucous celebration on the site of Imam Shamil's surrender, all of them enveloped in flames, along with soldiers storming Gimry village, Argutinsky's detachment crossing over the crest of the Caucasus, and the Russian encampment at Gunib... Splinters flew up in the gray, ashy air; oil paint formed bubbles and dripped down flaming canvases like tears.

"Look! Look there!" yelled the boys.

"Thugs!" the women said under their breath, spitting in disgust.

"Better hide your family photos," anxious fathers whispered to one another.

Arip walked past the fire without stopping, like a man intoxicated, suppressing the fury that was welling up inside him. Young men in camouflage watched him sullenly: "*Le!* Why so grouchy? Painting the living human form is *haram!*"

Arip's feet buzzed like loose piano strings, but he walked on, avoiding the staring eyes of the men in camouflage, his face a stony mask.

3

The little cellar café, which had by some miracle managed to stay open, hummed and whispered, and the air, stirred by the fan, was thick with sighs. Arip looked at the widened pupils of the people huddled together in a living, quivering cluster, sharing quiet, terrifying news.

Everything, all the shops, bakeries, hair salons, shoe stores, music venues, and movie theaters, had been closed, their doors nailed shut, their owners intimidated. Amina, who had sold home-baked goods, had been cleaned out by the beards and ruined. She'd started wearing a dark *khlamys*, and wrinkles had spread over her face overnight.

She looked like an old woman.

The beauty salons had been destroyed; men lay in wait for their proprietresses on the street and dashed foul-smelling swill over them as they passed.

The café patrons passed rumors back and forth. A group of girls who had for some reason dared to show up on the main square in cami tops had barely managed to escape with their lives from fanatical Arab public-morals militiamen.

Female singers had either gone into hiding or had fled the country, and those who remained hid themselves behind the niqab and hastily married influential *mujahideen*. Weddings were celebrated without dancing or music, with no one present except for the religious officials. Two young *mujahideen* were caught dancing the lezginka, brought to trial, and sentenced to be flogged.

Glossy magazines with advertisements for wedding salons, videographers, and photographers were destroyed, along with the flyers and posters announcing concerts that used to be everywhere on the streets. The old Philharmonia concert hall was taken over by the sharia office; cellos and harpsichords went flying out the windows onto the railroad tracks, and the tracks themselves were blown up and lay crumpled on the ground.

The rumors assaulted Arip's ears, and he sat down next to Shamil in shock, as the latter shifted back and forth on his chair.

"Arip, this is Lena, Kusium, Sharapudin Muradovich, this is…"

The customers in the café exchanged greetings and resumed their arguments. A middle-aged man in a brown jacket whirled his yellow fists in the air and, stammering with the effort, harangued his listeners: "It's the Islamic crusades, that's what it is, the east taking over, it's the end of democracy! We're going backward, degenerating!"

"The east isn't the problem, that's not the issue," a balding little man with protruding ears angrily interrupted him.

"What has the east got to do with it? We ourselves are to blame! And western special agents with all their conspiracies! They've done everything they can to incite mutual hatred between the Caucasians and the Russians, to tear the country apart. Bet they're gloating now!"

"Don't make me laugh, Ali!" Kusium, made up and dressed in her finest, rapped on the table and tossed back her lush curls. "Like America needs to cultivate Islamic *mujahideen*. Think what you're saying!"

Yes, Kusium was wearing a fashionable suede skirt and her lips were gleaming, as though there was no chaos on the streets, no *kufr*, no *fetva* or *gazavat*; the cappuccino foam in their cups featured designs of hearts and flowers, as though oil-painted mountain dwellers and soldiers were not going up in flames just outside the door. Arip asked the young woman who owned the café to bring him some spiced tea, and fixed his eyes on his own fidgeting fingers.

"They've knocked Lenin down! That's the problem—it's punishment. Under the Soviets we had friendship of the peoples…"

The man in brown again interrupted the bloated communist: "I remember that so-called friendship of the peoples! I'm here to tell you, enlightened Islam is a thing of the past, what we have now is hordes of primitive sectarians. You know what they do with Nakshiband sheikhs when they get their hands on them?"

The man whispered something, grimacing. Lena dropped a teaspoon.

"Still, you have to understand, we shouldn't be too pessimistic," wheezed Sharapudin Muradovich. "Our republic is the center of ancient civilizations, the cradle of the very first democratic societies. The oldest production economy, metallurgy, the location of the first cultivated agricultural crops! We can't just lose it all in one go.

They'll shoot for awhile, then they'll calm down."

The fan was blowing in Sharapudin Muradovich's ear, and his hair waved in the air like soldiers surrendering.

"And all because of the federal authorities," said Shamil quietly. "Because of the Special Forces. They made a nice living on our corpses, and then they abandoned us, like, 'Now you can rot in hell.'"

"What do you mean?" asked Lena.

"They were paid twenty thousand for each hour of special ops. So they dragged out for days what they could have dealt with in a matter of minutes. They set up an entire convoy of armored vehicles to deal with just three *Wahhabi* Kalashnikovs."

"We know that already," Lena waved her hands in the air.

"And who died?" continued Shamil. "Ordinary cops, Dagestanis. They unleashed a war here, brother against brother…"

"We've known that for a long time," declared the little man with the big ears. "But why did they stop? Why did they give up such a profitable spot? They could have stayed and kept on feeding their faces…"

"I know why," said Arip, "it's just a tactic. The fascists have taken over there. So now they feel they have the right to send planes in here to bomb us. To them we're just a nest of bandits."

"But not everyone is a bandit. There are even some decent *Salafis*!" whined Kusium.

"So there are," agreed Lena. "My neighbor has a business. The men from the woods demanded money, they threatened him, and then he went to one of their bosses and asked him to step in. And he did, defended him from his own men. And that's just one example."

"Where I live, there were hardly any of those fundamentalists. We lived peacefully together, no one ever complained!" Sharapudin Muradovich interjected. "But in other places they've been following their own law for a long time."

"In Unstukul they've had all the state officials dancing to their tune for years," Shamil confirmed.

"Your sister's husband," Sharapudin Muradovich addressed Shamil, "started an opposition movement up there in the village, have you heard? He's publishing a newspaper, with the support of the local Sufis. He has Sheikh Gazi-Abbas's blessing."

"In Russian?" asked Lena.

"It's bilingual," answered Shamil and lowered his eyes.

It was true. His brother-in-law had been extremely active in Cher. Out there, power changed hands practically every day, and the hostility between the lower and upper mosques was on the verge of tearing the *tukhums* apart, with the two warring sides poised to claim whatever shreds remained.

Patimat, Shamil's mother, had supposedly gotten into a feud with the family of her cousin once removed, who had taken the side of the *Salafis*, and had broken with them. Meanwhile the cousin had broken with his own parents and divorced his headstrong and perhaps overly clever wife, who had been unreceptive to his moralizing.

So the cousin's wife had broken off ties with her elder brother, who had renounced his former government career, and had turned over his waterfront estate, built on bribes he'd collected during his years of service, to the *vilayat* authorities.

Meanwhile, his colleague, a ministry official and a recognized poetess, had composed a long ode, "To the great emir, warrior of Allah, the All-merciful and All-charitable," which the emir, strange as it may seem, had accepted with great pleasure.

"By the way, on the subject of odes," said one of the customers. "Did you know that Makhmud Tagirovich Tagirov wrote a novel before he died? It's pretty interesting. Very relevant to our times. 'Course it's not perfect, the prose limps a little, but when I read it, it really gave me a feeling, something I can't explain..."

"What's it about?" asked Lena, with some enthusiasm. "Where can I get a copy?"

Shamil looked at Lena and thought about Madina. About the expensive gifts he and Uncle Alikhan had taken her, about his mother's plans to decorate the cornices in the apartment before the wedding, about his aunts rushing to reserve the banquet hall. Over the last few days his only dream had been to ferret out the odious Otsok, insolent, obnoxious Otsok, who had seduced the impressionable girl with distorted interpretations of the *suras*. Otsok, who had taken on the name of Al-Jabbar, must have known that Madina was engaged. He had known and had come sniffing around anyway!

That morning Shamil again had gone to the deceiver's home and had learned that she'd moved out, and that her disgraced parents, after their daughter had appealed to them on their behalf, had been presented formally to the new authorities, and were even receiving a special ration of meat, grains, and vegetables.

Old ties continued to fray; people's demeanor and behavior changed with restless rapidity. In a personal effort to postpone the collapse of his world, Shamil sought out forbidden DVDs of non-Muslim films, intensified his workout schedule, and went around visiting his relatives. They fought their anxiety and remained steeped in everyday routines and cares: changing diapers, counting money, repairing their homes. Despairing of ever making sense of it all, Shamil then took to visiting long-forgotten girlfriends.

The first was named Djeiran. He'd first noticed her one winter day, windy and slushy like all winter days in Makhachkala, standing outside the downtown department store with her girlfriends. She was wearing a modest skirt and a silvery jacket with a fake fur collar, and shiny, beaded, spike-heeled boots. Still, her white teeth, dimples, and mischievous, laughing eyes gave her a playful look.

Shamil went up to her and wouldn't leave until Djeiran, laughing and flashing her dimples, gave him her phone number. That evening he called the number and some hoarse old man's voice answered the phone; his new acquaintance had obviously just given him some random numbers. He already knew where she went to university, though, and, sure enough, he tracked her down after class one cold, windy day:

"You think you fooled me? See, I found you anyway."

Djeiran just fluttered her eyelashes and showed her big white teeth. That was how their semi-secret encounters began. He went out walking with her in a park, along the paths overgrown with honey locusts and white acacias, walked her home afterward, and barraged her with silly poems he found on the Internet:

> Sleep, little bunny, sleep, mousie dear;
> Sweet dreams, my little baby bear.
> We'll be together up in heaven,
> I will see you there.

Djeiran gradually yielded. She moved to the city from her village and rented an apartment with two of her classmates. Every month her parents sent money for her living expenses, and the new-fledged student spent hours in front of the mirror fixing her smooth black hair. So spring passed, and when Djeiran's summer session began,

Shamil saw her looking thoughtful for the first time. Her dimples disappeared and her pupils darkened like two overripe plums. He gave her the money to pass a test, and then the next one too. Then he paid for her final exams.

"Too bad we're from different ethnicities and can't get married," sighed Djeiran slyly, giving Shamil a chance to prove her wrong.

"If it weren't for that, I'd have proposed long ago," lied Shamil, stroking her big pink palm, and immediately changed the subject.

At the end of the term he took her to an empty apartment that belonged to one of his friends and helped her shed her modest skirt. She didn't resist, only giggled into his shoulder: "Don't, Shamil! Shamil, stop it!"

Afterward they had coffee in the kitchen, and she planned their future life together.

"You need to start teaching me Arabic," she said with a naïve smile.

They kept seeing each other for several years, though Shamil didn't exactly avoid the company of other women during that time—nice-looking, more mature, and less inhibited women.

At one point Djeiran found out about one of them. She bit her lip, then burst out laughing, like a child. "Like she has a chance! You're only sleeping with her, but I'm the one you love!"

Shamil concurred.

One day Djeiran told him that her family had started looking for a husband for her, and gave him an inquiring look.

"You'll have to get married. Just don't forget me," said Shamil.

And Djeiran cried.

On the day of her wedding he managed to sneak into the banquet hall and even participated in the ceremonial dance around the bride. While the guests were trying to figure out who this dancing stranger was, and which side of the family he represented, Shamil showered the already deflowered bride with the fresh banknotes that he'd gotten at work from Uncle Alikhan. She flushed scarlet and looked down at the floor.

A few months later he met Djeiran on her way to the market. She recognized him and blushed, but then turned immediately and crossed the street. Shamil followed her, noticing the new fullness in her belly, all the way to the market stalls, and within an hour they were lying on a bed in a hotel room, next to a bag of potatoes she had bought.

"What did you tell your husband?" asked Shamil, when it was over.

"I said that I was injured in gym class on the vaulting horse."

"Did he believe you?"

"No," answered Djeiran and flashed her dimples. "But he pretended to. Who needs trouble? But now he's really jealous, he won't let me leave my hair down…"

They got together a few more times, and then Djeiran disappeared. So now, when he went up to her house and stood in front of her balcony with its laundry neatly pinned to a clothesline, the woman who eventually came out onto the balcony was someone he didn't know, and didn't look at all like Djeiran. She was in a hijab.

Next was Marina. She was a young, sassy woman who worked as a masseuse. She lived in the same house with Uncle Alikhan—the uncle who had now disappeared—and was friends with his wife. Uncle Alikhan had asked Marina to treat his ailing back, in a neighborly way, and took her with him on his trips with his family to the seashore. After a while they started to go alone, just the two of them. Their romance began during the month of Ramadan. Toward evening he would tuck her into his Ferrari and take her to Kaspiisk. There they would wait impatiently until the sun went down, then, as the last rays melted away, their lips would meet and they would surrender to the inevitable.

After each tryst Uncle Alikhan would give Marina a significant amount of cash, but soon she rebelled: "Leave your wife, or I'll tell her everything!"

At that point Uncle Alikhan turned the hazardous masseuse over to his nephew. Shamil accepted the burden with pleasure and savored Marina's art to the fullest. Later, right when her energy was getting to be too much for him, she conveniently decided to marry an old widower and complied with the man's request that she take the veil.

Shamil went up to the widower's cement-plastered house and knocked on Marina's window, using their private code. He didn't recognize her at first. A black wart had sprouted on her tender cheek, and she wore no lipstick. Her chestnut hair was tightly covered with a scarf.

"Is your husband home?" asked Shamil.

"I have a different husband now. The last one died. And you'd better not tangle with my new one. And keep your distance from me too, while you're at it."

"All right," said Shamil. "What are you getting all worked up for, Marinka?"

"I'm not Marinka now, I'm Marzhanat."

Shamil frowned.

"And if you call me Marinka," continued the metamorphosed masseuse, "I will inform on you to the sharia court. They'll scoop your guts out while you watch."

Whereupon Marina-Marzhanat made her exit, slamming the wrought-iron gate behind her.

"Shamil, will you let me read it later?" asked Lena, bringing his thoughts back to the present day, in the cellar cafeteria.

"Give you what?"

"Makhmud Tagirovich's novel. They say you have it."

"I didn't take it for myself. I'm going to give it to my brother-in-law—maybe he'll publish an excerpt in his newspaper," said Shamil.

When they got outside, Arip told him, "Remember, Shamil, how you asked me about that village in the mountains where we fell asleep? And I said that I didn't remember?"

"Yeah?"

"I do now."

4

The bread line snaking around the brick booth swayed, shifted, and settled. Despite the heat, the women had wrapped themselves in long shawls, just to be safe. The men stood grumbling. Shamil was last in line, a hundred back, itching with impatience. The folder with white cord ties that he had been given in the café kept slipping out of his hands. He fumbled with it for a few minutes, then opened it up and leafed through the pages of Makhmud Tagirovich's thick manuscript.

> Your Makhmud, dear readers, is not a bookish man, and so he will start by following the promptings of his simple heart. I had intended to begin with the founding of the village, but Khandulai grabbed me by the hand and demanded that I start with her.

"Page twenty, and he's finally getting to the beginning," thought Shamil.

From her earliest childhood Khandulai, sturdy and round-cheeked, raised on the finest grains, meat, and milk, was always in a hurry. Springing down the terraced rooftops, with metal rings flashing on the temples of her colorful *chokhto*, she skipped along the streets of the village doing errands for her mother; she whirled down the stone stairways to the women's quarters, where bronze basins clanged against each other, and where twisted metal jewelry languished in intricately carved wooden chests; she sped like a bullet into the dark barn, whose thick walls kept out the sun; she climbed, slipping and sliding, into wooden granaries, dashed outside the village to the two-story awnings of the communal barns and haylofts...

Years passed, and Khandulai did not marry, though abundant, rich farmland was to be given as her dowry, and her skin was as white as a partridge. Mothers of young sons came to her house to chat, and when they departed, they would leave ten loaves of bread. But the next time they came the loaves would be returned to them, unsliced.

"Time devours all pride," said the old women enigmatically when they gathered at the village's oven, casting sidelong glances at Khandulai.

All the women of the quarter would take their grain, flour, and fuel to the communal oven to gossip. They covered all imaginable topics, everything they heard when they were out and about. Loudest of all was the widow Khurizada, who was a regular at all the bazaars in the district.

"They say that in Tsudakhar," whispered she, browning wheat flour in a pan. "No one will marry a girl unless she

has copper dinnerware. And in Burkikhan a bride howls
and sobs like a madwoman all the way to her new house,
so loudly that they can hear her in the next village! And in
Mugi, picture this, the groom's mother pours warm oil over
her new daughter-in-law so that it stains her clothes. And
the Gimrin grooms have to gather enough firewood for the
whole winter for their fiancées. And in Urkarakh a whole
day goes by before the bride has taken even five steps to
her future husband's house; she'll take one step forward,
stop and dance, then will take a step back, and dance again!
And the Laks, if it's raining and flooding, they'll catch a frog
and dress it in men's pants to make the rain stop."

Khurizada had no end of stories. About the Andiits'
burkas, the Balkhars' clay dishes, the Kubachi silver bracelets.
The singing competitions in Kuba and Derbent. About the
Tsovkra-dwellers, who walked on cables stretched across
bottomless abysses. And about the unions that free societies
formed against powerful khans, *shamkhals*, *nutsals*, and *utsmis*.

Much did Khandulai learn at the communal oven. About
the origins of each *tukhum*, and why Tsob thundered across
the sky. And so many love songs, so many poems did she hear
from the women.

"At last the Gergebils and Kudalins wreaked their revenge
on those Kulibs," said Khurizada. "They taught those bandits
and plunderers from the high road a lesson!"

"What do you mean taught them a lesson? The Kulibs
capture everyone with weapons who gets anywhere close
to their homes and toss them straight into their turbulent
Kara Koisu!"

"Here's what happened. The Gergebils and Kudalins come to the Kulibs and they say: 'You attacked us, but we want peace. You're invited to a banquet!' The Kulibs are glad, but they are afraid to let the strangers near. 'Tell you what,' they say, 'let's have a feast outside our village. But come unarmed.' So the Gergebils and Kudalins come with just belts on, no daggers—but they've hidden their daggers in the wine ewers. At the height of the feast one of them says, 'The grain is ripe, time for the harvest!' And they slaughter all the Kulibs with their daggers!"

"*Vakh, vakh, vakh...*"

That's the kind of thing they talked about at the oven. But mostly they discussed domestic matters and their work: which fields to irrigate when; the varieties of hard wheat and white barley; the maintenance and seeding of the terraces; the coming of the thaw.

"The Gazalovs started planting before everyone else!"

"Yes, and they've already had to pay a penalty for it— one sheep."

"And Itin's wife had to pay two measures of rye for doing her laundry in the common spring..."

Khandulai throws on her sheepskin coat and leaves the oven with her friends, heading for home. The walls on all sides are tall and thick—no one can get close to the village. Under her scarf the *chokhto* flows down her back, and huge silver spirals dangle on either side, and each one has a bird in it, or twinned saplings, or two horses mirroring each other, and such long, heavy earrings that her lobes can't hold them, they need to be sewed to her *chokhto* with string.

At the edge of the winter village the bachelors feast around bonfires. They live in the fortress, whose walls are ornamented with spiraled labyrinths, sacred lines, and pictures of horsemen at full gallop. From the fortress building underground passageways run all the way to the guard towers. They live there without women and call themselves the Union of the Unmarried. They engage in swordfights and in battles with or without spears; they engage in hand-to-hand combat, they build up their muscles, shoot arrows from their bows and drink wine. Among those bachelors is the daredevil Kebed, who has long been in love with Khandulai...

"Look what it's come to, lines like under the Communists."
"*Le*, get a move on!"
The human chain winds round and round the booth.

...in love with Khandulai. It happened during the last spring celebration—on the Red Day holiday. When burning hoops were rolled down from the roofs, and bonfires were lit on the flat rooftops, and the men jumped across them, chanting, "Into the fire, illness! Into me, strength!" Or maybe it was later, at the beginning of summer, when the young *dzhigits* and girls put on their best holiday clothes, tuned their *chungurs* and *pandurs*, packed food, and went out into the mountains at night with torches.

They danced the whole way, illuminating the path as they went, laughing and singing songs, led by the most energetic and playful of their number. At dawn they arrived at the meadow, and there they danced amid the fresh blossoms,

gathering bouquets and weaving flower wreaths. They
collected edible greens for pies, competed in races as well
as the long and high jumps, and climbed the cliffs. And there
it was that Kebed was pierced to the marrow by the white-
skinned, fleet-footed Khandulai, whose sharp wit eclipsed
even that of their merry, flower-draped conductor.

In the evening they came back to the village and gave
their flowers to the old people who had come out to greet
them; they organized dances on the village square, and again
Kebed could not tear his eyes from Khandulai's face. Did he
suspect that Khandulai from the upper quarter would refuse
him just like the others? That Kebed, dashing though he
might have been, was too simple for her, his clan too meager
and poor? Kebed's mother came back to her son emp-
ty-handed, and Kebed's soul darkened with injured pride.

"There's no slave blood in me!" he said to his mother.
"My ancestors served no one. They had the right to bear
arms! I may not be rich, but I'm a free *uzden*; how dare this
haughty she-wolf insult me!"

And mounting his steed, he headed out to the lowlands
with his friends to make war upon the neighbors who had
dared defy him.

Ultimately the elders had enough of Khandulai's
willfulness. They gave her a piece of ox hide and ordered
her to choose a husband right then and there. Khandulai
came out to the village square, went up to the tall, handsome
Surakat, and struck him on the shoulders with the ox hide.
Surakat stood and realized that there was no escape. They
began to make preparations for the wedding.

The courting, the wedding ceremony—during which the groom was made to stand on one foot on an unsheathed saber blade laid flat on the ground—and the celebration that followed, which went on for many days, with all manner of delicacies, competitions, processions, ritual songs, and costumes…it all spun around Khandulai like a multicolored whirlwind. She herself spent practically the whole time in a special room with her girlfriends, sitting on a big sack stuffed with grains and covered with a sheepskin.

Her mother dressed her in a special wedding dress, with a purple forehead cloth over the headdress, and with coins, spangles, chains, and river pearls sewed on, arranged in triangles, swastikas, animals, sunbeams, and circles, signifying all of Creation. Sukarat feasted in a separate room with his friends, whose task it was to guard him vigilantly from potential playful kidnapping attempts. Kebed drained goblet after goblet and pretended to be celebrating along with everyone else.

At last, on the third day of the wedding, Khandulai was taken to her uncle's home, and at midnight her new husband stole in. They were left alone in the house, but pranksters went up onto the roof to make noise and shout back and forth, and joking and laughter could be heard from outside the closed door. Surakat's friends were spying on the couple, following the course of this first nuptial encounter.

Khandulai was more than prepared to get through her wedding night: the battle began at midnight and continued for several hours. The new bride had enough strength to prevent her husband from cutting her woolen girdle with his

dagger, and she managed to hold out till morning. Surakat
had been made weak by the wine he'd drunk, and his new
wife resisted his efforts—to pin down her strong white arms,
to gain his prize—with such ferocity and violence that
ultimately she wore him down.

Hearing the sounds of the battle, his friends guffawed
and egged him on: "Come on, Surakat, come on! How can
such a *dzhigit* fail to saddle his mare?"

Come daybreak, the defeated Surakat collapsed on the
floor, his wife's innocence intact. His friends took a roof
roller and, still merry, stood it vertically on the rooftop.

When the villagers saw the roller poking up on the newlyweds' roof, they chorused: "Victory goes to the wife!"

"She could have given in, that's the done thing, she didn't
have to disgrace that fine young man," frowned the widow
Khurizada, inserting some snuff into her nostrils.

"When will it be our turn? The goddamned beards!"

"Shhh, quiet! Shhhhh!"

"They've already renamed the city, you know. We're now living in
Shamilkala."

"Shh, quiet! Shhhh!"

Shamil shifted his feet and leafed ahead a bit:

Many years have passed since Khandulai married Surakat,
and since Kebed killed him. Years and years since the
Council exiled Kebed from the village and turned him
into a forest *abrek*! And poor Makhmud still can't get to
the denouement. Let us turn away from the villagers

and take up the story of my father.

My father used to call me over and ask: "Tell me, Makhmud, what is small and big at the same time?"

"I don't know, Father," I would answer.

"Dagestan," my father explained. "Just think how small it is, and yet how many peoples and customs, languages and arts, animals and plants, coexist here. In tiny Dagestan you can see sand hills and tropical brushwood, eternal glaciers and mineral springs, arid plains and fertile alpine meadows, sea expanses and mountain canyons so deep you could fall for half a day and still not reach the bottom! We Dagestanis, all of us, are very different, but we are alike in our honesty, hospitality, our need for justice. Remember that you are Dagestani, my son, and don't exchange that honor for any worldly gold!"

Poets used to come visit my father. They told of their songs, how they'd made people sad or happy, had reconciled sworn enemies, sparked the hot flame of love in young hearts. I vividly recall one epic poem about a mountain, a mountain of celebrations; its name is Rokhel-Meer.

"Is that a legal document? Some kind of petition?"

A man waiting in the line behind Shamil was peering curiously over his shoulder at the manuscript.

"Where do we take legal papers these days, anyway? To sharia court?"

"I don't know—this isn't anything official," Shamil said, and mechanically flipped back several pages:

Khandulai's waist thickened and, as was the custom, she concealed her condition from everyone. But her belly swelled and became huge, like a gigantic pumpkin, and prevented her from taking out livestock and helping with the harvest.

Recently she had been avoiding visiting her parents, and when evening fell, she would press a piece of bread and some cheese to her chest.

"What's Surakat's Khandulai got in there, anyway?" Khurizada asked the women gathered at the spring. "I've never seen a belly like that in my entire life."

"She should have given birth long ago, but she's still dragging it out," the mountain women wagged their heads.

Finally her time came, and brave Surakat's aunt, red-handed, droopy-chested Zaza, the village midwife, rushed lickety-split along the November streets. The men had abandoned the house. There, on soft bedding that had been spread for her on the floor, writhed Khandulai, her teeth chattering.

"Open all the trunks!" commanded Zaza. "Tie a rope to the roof beam and make a loop at the end. Let her hold onto the loop, poor thing. Grab on, Khandulai, pull yourself up, now release. Pull, then release. Come on! Where do you think you're going, Bakhu? You can't come in, there's a woman in labor in here! Quick, tear Bakhu's dress!"

Zaza kneaded Khandulai's gigantic, swollen, naked belly with her red fingers, issuing and repeating commands: "Sprinkle grain around the bed!"

Khandulai's mother-in-law hastily cut a lock of hair from the crown of Khandulai's head and ignited it, whispering spells, sending a cloud of smoke over her daughter-in-law. Surakat's sister scurried around the bed sprinkling grains of wheat from a wooden measuring cup; the jaws of the intricately carved trunks and chests on the shelves gaped open, inviting Khandulai's loins to do the same…But the fruit would not come.

"Well, sister," Zaza commanded the suffering woman's mother-in-law, "sprinkle salt on the hearth! Let the sparks scorch the eyes of the mother of the *iblis*, make her flee to her cave!"

The mother-in-law tossed a handful of salt into the fire, salt which the villagers themselves had collected nearby, and at that exact moment Khandulai emitted a terrible cry and her loins spewed forth, one after another, three infants, all of them female.

The midwife gasped.

"*Vababai, vadadai!* Triplets, and not a single son! Surakat will be so upset!"

They immediately set aside the umbilical cords to be dried and made into a decoction to give the newborns later when they suffered illness or insomnia. They filled a basin with salt water, and tossed in some burning coals, a set of metal tongs, and three silver rings, and washed the babies in it. Khandulai's sister-in-law rushed to Surakat with the news.

Soon guests came to see the newborns, and along with them Khandulai's mother, bearing a marvelous cerated birchwood cradle with a charm to protect the babies.

"Who would have thought that we'd need three cradles!" She shook her head, contemplating the babies with amazement and joy.

An aunt brought a second cradle, and a third was

delivered by the new mother's grandmother, who, having treated herself to some sweets, ensconced herself upon a three-legged stool and set to swaddling the infants. She tucked her great-grandchildren into the cradles on crackling mattresses embroidered in a crisscross pattern, and with a pair of sharp scissors underneath each one. She lifted them across a kettle full of watery kasha, black as night and steeped with sprouted barley grains, and then sang a lullaby over the cradles:

> *Lai-lai-dalalai,*
> *May your brothers be many,*
> *Your parents be proud,*
> *May your clan respect you,*
> *Love and protect you;*
> *May Beched bless you with health*
> *And shower you with wealth!*
> *Lai-lai-dalalai…*

They named the first girl Khorol-En, which means Ear of the Fields; the second—Marian, in honor of the crucified Isa's mother; and the third—Abida, Arabic for "She Who Worships."

And from that day on the women of the village started bringing their sick children to Khandulai.

"You gave birth to triplets," they would say, "You have magic powers. Bathe my sick child and cure him…"

The line weaved on and on. The queue wavered but did not break.

"It's only a temporary shortage. Soon there'll be work for everyone. I heard that they're printing new money, colored green for Islam."

"Dollars, you mean?"

The line tittered and chattered quietly. Shamil flipped ahead again:

...and though they begged Khandulai to marry Surakat's brother after Surakat was murdered by the scraggy outlaw Kebed, she dug in her heels.

"How can you, where's your conscience?" her mother asked. "You have three daughters. Who's going to feed them? Who is going to defend their honor when they grow up?"

"There are enough men in the *tukhum* to defend my girls," Khandulai would say, adjusting her pendants proudly.

Meanwhile the girls grew. When Khandulai sat down to work on her felt rug pad, Khorol-En, Marian, and Abida would sit in a little row with needle and thread and mend clothes. Khandulai would tell them about the gods who lived at the peak of Rokhel-Meer, about their terraced fields and houses, their bows and arrows, their toothpicks.

"Don't forget to leave three spools of thread for Gamalkar," Khandulai would say, rhythmically working the rug press. "Or he'll come take you to live with him."

"What's he look like?" asked Khorol-En.

"He has no arms or legs, and he goes around with a leather bag full of wool," answered Khandulai.

"Let him take Marian," frowned Abida, who was always in a bad mood.

"No, let him take Abida," whimpered blonde Marian.

"Let him take them both," laughed black-eyed Khorol-En. "When we were having apricot compote with oatmeal today, Abida and Marian didn't share any with father's spirit."

"We forgot to."

"How could you forget?" Khandulai shook her head. "If you don't share with your late father's spirit, he will turn into a Hungry Ghost and will show up here in the village. He will be very, very angry and will take revenge on us for not sharing with him."

"Will the Ghost look like Papa?"

"No, he would be enormous, as tall as the sky, and black as soot."

"Khandulai's father-in-law, overhearing her stories one day, flew off the handle: "What is the matter with these women? Haven't our scholars taught them that there is one god, Allah?"

"Have you forgotten how you yourself used to sacrifice goats to Saint George?" mumbled Khandulai's mother-in-law. And she told Khandulai about the time she had run into Untul Ebel in a distant village.

"Vai-vai," her sister-in-law's mouth fell open. "Untul Ebel! Is it true that she's as tall as a tree, and has holes in her face where her cheeks should be?"

"And she has a really, really long nose and you can't see her eyes under her red hair?" Khandulai joined in.

"Not at all! She didn't look like a woman, she appeared to me in the form of a baby, completely naked. This baby is walking along, and its skin is as coarse as bark. The baby is groaning—I hear this groaning sound, and it's at night, so I say, 'Run up the mountain, down along the river, cross over onto the land. I will give you oil to rub on the cracks in your hands and feet!' I gather up some old things that are lying around: worn-out trousers and old shirts, work shirts, I take them and leave them out behind the garden; let Untel Ebel pick them up there...Oh, oh, my poor Surakat!"

One summer Khandulai went to collect ice in a cave where the walls were frozen even in July. When she started to chip at them, the elders ordered the entrance closed off with a big boulder.

"May the ears of grain multiply in your field!" exclaimed Khandulai. "Why have you locked me up in here?"

"Give us a name! Anyone—widower or handsome young man, whoever you want!"

"Why should I get married?" Khandulai stood her ground. "I've already got three daughters!"

"Just give us a name!"

"But why?"

"A name!"

And they kept her locked up in the icy cave until Khandulai was chilled to the bone and finally shouted to the people outside:

"Chantilav!"

"Chantilav? Do we have a Chantilav living in the village?" the elders asked skeptically.

"There's this loner named Chantilav, a *chanka* who lives on the outskirts. A conspirator who was exiled from the neighboring khanate. He has *kunaks* from Mesedil *tukhum*, in the middle quarter of the village. They have accepted him here."

They sent some boys to inform Chantilav that he'd been selected to marry Khandulai. And so she acquired her second husband. After a whispered consultation with the mullah, she moved to a different part of the village, leaving her daughters in the home of her first husband...

Shamil skipped ahead:

The outcast Kebed, whose hair had grown wild and matted, heard that the haughty girl who had rejected him was again living with a man, and he came up with a devious plan...

Shamil skipped several more pages:

Trembling all over, bloodied, Chantilav fell onto his mighty chest.

"How can it be?" they asked later in the *godekan*. "Chantilav gathered and armed a group of his friends, crept back to his native village, and overthrew his half-brother, and after all that, what happens? Some stinking outlaw lies in wait and sticks a knife into him!"

Khandulai, who had grown up in a free society where an assembly was called to discuss every last little thing and no one paid tribute to anyone, now found herself the absolute ruler of an alien khanate. Envious people, old dignitaries, and Chantilav's former comrades-in-arms all sharpened their daggers against her, and her Turkish bodyguards demanded incredible fees.

"If the child I am bearing under my heart is a boy, then there will be an heir and I am saved," thought she at night in the palace. "But if not?"

So then Khandulai decided to appeal for help to the cursed murderer, her rejected suitor Kebed...

Flip, flip, flip: "Twice a widow," he read, "Khandulai..."

He smirked. "Really, it's getting to be a bit much," he said to himself. "This Khandulai woman is a regular Black Widow."

The booth was finally just ahead. Shamil took a quick look around, then turned all the way to the last page:

I was taught from childhood that there is no God on earth. But now that I, Makhmud, have lived my life, I can state absolutely that He exists. And I can even tell you, dear readers, where souls end up after death.

Our souls end up at the top of Rokhel-Meer, the Mountain of Celebrations. And there, on Meer, will be a place of purity, where there is no poverty, no scarcity, no want. There will be a great village there with tanneries, armories, and stone workshops. Its dwellings are part of the very cliffs; there, benign white spirits will feast together with the people, and the celebration will never end. There too, I hope, will dwell your Makhmud, he will drink fresh *buza* and watch as the dove-gray steam rises above the green-white-blue peaks...

"Break it up, go on home! There's no more bread!" howled someone in a crude bass.

The line fidgeted and dispersed.

5

So Shamil didn't get any bread. He headed morosely off, but noticed a chartreuse-colored cloud, a light expanse of cloth billowing in the wind amid the hushed crowd, barely touching the earth.

"Asya!" exclaimed Shamil, discerning her familiar little nose in the waves of undulating cloth.

She smiled and floated toward him.

"What is that thing you're wearing?" Shamil snickered, looking over Asya's turban with its strangely flowing sail, and at all the gauzy material lightly enveloping her figure.

"I'm covering my *avrat*."

"That may very well be, but you're actually attracting attention."

"You're not the first to tell me that. They said that your external hijab needs to reflect your inner hijab." Asya looked around guiltily. "I simply wanted to cheer myself up," she said. "With everything that's going on around here...you can't make any sense of it."

"Why aren't you in Georgia?" Shamil got in a little jab. "Bearing in mind that I have no intention of leaving town."

"Forget the letter," Asya snapped, and then asked, "You're not going to make fun of me just because of that, are you?"

"Anyone in my position would."

"But you're not just anyone," objected Asya with uncustomary haste.

"Where did you get the nerve?"

"You try to live in a house without water or light for a whole week! What's it going to be like in the winter? We're going to have to get ahold of some kerosene lamps."

Asya had spent the last few days hauling buckets to the neighboring quarter to get water from the people there, who still had some utilities running. In the evenings people locked themselves inside their homes, lit stearin candles and huddled there quaking at the slightest sound. The women covered themselves completely from head to toe, cowering from the ferocious guardians of morality patrolling the streets, while the older men glowered, fiddled around with the felled telephone lines and their mute televisions, grumbling under their breath.

"Can you imagine, Asya? Some Jordanian guy broke into Umukusum's apartment and nearly shot her. She'd covered her arms, but her skirt only came down to here, just below the knees, you know," babbled Asya's neighbor, whose big, strong, gray-eyed son had disappeared during the winter, but who had quickly seen the error of his ways and had been pardoned by a special commission. Now the neighbor was afraid that her wayward son's former comrades would take revenge on him, so she had sent him away to a distant *kutan*.

"And Sultanov, the one who lived in that red mansion, he's from the same village as the mayor…he couldn't get away in time. He pasted on a fake mustache, changed his clothes, abandoned the house, tied a green sling across his chest, and went into hiding at a fish-canning plant. They found him there and put a lit match to his mustache. Without thinking, he immediately tried to peel it off, that's how they got him…"

There were a lot of stories like that making the rounds. People told about soldiers, policemen, government workers, judges, prostitutes, and bribe-takers who had tried to hide, but had been caught and executed.

Ultimately Asya and her brother had moved in with relatives in a cramped but clean little house in a neighborhood where there was still electricity. They turned on the only working channel, listened to the gray-haired emir in military uniform making promises on the screen, and in hushed voices discussed the video clips showing people in Dagestan and neighboring republics ecstatically celebrating the new emirate and hurling cobblestones at the abandoned police departments and government offices.

Shamil accompanied Asya to that little house. They walked down empty streets, plastered with triumphant proclamations, summons, and direct threats aimed at the infidels.

"Come along on Thursday, Shamil," said Asya. "It's dangerous to be out driving alone. There's unrest everywhere, and there are a lot of checkpoints on the highways. We're getting together a big group, there will be twenty cars. We'll go to Ebekh, where our parents are. And from there we can go to Cher, it's very close. We can think, decide what to do next. The people won't just sit by and let this happen…"

"There are people on the other side as well," answered Shamil.

"Yes, including Madina, but our people outnumber them…I'm sorry to be so direct, but I know why you stayed here and why you didn't go with your mother."

"I had things to do. I was looking for Uncle Alikhan."

"Uncle Alikhan is long gone! He's undoubtedly been killed!" exclaimed Asya so loudly that a figure lurking under a tree emerged and began following them, carrying an automatic rifle.

Shamil frowned. "Wait, what are you implying?"

"That you want to kill Otsok, Madina's husband. Everyone's expecting you to do it. Not me, of course," Asya broke off. "Well, not expecting, exactly, but everyone thinks you're capable of doing something like that."

"Everyone who?"

"They were talking about it yesterday at Uncle Eldar's, I heard them."

Nearby in the road a pile of trash smoldered, sending up caustic

ALISA GANIEVA

smoke. The windows of gutted stores gaped, their glass shattered, and in the place where the café had flourished, a dark sign now read: ADVANCED TRAINING CLUB FOR TRUE MUSLIMS.

"Why do they think I would?"

"What do you mean?" Asya's eyes grew big and round. "To take revenge! I'm opposed to murder, naturally, but honestly I assumed that you were simply waiting for the right moment. They say that you've figured out where Madina is living."

"That's..." Shamil sputtered, "that's ridiculous! Why..."

They were standing outside the neatly whitewashed gate of the house where Asya had been staying. Her relatives had noticed she was gone, and had sent people out to look for her. They stood on the terrace muttering to one another: "*Vakh, vakh,* where did she run off to, all by herself?"

"I'm sorry, I seem to have said some *khapur-chapur,*" said Asya, her voice dropping to a near whisper. "Come in with me and get some bread for yourself."

She pulled out a loaf of bread and handed it to Shamil. Her fingers were cold, in spite of the hot, humid air.

"You there!" The voice, rude and self-righteous, came out of nowhere, right next to them: "Why are you out alone together? Did you just touch each other?"

They turned and saw the figure with his automatic rifle.

"She's my wife," Shamil answered curtly, with a sense of burning irritation. Asya gave him a surprised look, waved her hand, and disappeared through the gate. The meddler looked at Shamil silently for a second, then growled, "You better look out, we can check," and turned away.

Shamil didn't follow Asya in, but continued on down the demolished street.

His thoughts were disjointed. "They're all waiting for me to...well, perhaps...or maybe not..."

Then he stopped in the middle of the road. "To hell with her, the bitch," he said to himself. "See if I ever get my hands dirty with the likes of her again!"

The disgust that he had felt toward Madina had cooled; he had become almost indifferent to her. And then he realized that he had just now called Asya his wife.

"Shamil! *Le*, you with the folder!" someone shouted.

This voice belonged to a young man of average height, dressed in loose trousers and a strange, faded T-shirt with a half-moon on the front. Shamil didn't recognize his friend right away. The last time he had seen him was that night when they'd gone to the Padishakh nightclub with those two girls.

"Arsenchik, what's up, how are things?"

"No worries. Though we're in deep shit, let me tell you. The old man sold the flat, he bailed, wanted to take me along..."

Shamil cast a skeptical look at the halfmoon and nodded vaguely. "So why didn't you go?"

Arsen grinned: "What, get in with those wackos from the woods? No way. This guy I know, he says come to Chirkei. I'm out of here tomorrow morning. My mom's losing it, but I'm going no matter what. They have a bunker, they're digging trenches and what-all, they're getting down with some major firepower, let me tell you."

"To use against who?"

"Against those guys, the *mujahideen*, I mean. Serious shit, the sheikh is right in the thick of it."

"You didn't use to have anything to do with the sheikhs, as I recall," smiled Shamil.

"*Le*, bro, good luck handling it some other way. The sheikh is where the power is! He'll give those *Wahhabis* a real kick in the ass. How about you come along? Everyone's going to get grenades and a sidearm. Their guys had some heat left over from '99."[§]

"I already agreed to go home with my relatives, to our village. We have our own sheikh up there, if he hasn't been rubbed out yet."

"*Ai saul*, bro!"

"Listen, where's Nariman?"

Arsen frowned. "Rashik said that they offed him. Him and his folks, and his sister too. Burned their house down."

"Who, the beards?"

"Who else? His old man worked in the tax office, ripped everyone off right and left. You know yourself the kind of dough he was slinging around."

Arsen spat on the street without listening to Shamil's muttered complaints.

"Right, then, bro! Don't take it wrong, they're waiting for me."

"Good luck! Don't worry. With luck we'll see each other again," said Shamil, slapping him on the shoulders.

"*Saul* to you! Here, take this rag, I don't need it. It's from the Emirate."

Shamil tucked both Asya's loaf of bread and the folder with Makhmud Tagirovish's novel under his arm, and took the tabloid with his free hand. It was covered with Arabic script and had a black flag with a white saber and the *shahada* on the masthead.

Shamil crossed the railroad tracks directly over the ties, then descended the sandy steps and sprang down onto the beach, which was deserted and seemed unusually broad in the evening light. He took off his shoes and breathed deeply, filling his chest with air, then

---

[§] The year of the invasion of Dagestan by Chechen militants.

started walking across the warm sand alongside the thundering, restless sea, past the orphaned lifeguard tower.

Shamil tucked the things he was carrying under one arm and opened the newspaper. The wind wouldn't let him open it out flat, but he persisted. By the booth where they'd been selling cotton candy just a month ago, some big hulking guy was standing on guard, his chest lined with bands of automatic rifle shells. He scrutinized Shamil, but did not budge from his spot.

6

The waves choked in their own foam. Gagging on fragments of seashells, they hissed and dissolved in the swelling sand. Shamil unfolded the Emirate's tabloid. The front page featured an address by the emir, framed in a graphic of unsheathed sword blades:

> Praise be to Allah, the Lord of the Worlds, Who created
> us Muslims and Who blessed us with jihad, giving us the
> opportunity to earn Paradise. I praise Allah for the events
> that are taking place among us. A new independent state has
> come into being in the Islamic world. It has overthrown the
> Russian *tagut*, who was wallowing in vice. Guided only by
> the law of sharia, it will overcome the troubles of our time!
> The path to the Emirate was long, hard, and bloody.
> I recall the beginning of negotiations with those who are no
> longer with us and who, *inshallah*, have been martyred. It was
> a difficult time. People came to us bearing banners of Islam,
> but this was only a disguise. They masked themselves with

the letter of Islam, while in fact they were struggling for Ichkerian independence, taking revenge for a murdered brother, or were simply out to make a profit…

A new day is dawning. We will purge our ranks of casual warriors who lack *aqeedah*. We have no need for young romantics or men who only want to swagger and show how brave they are. We need only true servants of Allah, prepared to die at any moment. *Mujahideen* who love the Messenger and Paradise.

Alhamdulillah, now we see how our *umma* is coming together, is becoming firm; now the *munafiqs* and *kafirs* face retribution; they will be hunted like rats. But that does not mean that we can lay down our weapons or can loll about in the palaces confiscated from the thieves! *Gazavat* will continue so long as we face an external and internal threat.

Forget about filial or family attachments. If your brother, friend, or dear one does not believe in Allah as he should, if he indulges his *nafs* and refuses to accept your teaching, let nothing and no one hinder your way forward on the correct path…

Shamil set the newspaper aside. Darkness was settling in. He stood listening to the roar of the surf. A huge, gray mass, it rushed clumsily toward the shore, tumbled, fell, seeped into the sand, then swelled again. The sea heaved and devoured the last sliver of the scarlet sun. Shamil recalled Asya's chartreuse robe and smiled to himself: "*Vababai*, Shamil, fallen in love, have you?"

He tried to chase away thoughts of Asya. Then, he lifted the fragrant, crusty bread and sank his teeth into it.

"*Salam*, Shamil!"

Shamil started, turned, and saw a kind of shadow under a pile of boulders. A man was sitting literally two paces behind him.

"Well, young man, what are you doing sitting all alone out here after sunset? It's not safe."

"*Vaaleikum salam*," murmured Shamil, standing up and extending his hand.

"I must have said my name out loud, somehow?" the thought flashed through his mind.

Shamil felt awkward holding the bread with the piece bitten out of it, and he settled down on the sand again and sat half-turned toward the stranger. The man gave a friendly smile and took a folded plastic bag out of his pocket.

"Come on, put your things in here, why carry them in your bare hands? It could be dangerous to show people that you've got a loaf of bread. The times we're living in…"

Shamil took the bag gratefully and tucked the folder, the bread, and, after some hesitation, the half-read newspaper inside. Meanwhile the stranger leaned his head back and started chanting the constellations as they appeared in the sky: "Ursa Minor, the Dragon, Hercules, The Big Dipper, Boötes…Are you planning to stay in the city much longer? Aries, the Triangulum, Perseus, Cassiopeia, Anvar, Yusup, Kerim, Makhmud…"

Shamil listened in amazement. "I don't know, we'll see how things work out," he answered at last.

"The things they've gotten up to!" the man chortled. "No light, no water…like during wartime! But remember, you never know how things will turn out. Say a man goes up a mountain, thinks there's a village with people there at the top, and it turns out there's nothing but ruins. Or he goes up again and thinks, it's ruins, but all he sees are bare cliffs. Someone rushes to see Pakhriman but ends up at Khalilbek's. Someone wants to get married and dies instead, and someone dies and…gets married."

They could hear shots in the distance. The sea groaned and heaved.

PART IV

I

The thing that bothered Madina the most was that the blessed world of truth and justice that had been promised to her never came into being; instead, every night she was awakened by the sound of shots and screams, and by the red glow rising from burning homes. Once they had destroyed the bankers and policemen, the imams of mosques and the teachers at the new theological academies, the *mujahideen* started in on their former neighbors, relatives, and classmates.

"Brother Muslims!" she read on leaflets that fell out of Otsok-Al-Jabbar's pockets, "collect *zakat* from everyone who is obliged to pay! If a man refuses, take it by force! And if he denies *zakat*, then take *dzhizia* from him, and fight him mightily, as with a *kafir*! Burn his property! Destroy his fields! Kill him in the name of Allah, and let not your hands falter!"

So long as the cause was taking revenge on murderers in the security forces, corrupt officials, and thieves, Madina passionately supported the calls for violent action; she knitted warm socks and sweaters for jihadists and was prepared to share everything she had with the *umma*. But then things changed. First the *mujahideen* murdered her uncle, her father's brother, for some incautious remark. Her mother ran to Madina cursing, hurled the bag with their rations from the Emirate at her, and grain had spilled out and scattered on the floor.

"It's all because of you!" screamed her mother in her native language. "Because of you and your *abrek* we've become nothing but rotten meat! Our whole family has turned against us! We shouldn't have supported you, you bitch. I should given you a good beating and thrown you out on the street the day you put on that veil!"

Madina bit her lips wrathfully and said, "Go away, then, leave!"

Her mother left, but rumors kept coming; more and more friends and family members were being killed by the *mujahideen*, and Madina couldn't sleep or focus on her Koran and *hadiths* readings or her Arabic studies.

"What is going on, Al-Jabbar?" she would ask her husband. "Filth everywhere, there's no running water or electricity, and they're out persecuting perfectly innocent people."

"Innocent?" snapped Al-Jabbar. "Those so-called innocent people tormented my brother and drove him into the woods with their slander and denunciation, and they were about to drive me out there too! Those people reject the teachings of Allah, Madina! They are ignorant and deaf and do not follow the holy sharia law. They paid the *kafir* state for electricity, gas, and water, and the *kafir* state used that tax money to destroy us…"

But Al-Jabbar's voice wavered. People didn't take him seriously when he spoke at *dzhamaat* assemblies and excluded him from important work assignments.

"Your husband," the black widows and *Salafi* wives said to Madina, "hasn't killed a single *murtad*! He never lived in the forest! Just giving food to a brother *mujahid* is hardly some major act of heroism."

"But he follows Islam," Madina said, trying to defend him.

"Follows Islam!" snorted the women, "Some hero you've found! Does he teach others? It's not enough to live a righteous life—

the earth must be purged of the unrighteous."

Madina sulked and stroked her belly; she hadn't yet begun to show.

The people of the Emirate grew restless. They fled south in convoys, hauling their earthly goods to the other side of the Samur. There they encountered columns of the newly founded Belokano-Dzharsk *dzhamaat*, whose members dreamed about joining the Emirate, heading north.

Madina heard stories. There was a woman in Izberbash who murdered an emissary who wouldn't let her get behind the wheel. A vintner from Derbent with the strange name of Peak had tracked down the men who had destroyed his cognac distillery and had mowed them down with a machine gun. In many regions the local people had disbanded the sharia courts.

"Still," said the women, "there are a lot of people around who support the strictest Islam. And what was it like before? It was all about money—give money. Give money here, give money there, bribe your way into the university, pay off your teachers and your kids' teachers. Now everyone will live honestly…"

But people still grumbled, even in the *dzhamaats*, which were bursting at the seams with new recruits.

"Half of our leaders spit on Islam, all they care about is making money!" whispered the young *mujahideen*, flashing their fanatical eyes.

And indeed, many of those who had taken over the converted government building had moved into confiscated government villas, taken former debauchees as their wives, sometimes several at a time, and under the banner of *tawhid* had taken up racketeering and banditry. When any of their confederates objected they answered, "Have you heard our emir's instructions? We are to free ourselves of romantics and idealists, of the people who went off into the woods to fight for justice. We must struggle not for some abstract justice, but for faith in the

Prophet, *salallakhu alaikha vassalam!*"

This intimidated many former *gazavat* warriors. A few of them, after some hesitation, ran off and joined the burgeoning Nakshiband opposition. And one morning a group of armed young men attacked some *mujahideen* who were holding a meeting in a former school, and in the ensuing scuffle killed one of the *naibs*—a deputy of the chief emir.

Madina and her girlfriends were approaching the *madrasa*, when Zariat, wearing a black niqab, ran out and shouted, "The Sufi polytheists are attacking our men at the gas station! It's a total bloodbath!"

"Al…Al-Jabbar," Madina was shaking, close to tears.

"Say a *sabur*, sister, your husband isn't there right now, he's at the seashore. Some guys came up from the sea and just started shooting."

"What, they came by sea? Who is it?" Madina was gasping for air.

The rest of the Muslim women ran up to them, waving their arms.

"It's the damned *dzhakhils*, on account of the wine! They're coming from Kizlyar, not the sea!"

"*Astauperulla*, sister! What wine are you talking about?"

"Our brothers destroyed the Kizlyar wine cellars, and the *dzhakhils* got all worked up. They said there were rare vintages there."

"*Auzubillah*, may Allah save us from those ignorant *murtads!*" wailed Zariat.

Madina turned and ran, she had no idea where.

2

She ran toward the sea, past people covered with dust and tormented by fear and uncertainty. She ran past silent clusters of terrified girls dragging barrels of water.

"*Munafiqs*! Hypocrites! They put on the hijab to keep from being murdered, while living in *nifaq*! They enter Islam from one side, and come out the other!" she muttered, watching the girls: anything but think about her husband.

"Hey, stop! Where do you think you're going?" an armed man shouted to her from around the corner.

"To join the battle!" Madina flew past, amazing the timid onlookers.

She rounded the corner and there was Shamil. He was walking along, taking big strides, a heavy rucksack bouncing against his back. Madina remembered the games they used to play as children in Ebekh; she recalled their dance at a wedding in Kaspiisk, his confession of love, their courtship, and she recalled the all-encompassing loathing, the scorn, even, that she had come to feel for this rudderless hypocrite.

"Go on, keep walking," she whispered, "Just keep on walking with that rucksack of yours. If I had married you I would have turned you over to the *shaitan*! Al-Jabbar is handsomer, stronger, smarter, better, closer to Allah."

She stopped to catch her breath, but Shamil had vanished. He hadn't seen her.

Shamil was on his way to the house where Asya was living. They would load up their things and join an armed convoy heading for his home village.

"I should have gotten another weapon. Here I am like some fool with my rubber-bullet gun…"

For the first time in many days he felt at ease and even happy. The obsession with Otsok that had taken root in his head was gone, and instead something tender, something gauzy and chartreuse, had taken its place.

"Asya," he said to himself quietly, and before he could even be surprised at himself for saying her name, something buzzed in the sky overhead, then it hummed, then it growled, then it roared.

The shadow of the thing in the sky sped along the ground and across the building façades, and the roar became a deafening howl. Then within the howl there arose another sound, something excruciating, piercing, and thin. At that moment there was a tremendous explosion behind the nearest houses, and everything was engulfed in hot smoke. Shamil fell to the rumbling earth, clutching at his aching ears. People came running out of the smoke, covered with blood, their mouths distorted with panic.

Shamil tossed away his rucksack and rushed into the smoke toward the wounded people. The street itself was maimed, strewn with fragments of glass and cement dust. Shamil coughed. "Where are they?" he repeated to himself, over and over. His people were waiting there, with Asya. But the buildings were unrecognizable, their shredded, shattered contents jutting into the scorching, smoky air. On the ground, people writhed in agony, dying.

There came another roar, something exploded and thundered, now from some other direction. Shamil braced himself against a wall that had been left standing. Behind it, in what had been a private home, weak groans could be heard. The world wavered and floated before his eyes. With a mighty effort he pushed away from the wall and staggered on in the direction of the house, which was gradually becoming engulfed in smoke. On both sides the buildings stood with their roofs turned inside out, their paneless windows gaping.

"*Vai alla, vai alla!*"

Shamil wanted to add his voice to the chorus of howls, but he restrained himself and pressed on, flexing his limbs as he went, bumping into bewildered, panicked people, all of them rushing somewhere. On he went, on and on and on, and he lost all sense of time and no longer understood what was going on around him.

On the corner of some endless street he came upon a demolished antique shop. Out of the remains of its ruined wall bulged a chaos of antique kettles, wooden chests, and engraved bronze plates that had tumbled down from the walls.

"They're bombing the port!" shouted a man, his face stained with ash and blood. "The docks, the warehouses!"

Shots whooped from the sea. A *mujahid* draped in a black flag with a white horizontal saber on it had climbed up onto the roof of one of the surviving houses with his automatic weapon and had begun strafing the street. Everyone lurched and fled, Shamil among them. The shattered streets belched up cursing people, and a terrible, thundering crash was heard. A dog tore past, leaping across the splayed metal fittings and the fragments of adobe bricks.

"Where's their house?" Shamil asked and asked, and no longer understood what he was asking.

Cement dust rose in a column above the street, blinding him; there was a buzzing in his ears. Up ahead a man was running, showing the rubber soles of his shoes. Shamil ran after him, slipping on plastic bags scattered on the ground. Rounding the turn, he saw several more people running. On a rooftop someone was shouting hoarsely, "*Tokhta! Tokhta!*" Behind them something heavy lumbered across the roof, sending tiles crashing to the ground, but the people ran on, seeking shelter from whatever it was making that terrible roar. Shamil rounded one last corner, then heard nothing more...

EPILOGUE

Laughing, Anvar ascended the stone steps and, springing up onto the flat roof, sat down next to the women to watch the dancing. Above the newlyweds hung an aurochs head, adorned with colorful ribbons, and wedding silver jingled on the bride's forehead, the back and crown of her head, her neck, temples, chest, belly, and the hem of her dress.

A man wearing a goat-head mask poured wine out of wineskins into goblets made of animal horns, and teased and joked with the people dancing. Between the *zurna* players and the drummers a bright-eyed girl stood tapping a tambourine. She sang about eternal snowcapped mountain peaks and spring thaws, about lovesickness and mourning doves, about unfaithful lovers, and about death, which did not exist.

They danced: Kerim and Zumrud, Dibir and Madina, Makhmud Tagirovich and Khandulai, Yusup and Abida, Otsok and Marian, Maga and Khorol-En. The women and children clapped from the rooftops, and the young people went around with wooden trays serving *khinkal* and hot meat.

Shamil took his place in the groom's seat. He could hardly recognize Asya's features in the face that the timid bride was trying to conceal from him, or his near and distant cousins in the merrymakers who had organized "wolves' games," competitions with people dressed in wolf costumes, to entertain the villagers.

The ornamentally carved window shutters had been flung open; they looked out onto the square, onto the faces of the people celebrating there, some of whom Shamil barely recognized. Among them one profile stood out, a man of fifty wearing a bright homespun shirt belted with a silver sash. The man watched the celebration with a sly smile.

"Khalilbek! Khalilbek!" someone called out, and the profile disappeared.

The goat-masked man rushed past, sprinkling Shamil and Asya with oat flour.

"May you have as many children as there are specks of powder in this flour!"

"May you have as much wealth as there are fibers in this burka!"

"May your faces be as festive as this Mountain of Celebrations!"

The dancers reveled, and the songs echoed to the snow-covered mountaintops that surrounded them. And the sky came down, touching the towers and the ancient houses, and the village was filled with light.

GLOSSARY OF WORDS, PHRASES, PLACES, & PEOPLE

A

Abdal (ARABIC) Literally "slave of God." Among the Avars it means "fool."

Abrek (GENERAL CAUCASIAN TERM) A person who has gone into the mountains, where he lives beyond the reach of the authorities as an outlaw and a partisan. Originally a man from the Caucasian mountains, exiled from his community for a crime, usually murder.

Adats — The traditional common laws that governed the free mountain communities.

Ai-ui (AVAR) Pandemonium.

Akhvakh and Chamalal — Two of the indigenous ethnicities of Dagestan.

Alhamdulillah (ARABIC) Praise Allah.

Aqeedah (ARABIC) The Islamic creed.

Aria-urai (AVAR) Hullaballoo.

As-Salaf-As-Salih (ARABIC) Righteous ancestors.

Astauperulla (ARABIC) Lord forgive.

Auzubillah (ARABIC) I turn to Allah for protection.

Avrat (ARABIC) Parts of the body that must be concealed from outsiders.

Ayat (ARABIC) A sign; a portent; a miracle. Each verse of the Koran.

Azhdakha (TURKIC) An evil monster.

Aziz yoldashlar (KUMYK) Dear comrades.

B

Barakat (ARABIC) Blessings.

Barkala (ARABIC) Thank you.

Bashlyk (TURKIC) A peaked cloth cowl with long ends that are wrapped around the neck, worn over headgear in inclement weather for protection against cold, rain and sun.

Bay'ah (ARABIC) An oath of allegiance.

Bida (ARABIC) A new practice bordering on heresy.

Bismillah (ARABIC) Shortened form of *Bismillah-ir-Rahman-ir-Rahim*: "In the name of Allah, the Merciful and Charitable."

Buruti (AVAR) Jug.

Buza (TURKIC) A fermented drink made from barley, oats, millet, or corn.

C

Ch'a (AVAR) Stop, wait.

Ch'anda (AVAR) Nonsense, foolishness.

Chanka (AVAR) A social class in Dagestan. Descendants from marriages between members of feudal households and local free Dagestanis.

Chchit (AVAR) Shoo! Scat!

Chokhto (AVAR) A headdress for Dagestani women. Nowadays only worn rarely, and only by old women in the mountain regions.

Chudu (AVAR) A Dagestani national dish, pancakes with various kinds of fillings.

Chukha (TURKIC) A shirt worn by mountain dwellers.

Chungur (DARGIN) A stringed, plucked musical instrument.

D

Derkhab (DARGIN) To your health.

Din (ARABIC) Faith, religion.

Dzhakhils (ARABIC) Crude people, savages, ignoramuses; apostates from the Muslim faith.

Dzhigit (TURKIC) In Central Asia and in the Caucasus: a horseman distinguished for bravery, endurance, hardiness, and expertise with horses and weaponry.

Dzhamaat (ARABIC) A group of comrades. The term has come to refer to militant Salafi groups active in the Northern Caucasus.

Dzhizia (ARABIC) An annual per capita tax levied in Islamic states on free adult male non-Muslims (with the exception of monks).

Dzhurab – A thick, knitted sock worn by the peoples of the Caucasus and Southwest and Central Asia.

F

Fatimids (ARABIC) A dynasty of Arabic khalifs (909–1171) who traced their origin to Fatima, the daughter of Muhammad.

Fitna (ARABIC) Chaos, discord.

G

Gada (LEZGIAN) Guy, man.

Gazavat (ARABIC) Among Muslims, the term for holy war with nonbelievers.

Godekan (DAGESTANI) A gathering place for men in Dagestani mountain settlements; originally serving as a local representative assembly.

Golden Bridge – A bridge over the river Samur on the Azerbaijan border. Called the "Golden Bridge" because of the huge amounts of bribes taken by border guards and customs officials.

H

Hadith (ARABIC) Accounts of the words and deeds of the Prophet Muhammad, as they pertain to religious and legal aspects of Islamic life.

Haram (ARABIC) Acts that are forbidden in sharia.

Hijab (ARABIC) In Islam any garment that covers avrat, that is, for women, the whole body except the hands and the face; for men, everything between the navel and the knees.

I

Iakh'namus (AVAR) A sense of shame, conscience.

Iblis (ARABIC) Evil spirit, demon.

Iman (ARABIC) Faith in the tenets of Islam.

Inshalla (ARABIC) God willing.

K

Kafir (ARABIC) An unbeliever, an infidel, one who rejects or does not believe in God.

K'akh'ba (AVAR) Slut, bitch.

Khabary (ARABIC) Rumors, stories.

Khakims (ARABIC) People in charge; rulers.

Khanafites (ARABIC) Followers of one of the legal religious schools of Islam, disciples of the theologian Abu Khanifa.

Khapur-chapur (AVAR) Nonsense, absurdity.

Khinkal (AVAR) Dumplings: lumps of boiled dough served with pieces of boiled meat or sausage, broth, and various gravies.

Koisu (TURKIC) Literally "sheep's water." The name of several rivers in the mountainous part of Dagestan.

Kufr (ARABIC) Unbelief, the lack of a moral core, a spiritual vacuum.

Kufr keepers (SLAVIC) *Kufrokhranitel,* a pejorative term used by Salafis to refer to policemen.

Kunak (TURKIC) In Caucasian mountain communities, a person bound by mutual obligations of hospitality. The institution of kunaks is similar to that of *xenia* (hospitality) among the ancient Greeks.

Kurze (TURKIC) A kind of dumpling.

Kutan (TURKIC) A populated area that falls under a regional mountain administration, but is located on a plain designated for livestock, in an area used for winter pasturing.

L

Le – A word used in Dagestan when addressing men.

M

Madzhlis (ARABIC) In Islamic states, a sort of parliament; in Dagestan, however, the word is used as a catchall term for religious gatherings, and is sometimes applied ironically, referring to any sort of gathering at all.

Magarych (SLAVIC) A celebration following the successful transaction of a business deal, thrown by whichever party profited.

Mashalla (ARABIC) According to Allah's will.

Masliat (ARABIC) Reconciliation.

Mavlid (ARABIC) The holiday in honor of the prophet's birthday. In Dagestan it also refers to any important event in the lives of the faithful.

Mazkhab (ARABIC) The school of sharia law in Islam.

Miurid (ARABIC) Broadly, representatives of one of the movements of Sufism. In the Caucasus, however, the word was used to refer to participants in the national liberation movement of mountain militants fighting for liberation from the Russian Empire.

Muchalas (DARGIN) Traditional Kubachi water pitchers.

Mujahid (plural: *Mujahideen*) (ARABIC) The term for one engaged in jihad.

Munafiq (ARABIC) A hypocrite, keeping the tenets of Islam while harboring doubts or disbelief.

Murtad (ARABIC) Apostate.

N

Nafs (ARABIC) In Islam, the animal passions in man that prompt him to do evil.

Naib (ARABIC) A second in command.

Namaz (ARABIC) In Islam a canonical prayer performed five times a day at strictly stipulated times. One of the pillars of Islam.

Niqab (ARABIC) A women's garment, usually black, that completely covers the face, with a narrow opening for the eyes. Does not fall under one of the mandatory dictates of Islam.

Nikiakh (ARABIC) Marriage within Islam.

P

Pandur (DAGESTANI) A Dagestani two-stringed musical instrument.

Papakha (TURKIC) Sheepskin or astrakhan fur headgear widespread among the peoples of the Caucasus, the Cossacks, and in Central Asia; worn as part of military attire.

Q

Qadi (ARABIC) A sharia judge.

R

Reduktorny – A district in Makhachkala.

S

Sabur (ARABIC) Patience.

Sadval (LEZGIAN) Unity.

Sag'rai (LEZGIAN) Good-bye; be healthy.

Sahk (AVAR) A measure of weight equivalent to four kilograms.

Sakhl-i (AVAR) An exclamation during toasts, the equivalent to "to your health."

Salafi (ARABIC) Derived from *As-Salaf-As-Salih*; a representative of a radical movement in Islam that calls for a renunciation of innovation and a return to the way of life of the Prophet and his followers.

Salallakhu alaikha vassalam (ARABIC) Peace be upon him. One of the standard, complimentary invocations to the Prophet Muhammad that must be spoken when his name is said aloud.

Sura (ARABIC) A chapter of the Koran.

Shahada (ARABIC) Islamic creed testifying to a believer's faith in Allah as the only god, as well as the prophetic mission of the Prophet.

Shaitan – In Islam, an evil spirit, hostile to Allah and to human beings.

Shamil, Imam – Leader of the long-lasting resistance to the Russian Empire in the Caucasus in the nineteenth century; ruler of Dagestan and Chechnya. Ultimately, the mountain dwellers themselves turned him over to the Russians, in 1859, because of his severe policies and imposition of sharia law.

Shamkhals, nutsals, and utsmis – Feudal titles used in different regions and among different peoples of Dagestan.

Sharia (ARABIC) Islamic religious law.

Shirk (ARABIC) Polytheism.

Subhanallah (ARABIC) Allah be praised.

Sunna (ARABIC) The path, the way. The words and actions of the Prophet Muhammad.

Sunnat (ARABIC) Circumcision.

Sura (ARABIC) A chapter in the Koran.

T

Tagut (ARABIC) Here, a criminal ruler who betrays the laws of Allah. A general term from the Koran, denoting "mutineer," "criminal," or "person who transgresses religious and moral boundaries." Used in the present day to refer to any anti-Islamic person, group, party or authority that supports secular and material Western values.

Takfir (ARABIC) Excommunication from Islam.

Tariq (ARABIC) A popular Sufi teaching order popular among Dagestani Sufis. Preaches a path of spiritual purification and enrichment, most commonly through asceticism, retreat from the world, and mystical practices.

Tashshakhud (ARABIC) A prayer read in a sitting position during *namaz*.

Tawhid (ARABIC) Monotheism.

Tenglik (KUMYK) Equality.

Tiuz (KUMYK) Right; true.

Tokhta (TURKIC) Stop!

Tukhum – In Dagestan, one's local community; a clan.

Tsaps (LEZGIAN) Literally, the manure of animals without cloven hooves in Lezgian. Some Lezgian nationalists, however, use the word to refer to Turks and Azeris.

U

Umma (ARABIC) A community of believers.

Uraza (ARABIC) *Uraza Bairam*, the Islamic holiday marking the end of Ramadan.

Ustaz (ARABIC) A teacher; specifically, in this context, a teacher of *tariq*.

Uzden (TURKIC) In Dagestan, a broad class of free people.

V

Vasvas (ARABIC) Possession by evil forces.

Vilayat (ARABIC) The major administrative territorial unit in several countries in North Africa as well as the Near and Middle East.

Vore, vore (AVAR) Come on, come on.

W

Wahhabi (ARABIC) The same as *Salafi*.

Y

Yo (DAGESTANI) A word used in Dagestan when addressing women.

Z

Zakat (ARABIC) A tax, or form of obligatory charity, consisting of 1/5 of a Muslim's personal revenue, paid to the poor, to mosques, etc.

Ziarat (ARABIC) Traveling to sacred places; also a term referring to these sacred places.

Thank you all for your support. We do this for you, and could not do it without you.

LIGA DE ORO ($5,000+)

Anonymous (2)

LIGA DEL SIGLO ($1,000+)

Allred Capital Management

Ben Fountain

Judy Pollock

Loretta Siciliano

Lori Feathers

Mary Ann Thompson-Frenk
   & Joshua Frenk

Matthew Rittmayer

Meriwether Evans

Pixel and Texel

Nick Storch

Stephen Bullock

DONORS

Alan Shockley	Christie Tull	Maynard Thomson
Amrit Dhir	Daniel J. Hale	Michael Reklis
Anonymous	Ed Nawotka	Mike Kaminsky
Andrew Yorke	Greg McConeghy	Mokhtar Ramadan
Bob & Katherine Penn	JJ Italiano	Nikki Gibson
Brandon Childress	Kay Cattarulla	Richard Meyer
Brandon Kennedy	Kelly Falconer	Suejean Kim
Charles Dee Mitchell	Linda Nell Evans	Susan Carp
Charley Mitcherson	Lissa Dunlay	Tim Perttula
Cheryl Thompson	Mary Cline	

SUBSCRIBERS

Adam Hetherington

Adam Rekerdres

Alan Shockley

Amber J. Appel

Andrew Lemon

Andrew Strickland

Anonymous

Antonia Lloyd-Jones

Ariel Saldivar

Balthazar Simões

Barbara Graettinger

Ben Fountain

Ben Nichols

Betsy Morrison

Bill Fisher

Bjorn Beer

Bob & Mona Ball

Bob Appel

Bob Penn

Brandon Kennedy

Brina Palencia

Charles Dee Mitchell

Chase LaFerney

Cheryl Thompson

Chris Sweet

Christie Tull

David Hopkins

David Lowery

David Shook

David Weinberger

Dennis Humphries

Ed Nawotka

Fiona Schlachter

Frank Merlino

George Henson

Gino Palencia

Greg McConeghy

Heath Dollar

Jacob Siefring

Jacob Silverman

James Crates

Jane Watson

Jeanne Milazzo

Jeff Whittington

Jennifer Smart

Jeremy Hughes

Joe Milazzo

Joel Garza

John Harvell

Joshua Edwin

Julia Pashin

Julie Janicke Muhsmann

Justin Childress

Kaleigh Emerson

Kenneth McClain

Kimberly Alexander

Lauren Shekari

Linda Nell Evans

Lisa Pon

Lissa Dunlay

Liz Ramsburg

Lytton Smith

Mac Tull

Mallory Davis

Marcia Lynx Qualey

Margaret Terwey

Mark Larson

Martha Gifford

Mary Ann Thompson-Frenk
  & Joshua Frenk

Meaghan Corwin

Michael Holtmann

Mike Kaminsky

Naomi Firestone-Teeter

Neal Chuang

Nicholas Kennedy

Nick Oxford

Owen Rowe

Patrick Brown

Peter McCambridge

Regina Imburgia

Scot Roberts

Sean & Karen Fitzgerald

Shelby Vincent

Steven Norton

Susan Ernst

Taylor Zakarin

Tess Lewis

Tim Kindseth

Todd Mostrog

Tom Bowden

Tony Fleo

Will Morrison

Photo by Susanne Schleyer · autorenarchiv.de

ALISA GANIEVA, born in 1985, grew up in Makhachkala, Dagestan. Her literary debut, the novella *Salam, Dalgat!* won the prestigious Debut Prize in 2009. Shortlisted for all of Russia's major literary awards, *The Mountain and the Wall* is her first novel, and has already been translated into seven languages. Ganieva lives in Moscow, where she works as a journalist and literary critic. Her second novel, *Bride and Groom*, was published in Russia in spring 2015.

CAROL APOLLONIO is Professor of the Practice of Russian at Duke University. Her most recent translation is German Sadulaev's *The Maya Pill* (Dalkey Archive, 2014). As well as an accomplished translator, Dr. Apollonio is also a scholar specializing in the works of Fyodor Dostoevsky and Chekhov and on problems of translation. She is the author of the monograph *Dostoevsky's Secrets* (2009).